THE SHERIFF OF SAN MIGUEL

ALLAN VAUGHAN ELSTON

SAGEBRUSH
Large Print Westerns

First published in Great Britain by Ward Lock
First published in the United States by Lippincott

First Isis Edition
published 2020
by arrangement with
Golden West Literary Agency

The moral right of the author has been asserted

A catalogue record for this book is available
from the British Library.

ISBN 978–1–78541–854–9

Published by
Ulverscroft Limited
Anstey, Leicestershire
Set by Words & Graphics Ltd.
Anstey, Leicestershire
Printed and bound in Great Britain by
T. J. International Ltd., Padstow, Cornwall

This book is printed on acid-free paper

To New Mexico's distinguished guest of the year 1879, one that remained there to become an entrepreneur of her pageantry and a nimble scene-shifter among the backdrops of her crimson mesas — the Atchison, Topeka & Santa Fe Railway.

List of Chapters

CHAPTER
ONE

The Sheriff Makes a Bet

The railroad hadn't come yet. New Mexico waited in sluggish suspense for it, and there were some who wanted it to come and some who didn't. Theirs was an old civilization, older than Virginia's, an empire of pueblos and ranchos where commerce was welcome only when it did not disturb the siesta.

Certainly there were some in the capital city who wanted to keep it that way. A broad trail carved by the hoofs of bullock and burro, rutted by the tires of stagecoach and freight wagon, already linked it to the East. The capital city had given its name to that trail and by it had been made famous. And now, they said, the coming of the railroad would kill the trail. And the killing of the trail would kill Santa Fe. For a whisper ran that the railroad, when it came, would miss Santa Fe. The Royal City of the Holy Faith, in its mountain bowl, was too high for rails. The steam wagons would be sure to follow a plains route, through Las Vegas.

Las Vegas, naturally, was for it. Their town, people said, would some day be a division point. Just now it was only a long, scraggly line of shops and saloons and adobe shacks strung along the trail. Great droves of

1

cattle and sheep plodded through it toward present railheads far to the northeast. A four-horse stage pulled out on regular schedule for Otero, Colorado. Bull-drawn wool wagons and caravans of burros kicked dust through Las Vegas. But some day it would be different. When? *Mañana*, the Las Vegans said. Meaning not tomorrow but some hazy, indifferent date in the future.

Mañana would come that thing which had already crawled across Kansas and deep into Colorado at the rate of a mile a day. And to that end speculators were already buying land in and around Las Vegas. Land for ranches and town lots for stores and housing for the families of railroaders. Drovers had come down the trail and told them of booms in Newton and Dodge City. And surely Las Vegas, already the seat of San Miguel County and trading-center for an area bigger than Pennsylvania, would outboom them all.

As to which railroad would come, Las Vegas didn't know and didn't care. There were two of them. One, called the Atchison, Topeka and Santa Fe, had gotten as far in this direction as Otero, Colorado. The other, the Denver and Rio Grande, had dropped a line south from Denver to El Moro. Both were ambitious to get into New Mexico. Each was determined to head the other off.

"Whichever one comes," murmured Don Alfredo Baca, "she will bring us much commerce and prosperity. Your cut, Señor Harper."

"Whichever one comes," retorted Colonel Cal Harper, "it'll bring us a pack of damnyankees. Sodbusters and damnyankees. Odd or even, Alfredo?"

2

They were seated at a table in Las Vegas's leading palace of chance, the Buena Suerte. It was an early afternoon of February in the year 1878, and the place at this hour had only a few customers. Dancing girls were asleep upstairs, to be fresh for the rush of night patronage. So were the dealers and steerers and spotters. It didn't pay to open up the house games this early. Back of the bar old Pedro Gonzalez was serving a few dusty, dry-throated drovers. No gambling of any kind was in progress except this one private, friendly game between Alfredo Baca and Calvin Harper.

"Odd, *señor amigo*," purred Alfredo.

Colonel Harper cut the cards, exposing an eight-spot.

Alfredo sighed. "*Que mala suerte!* So I owe you another fifty steers." He made a note of it on his cuff.

But on the next cut he won them back. It was a simple game which they called "Odd or Even." For years they'd been at it, these two. Harper had had a little of the best of it, but not much. Luck in the long run had nearly balanced.

They continued, now, to while away the time at fifty steers per cut.

Each could afford it. Each owned vast herds and acres. And through the veins of each ran generations of an impulse called sporting-blood. Alfredo was a Mexican of the ruling class, directly descended from the original Conquerors. He was only twenty-eight years old, with a face smooth, olive, and gentle, a mustache thin and black, flashing dark eyes, and mellow, courteous speech. In build he was slight, in feature delicate, in dress quietly elegant. Nothing visible to the eye gave evidence that he was sheriff of San Miguel County. Being a scion of *los ricos* and the owner of a great rancho, he had no need for the pay of a sheriff. But he liked hazard and excitement. That, too, was in his blood. His trimly fitting vest showed no badge. The badge was in his pocket, along with his cigarillos and watch. His slender waist showed no belt or gun. But a gun was on him somewhere, and upon occasion Alfredo Baca had been known to produce it with eye-baffling celerity. His real weapons were dignity, self-confidence, and a reputation for being utterly fearless. Once he'd walked into this very bar to arrest an outlaw. Showing no gun, he'd merely taken from his pocket a sheriff's badge and exposed it in the palm of his hand. "I am Alfredo Baca. You will follow me, señor." Whereupon, taking obedience for granted, he had turned his back on the outlaw and walked three blocks to the *carcel*. "After you, señor." And the wanted man, two guns and all, had marched sullenly in.

That was Alfredo Baca.

Facing him now sat his crony, Colonel Calvin Harper. Grizzled and sixty, tall, lean, white-thatched, goateed, and blizzard-blistered, Calvin Harper had migrated from Texas after the Mexican war, bringing with him, together with a great herd of longhorns, a taste for plunging and a mind seamed with prejudices. Most deeply rooted of all were his prejudices against damnyankees and homesteaders. And since the Atchison, Topeka and Santa Fe was a damnyankee railroad born in Kansas, and since the Denver and Rio

4

Grande was another damnyankee railroad, and since whichever one came in was certain to bring a lot of damnyankee settlers to spread like ants over his own grama grass range, Cal Harper was implacably hostile toward both lines.

He expressed himself vigorously to that effect as Alfredo Baca reshuffled the cards.

"Odd or even, señor?"

"Even," said the old cattleman, and lost when the cut exposed a king.

A broad, square-cut man came in and strolled toward the rear. His white collar, bow tie, and double-breasted coat of black broadcloth identified him as a prosperous merchant rather than a rangeman. As he passed the odd-or-even game he paused to watch for a moment. His face was smooth-shaven, well-featured, and shrewd. It creased in a tolerant smile. "Keep that up, Cal," he predicted, "and some day you'll own the Linked Hearts, every hoof, horn, and acre."

"It's more likely," Harper growled, "that Alfredo here'll own the Rafter Cross."

Rafter Cross was Harper's brand and Linked Hearts was Alfredo Baca's.

"Will you join us, Señor Vogle?" invited Alfredo.

Adam Vogle grimaced and shook his head. "No, thanks. Fifty steers a cut's too steep for me. I'll stick to selling singletrees and saddles."

Vogle was the town's leading merchant. He was also its leading landlord and the owner, people said, of nearly a third of the realty in Las Vegas. For the past year he'd been buying up buildings, lots, close-in

5

acreage, with the idea of tripling his money when the railroad came. No one had ever seen him take a drink or riffle a card. A solid, sober citizen was Adam Vogle, and his only errand now in the Buena Suerte was to collect the rent. For that purpose he moved on into the office of his tenant.

The game continued, Alfredo occasionally taking a sip of wine and the colonel at intervals refilling his whisky glass. Finally Alfredo consulted his cuff, announcing with dismay, "*Caramba!* We have wasted our time. The luck has exactly balanced."

Harper scowled. "So we're even Steven, huh? Well, I'm sort of fed up with this peanut game anyway. What yuh say we make one good stiff bet and then quit?"

Sheriff Alfredo Baca sipped his wine and his eyes narrowed thoughtfully. "I too have been bored, señor, with these trifling wagers. It has no excitement, no suspense. I cut and you win; you cut and I win. And we get nowhere. I think it would be more interesting, señor, if we make one big bet and then wait a long time before we know who wins it."

The colonel stared. "Whata yuh mean, wait a long time?"

"We will still play odd or even," suggested Alfredo Baca. "But not with cards. We throw the cards away, like this." He hurled the cards across the barroom.

"You'd ruther flip a coin, huh?"

Alfredo spread his hands in distaste. "No, señor. Tossing a coin is as dull as cutting cards. My people have an old saying — nothing is sweet except what we wait for. And when it comes one must taste it slowly,

6

like the fine wine. You flip the coin — you cut the cards — and it's all over in a wink. That is not good. Do you agree, *señor amigo?*"

"Agree to what? Talk sense, Alfredo."

Alfredo looked dreamily out a window, gazing northeast. "Some day," he murmured, "the railroad will come to Las Vegas. Perhaps this year, perhaps next. But it will surely come. Will it come on an odd day of the month, like the seventh, or on an even day, like the fourteenth?"

"Hell!" snorted Cal Harper. "You think I'd wait a year to win one lousy little bet?"

"The longer you wait, señor, the longer the tingle of suspense. And as for the bet, it may be as large as you like."

Colonel Calvin Harper, whose forefathers had raced horses and fought cocks, and who himself had never been known to turn his back on a fair wager, caught the genius of it. Here was a hazard where the chances were exactly balanced either way. A decision which would creep closer day by day, for weeks, months, years possibly. But inevitably on a certain day, odd or even, the railroad would come to Las Vegas.

"It is a cup we can sip for a long time, señor," purred Alfredo. "For any stake you like. Say for a thousand steers?"

"We'd have to make it foolproof," Harper insisted. "The grade could come one day, the track another day, and the first train on still another. Or it could come part way through town and stop."

"There is a big cottonwood tree just east of the Exchange Hotel," Alfredo said. "When the first passenger train arrives as far as that *álamo*, that instant we will say the railroad has arrived in Las Vegas. Then and then only. I say it will be on an *odd* day, Señor Harper."

"For a thousand steers," Harper challenged, "it'll get here on an *even* day, Alfredo."

"Shall we shake hands on it, señor?"

They shook hands and the bet was made.

There was no witness, but it made no difference. On certain counts Alfredo did not quite approve of Calvin Harper. Harper, he knew, was a roughshod cowman. His ranch crew, out on the Rafter Cross, was the backwash from Texas, gun-slung bullies many of whom had records which wouldn't bear inspection. Killers, some of them. Harper had hired them, Alfredo suspected, to make the Rafter Cross range unhealthy for homesteaders. Folks whispered that a standard order at the Rafter Cross was: "If you see anyone digging a posthole, take a shot at him." And that another was: "If you find a butchered beef, toss a loop over the nearest damnyankee nester." Just how true it was, Alfredo Baca couldn't be quite sure. He did know, though, that old Cal Harper looked upon post-hole diggers and plows as tools of destruction; and upon six-guns as tools of conservation, usable in righteous wrath against all despoilers of the range.

Yet whatever his sins, however warped his code of range practice, Alfredo Baca knew that on at least one count Calvin Harper was a gentleman of unsullied honor. And on that same score Harper had complete trust in Alfredo Baca. They were both right. Neither of them would ever welsh on a bet.

CHAPTER
TWO

Dirty Work at the CLC

The Linked Hearts lay west of Las Vegas in the Glorietta Hills. Far to the east, where Conchas and Red creeks came together to make the Canadian River, lay Cal Harper's Rafter Cross. In between them, on an easterly fork of Gallinas Creek and reaching down to the Pecos, sprawled the widely scattered holdings of the Crown Land and Cattle Company, Limited, of London.

These were the days when England was banker for the world. Just as British capital often controlled mining properties in South Africa and tea plantings in Ceylon, so also were there vast cattle ranches in the American West whose every stockholder was a resident of the British Isles.

In the case of the CLC, in San Miguel County, New Mexico, an experienced stockman named Charles Swift was employed as manager. Charlie Swift had complete power of attorney to buy or sell cattle. He picked his own crew and made all operating decisions. The London stockholders asked only that he produce cash dividends or at least show profit on the hoof. Once a year they sent a representative to inspect the property and make an inventory of stock on hand.

An inspector from England was on the ranch now.

"We got one more bunch to look at, Mr. Templeton," Charlie Swift said.

"Righto." Archie Templeton climbed into the CLC buckboard. This was Thursday and his fourth day here. He was anxious to get started home.

Charlie flicked the reins and the team was off at a fast trot up the creek valley. In the bed of the vehicle was Archie Templeton's luggage. If the bunch up this way tallied out all right, he could drive straightway on to Las Vegas and catch the afternoon stage north. By ship, rail, and stage Archie had come, on this annual inspection for the London owners, and by stage, rail, and ship he must return home.

He grinned wryly. "Dashed long way to come just to count eight thousand cows. What?"

Charlie Swift nodded amiably. Deftly, holding the reins in his left hand, he twirled a cigarette with his right. "But cows ain't all you can report, Mr. Templeton. This here country's right on the edge of a big boom. Land's goin' up already. So's cattle. When the railroad comes, the CLC'll be worth twice what it is now. We won't have to drive all the fat offa steers gettin' 'em to market. We won't have to peddle 'em around to the Indian reservations. We can just haze 'em into cars at Vegas, and then sit back and wait fer the check."

Archie Templeton looked off across a sea of sagebrush which flanked a thin line of cottonwoods along the creek. "Are we on CLC land now?" he inquired.

"We're on CLC range," Charlie said. "If you mean do we own it in fee simple, we don't. We own a section or two where the house and corrals are and we own four groups of water holes, one south, one east, one west, and one north. In between is government land. We graze it free. So what's the use payin' taxes on it? Cattle's what counts. Beef on the hoof."

Archie consulted a leather-bound notebook which the manager had handed him on his arrival last Sunday. It was the CLC tally book. Thumbing through it, the Britisher saw that the present tally at the CLC was 8,084 head.

"That's everything but unweaned calves," Charlie explained. "We don't count 'em till we brand 'em."

"About this government land in between our water holes," Archie worried. "Won't settlers come in some day and claim it?"

Charlie laughed scornfully. "A few'll come in, maybe, but they won't stay long. This here's a cow country. A doggone good cow country but it ain't fit fer farmin'. Dry season's too long. It burns 'em out, those there nesters, and they soon leave."

"Do the other ranches around here operate the same way? I mean, by controlling land instead of owning it?"

"Sure they do. Take old man Harper out east o' here. He's got fifteen thousand head and don't own much land except a few scattered water holes. Same goes for Alfredo Baca up in the Gloriettas."

Archie saw a copy of the current CLC payroll in the tally book. Besides Charlie Swift's, there were only four names on it. "I didn't meet this man Lindsay, did I?"

"Mark Lindsay? Nope, he's down on the Pecos lookin' fer strays. A new hand, he is. Sorry you missed seein' him."

"How can you look after eight thousand head with just four men?"

"Four's plenty except fer spring and fall brandings. At them times we take on a few more. The way we run 'em, Mr. Templeton, it's easy. We keep 'em in four bunches 'bout the same size. One bunch we run south down around Gallinas Springs; that's the bunch you checked Monday. Another bunch we run east along the upper Conchas; you tallied them Tuesday. Then there's the herd you looked at yesterday, east along the main Gallinas. This bunch we're headin' for now, north up this creek, is the last of 'em."

A few miles farther Archie began to see cattle. He noted a big CLC on the right flanks. "Here's our first chunk o' salt up this way," Charlie explained, thumbing toward a block of rock salt on the creek bank. "We got a chunk about every half mile from here on. Cattle stay purty close to the salt you put out fer 'em."

It made the count fairly easy. Standing in the bed of the buckboard, Archie Templeton counted one hundred and seventy-five head. He made a note on a pad and they drove on. At the next salt block he counted more cattle, some close by, some grazing off toward the horizons. They continued on up the valley, Archie counting by tens. An approximate tally would be near enough.

By the time the cattle petered out, he had counted nineteen hundred and eighty head.

"Close enough," he exclaimed brightly. "About the same size as the bunch we rode through yesterday. Now what about making that stage?"

"You'll be on it," Charlie Swift promised. He cracked his whip.

An hour later the buckboard was kicking dust up the main street in Las Vegas. Charlie drew up at the stage station. The stage was there, ready to pull out for the railhead in Colorado. Charlie Swift transferred his guest's baggage to it. "Sorry you got to rush off, Mr. Templeton." He winked at the stage driver. "Stick around and I'll give you a job breakin' colts."

"Cheerio!" Archie Templeton shouted back as the stage rolled away.

Spurs clinking, Charlie Swift walked a few doors up the street to the Buena Suerte. He went in and said, "The same, Pedro." Pedro Gonzalez served him a rye highball.

The CLC manager sipped it, listening idly to talk along the bar. A pair of bell-hatted vaqueros from the Linked Hearts were there, and beyond them a couple of gun-slung punchers from the Rafter Cross. Swift heard one of the Rafter Cross men mutter to his companion, "The old man must be loco, makin' a bet like that!"

"Ain't it the truth, Buck? Me, I'll take three-card monte every time. Who the hell ever heard o' bettin' on a railroad? A thousand head, huh?"

A dark girl with a high comb in her hair came up to Charlie Swift. She hooked an arm through his and

14

pouted. "Where have you been all these time, *querido?* Will you buy me a drink?"

Charlie nodded to Pedro, who set out another highball. "I been busy, Carmencita. Bring me up to date. What's all this about somebody bettin' on a railroad?"

She told him of the bet between Colonel Harper and Alfredo Baca. The whole town was talking about it by now. "Are they not the grand sports, Charlie? A thousand beef. But poof!" She snapped her fingers. "To them it is nothing. They are *ricos.*"

"But the winner can't collect till the railroad comes," Charlie objected. "That's too long to wait."

"Ah, you gringos!" Carmencita sighed. "You do not understand." She stood close to Charlie with her lips near his. "A thrill, to be sweet, must linger — like the kiss. See?"

He pushed her away. "Some other time, Carmencita. I gotta fog back to the ranch."

He left her and went out, crossing to the Adam Vogle Mercantile Emporium. A Mexican clerk came up. "Your pleasure, señor?"

"Wrap up a box of forty-five shells, José."

While José was filling the order, Adam Vogle himself stepped up. "Hello, Charlie," he greeted. "Everything all right?"

"High and handsome," Charlie said. His eyes met Vogle's and something passed between them. Vogle's face, which had been anxious a moment ago, now relaxed. To the clerk it seemed that his employer had merely inquired if a customer was being served with satisfaction and dispatch.

"That's fine, Charlie," Adam Vogle said. "Anything I can do, let me know." He turned away.

Charlie Swift took his merchandise to the buckboard and drove out of town. It was dark when he arrived at the CLC.

The bunkshack was lighted. He could see his three regular hands, Stites, Forgy, and Dalhart, eating supper in there. Charlie Swift didn't stop till he reached the manager's cabin, fifty yards farther on. He hitched his team there and went in.

He had lighted a lamp in the ranch office before he realized he wasn't alone. A slim, curly-haired cowboy in a red-checkered shirt, and with a .45 gun holstered against his right *chaparajo*, was standing there rolling a cigarette.

Charlie Swift gave a start of surprise. "What are you doin' here, Lindsay? Thought I sent you down the Pecos lookin' fer strays."

"You did." There was something odd and stiff in Mark Lindsay's tone. "But I decided to quit. Figure up my time and I'll pull out."

A glint in Lindsay's level gray eyes gave Charlie Swift a chill. Did this kid know anything? Why did he want to quit?

"Don't yuh like it here, Lindsay?"

"No. I been here twenty-six days. You can pay me twenty-six dollars and I'll go."

But if he knew anything, Charlie Swift didn't dare let him go. He stalled. "You got any complaints, let's hear 'em."

"The only complaint I got," Mark Lindsay said, "is that this whole layout's crooked. I don't work for crooked outfits. I got twenty-six day's pay comin', though; so I'll take it and ride."

Swift hadn't worn a gun today. He'd laid aside his usual armament in order to make a more sober impression on the Englishman. But there was a gun in the desk drawer. Charlie Swift edged toward it. "All right, kid. I'll get you your money."

He was reaching a hand into the drawer when Lindsay's voice cracked a warning. "Keep away from that gun. You're looking at one now."

Charlie Swift saw it pointing at his head. He backed away from the desk. "What's this?" he demanded. "A holdup?"

"All I want, Swift, is what's coming to me."

The CLC manager didn't in the least mind giving him twenty-six dollars. But he must find out just how much Lindsay knew. So he hedged. "I don't owe you a thing, kid, because you didn't obey orders. I sent you down to the Pecos."

"To get me out of the way," Lindsay amended, "while that Englishman was here. I was curious to know why. So I doubled back and camped out the last four nights close by. And what did I see? I saw you show that Englishman two thousand head south of here, Monday, and two thousand head east of here, Tuesday, and two thousand head west of here, Wednesday, and two thousand head north of here today. But it was the same two thousand head all four times. You had Stites and Dalhart and Forgy shift 'em

17

by night. The tally book said eight thousand head. And that's what you made the Englishman think you got on hand. You covered up a shortage of six thousand cows. What you did with 'em is none of my business. But I don't work for outfits like that. So pay me off, and I'll ride."

Ride where? He might ride straight to the sheriff. Prospect of that panicked Charlie Swift. Alfredo Baca wouldn't stand for anything like this. That cocky little Mexican had a stiff code of honor. A shameful treachery, Baca would say, to cheat trusting foreign investors. So Alfredo Baca would come with a posse of guns and drag the entire CLC crew to court.

It was a chance Charlie couldn't take. With a flick of his arm he knocked the lamp off the desk. The lamp crashed and the office went dark. In the same split second Charlie made a dive for Lindsay's legs.

The impact buckled Lindsay and the gun flew from his hand. It left Lindsay flat on his chest with Charlie holding a tackler's grip on his knees. Charlie's legs were free and he kicked savagely, scoring a thump on Lindsay's head. "Stites! Forgy! Dalhart!" Charlie yelled. Lindsay twisted clear of him and Charlie lost him, for a moment, in the dark. Then a kick landed in his groin and he knew the cowboy was up. Charlie groped blindly for him. Knuckles grazed his chin. The cowboy was swinging wildly. Charlie closed in, touched flesh, and clinched, feeling Lindsay's hot breath on his face.

Somewhere on the floor near them lay Lindsay's gun. When Charlie loosened his grip to grope for it, Lindsay squirmed out of the clinch. Again Charlie lost

18

him until a solid punch jolted his nose. He yelled again for the bunkhouse crew. A chair toppled as Lindsay, groping for Charlie, tripped over it. Then the chair crashed down on Charlie's head. It mashed him flat. His chin bumped something on the floor and he knew it was Lindsay's gun. The ranch manager gripped it, rolled over, got to his knees ready to shoot at the next sound.

All he heard was a labored breathing and Charlie fired in that direction. He knew he'd missed when Lindsay's left hand suddenly gripped his gun wrist. The cowboy's right arm circled Charlie's neck and a spurred boot raked his shin. Charlie felt himself being pushed back. His shoulders bumped the wall. A hoarse whisper came from Lindsay. "Drop that gun."

The grip on his wrist kept Charlie from shooting again. But he wouldn't need to. The bunkshack crew must have heard the shot already fired. They'd come on the run. Charlie stood there, rigid, helpless, his back to the wall, his wrist in a vise. The squeeze on his neck was strangling him. Then he heard steps outside. The office door creaked open. From the dark came Forgy's voice — "What's goin' on?" A match flared in the hand of Ed Dalhart.

Mark Lindsay's back was toward them. He couldn't turn around without releasing Charlie Swift. A gun barrel banged on his head and he went down.

Stites lighted a lamp. Charlie Swift leaned against the desk, breathing heavily. He looked down at the man on the floor and said bitterly, "He knows everything. Get rid of him."

Forgy asked, "Is he dead?"

Charlie Swift said shakily, "What difference does it make? If he ain't, one more sock on the head'll do it. Take him away and bury him deep."

Forgy's faded eyes met Dalhart's. Sweat gleamed on Dalhart's broad red face. He pushed his hat back and mopped with a bandanna. "How come he got wise, Charlie?"

"Don't stand there gabbin'. He knows everything. Stites, you fork a bronc and ride to Vegas. Tip Vogle. But tell him he don't need to worry. This guy won't ever see daylight again."

Stites, a beanpole on long, bowed legs, nodded and went out.

Charlie said, "Al, you and Ed toss this guy in the buckboard. It's still hitched in front. I want the guy hauled clear off the CLC. Savvy? Then plant him three feet under sod."

Ed Dalhart picked up Lindsay's legs. Al Forgy took him by the shoulders. They carried him outside and tossed him in the bed of the buckboard. "He's out cold," Dalhart said. "But he's still breathin'. Better tie him up, Al."

Forgy took tie ropes and secured Lindsay, hand and foot. Then he climbed to the seat beside Dalhart, and they drove away. They took a dark trail north up the creek.

For a mile they said nothing. Finally Al Forgy remembered something. "We forgot to bring a spade, Ed."

Dalhart rolled a smoke broodingly. "For a long time I been worried about this deal, Al. Now I see a way out. We won't need no spade."

Forgy gave him a vacant stare. "But Charlie said —"

"To hell with Charlie. Same goes for that smoothie in town, Adam Vogle. When the time comes for a divvy, I don't trust neither of 'em. Not as far as you could throw a heifer by the tail."

"You mean they'd leave us outa the pot?" Forgy echoed. "They wouldn't dare."

Dalhart brooded a while longer. Then: "Look, Al. We drive off six thousand cows. It was Vogle's idea, and it was him who found the markets for 'em. So he's in on it. Them cows brang sixty thousand dollars. Vogle claimed we could triple it by investin' it in Las Vegas real estate. We hold it till the railroad comes, then sell out and divvy up. *Bueno*. He talked us into it. Here we are waitin' fer the railroad to come. When the boom comes we cash in, split up, and fade. But all that real estate's in Vogle's name. We was afraid to put in our names because us bein' just plain cowhands, people might wonder where we got all that coin. So Vogle and Charlie could sell out and keep it all, couldn't they?"

Flint came into Forgy's pale eyes. "If they try that," he swore, "they'll eat slugs."

"But there's a easier way," Dalhart suggested slyly. "Suppose we keep this kid puncher on ice. Stow him away at Goff's place up in the Truchas. Goff'll ride herd on him, all right, for as long as we say. Which'll be till the railroad comes. Till we sell out on a boom and it's time for a divvy. Then if Vogle tries to cross us, we got

21

him. We got a livin' witness we can turn loose any time we want."

"That," Forgy agreed, "would sure build a fire under Vogle."

"*Bueno*. Stop at the creek, Al. We'll throw some water in this guy's face. Then we'll haul him to Goff's."

CHAPTER
THREE

On the Trail of a Girl

Two hundred and fifteen miles northeast of Las Vegas, at the town of Otero, Colorado, a train pulled in from Kansas. A tall, broad-shouldered young man got off and mingled with the crowd on the platform. In that crowd were cattlemen, sheepmen, homeseekers, boomers, gamblers, railroad construction men, and drifters. The broad-shouldered young man towered half a head above most of them. He wore a .45 gun and a cartridge belt. On his head was a high-crowned, triple-dented sombrero with two bullet holes through it. His chamois vest hung open, exposing a shirt of creamy silk. His pants were corduroys tucked into scuffed half-boots. His bold-featured face, handsome enough to be looked at twice by any woman, was the color of a saddle which the baggageman now threw off. With a baggage check the young man claimed the saddle. He picked it up, slung it over his shoulder by a stirrup strap, and strode off down the street.

He might have been a cowboy, a sheriff ranging far afield, or a buffalo hunter. At times he had been all three. Just now he was looking for a covered wagon pulled by four white mules.

At Otero's main livery barn he inquired: "Did you happen to notice an outfit with four big white mules pass through here last week or two? Covered-wagon outfit. Man and a girl."

"Covered wagon? They's been lots of 'em. They team through here every day. I wouldn't remember any particular one."

"You'd remember this one. It's not often you see four matched white mules in one team. And they were leading a calico mare."

The liveryman's eyes narrowed. "Sure. I remember. They stopped and bought a sack of oats."

The young man's face brightened. "They did? How long ago was it?"

"Can't say exactly. Ten days or two weeks, I reckon."

"Which fork of the trail did they take outa here?"

"How would I know? Maybe they turned northwest up the Arkansas, toward Pueblo. Or maybe they kept on southwest down the Santa Fe trail. I didn't talk to 'em 'cept to sell 'em a sack of oats and fill their water kegs for 'em."

"They wouldn't bother to fill their water kegs, would they, if they meant to follow up the Arkansas River?"

"Humph! Reckon you're right, young feller. So I reckon they kept on down the Santa Fe trail. No water on it this side of El Moro."

"In that case," the young man said, "I'll buy a good horse if you got one."

The liveryman took him to a corral out back. The broad-shouldered young man looked over a score of range horses there. He knew horses like a sea captain knows ships. In the end he selected a big rangy bay. He paid cash for the horse and left his saddle there. "I'll want him early in the morning. Make the bill o' sale out to Kirk Calloway."

When the transaction was complete, Kirk Calloway started out. At the door he turned with one more question. "This outfit with the four white mules. They didn't happen to mention what their name is, did they?"

The liveryman shook his head. He stared quizzically at his customer. "You mean you been follerin' 'em down the Santa Fe trail and don't even know who they are?"

Calloway grinned sheepishly. "That's it," he admitted. "I don't even know who they are."

He went back to the depot and claimed his other piece of baggage. This was a slim, compact blanket roll with a saddle rifle inside of it.

The train had gone on, leaving the platform empty except for a station agent. For on this twenty-third day of February, 1878, the railroad was already in operation as far as Pueblo. Otero, however, was the end of it in the direction of its ultimate destiny, New Mexico and points southwest.

"When," Kirk Calloway asked the agent, "are they goin' to build on down the main trail?"

The agent pointed to a fifty-six-pound frog leaning against the depot. "See that frog? They'll be cuttin' it in any day now. Construction foreman's already here with men and materials. He's just waitin' fer a wire from the old man. Then they'll be off, hell-bent fer Santa Fe at a mile a day."

"What's been delayin' 'em?"

"New Mexico politics, mostly. They's people down that way who don't like Kansas railroads. Then there's been money troubles. Top o' that, there's a fight on with the Rio Grande. Ain't room fer but one line over Raton Pass. But our crowd'll win out, brother, and you can bet your saddle on it. This here line was named fer Santa Fe, and it's sure as hell goin' there."

Calloway carried his blanket roll to the hotel and checked in. After freshening up, he sauntered out to the street just in time to see a stage pull in from the southwest.

At the first opportunity he accosted the driver. "Did you meet a four-white-mule team on the trail, *amigo?* Covered wagon with a calico mare on a lead rope."

The driver was tired and a bit gruff. "I don't keep books on trail wagons. I've met thousands of 'em, in my time." He turned away.

A passenger was getting off the stage. He was a neat little man in a tweed suit. "Howdy, neighbor," Kirk Calloway greeted him. "How far you been ridin' this hack?"

"I got on at Las Vegas two days ago," the man said. His accent was distinctly British. "And I'm dashed glad to get off. When's the next train east?"

"Tomorrow," Kirk told him. "Reckon you'll have to bed down at the hotel." The two strolled that way.

"By the way," Kirk chatted, "do you recollect meetin' a covered wagon pulled by four white mules? It was headin' southwest along that same trail."

"Didn't notice it, old chap," Archie Templeton said. "But part of the time I was asleep."

They separated in the lobby, and Kirk went to his room.

Later, after supper, he went out to look over the town. The barrooms were full, and Kirk Calloway ran into half a dozen men he knew. Trailsmen, buffalo hunters, and shippers. Some of them he'd rubbed elbows with in Newton and Dodge City.

Most of the talk was about the railroad. When would the Santa Fe cut in that frog and start building southwest from here? Who would win out in the feud between the Santa Fe and the Rio Grande?

"The way I hear it," one old-timer said, "they're gonna change the name of this town."

"What to?" Kirk inquired idly.

"La Junta."

They were in a crowded barroom with card games going on in booths at one side. About half the customers were Mexicans. The rest were the same mixture of railroad builders and rangemen that Kirk had encountered often during the last five years at booming railheads in Kansas.

Through a gap in the crowd he caught sight of the Englishman who had just come in on the stage. He was engaged at two-handed stud with a swarthy, overdressed man whose sleeves were rolled to the elbows. This man's narrow, dark face was uncommonly handsome, and his black, crinkly hair hung in deep sideburns. A bulge at his left breast told Kirk that a gun nestled there.

Kirk shifted a little way down the bar to watch the Englishman's luck. Judging by the chips in sight he had already lost heavily. The eyes of the other man, and the deftness of his fingers, convinced Kirk that he was a professional sharper.

The Englishman lost three more pots in succession. *He'll be sheared like a lamb*, Kirk thought. His impulse was to warn the Englishman. He didn't because it wasn't any of his business. This was a country of raw individualism where every man was on his own.

The sharper shuffled expertly and offered the deck for a cut. The Englishman made the cut. But as the other man picked up the deck Kirk caught a flash of something palmed in his left hand. Kirk had a feeling that there were now fifty-three cards in play.

The sharper dealt two hole cards, face down, one to his opponent and one to himself. Then came a face-up king to the Englishman and a face-up queen to the dealer.

"King bets a blue," the Englishman said.

"Raise you a blue."

Kirk watched closely. With cheerful confidence the Englishman made a bet at each card dealt him, the sharper hiking him every time. When the deal was completed, the Englishman's four exposed cards were two kings, a nine and a queen. The sharper had two queens exposed with a jack and a five.

The sharper bet stiffly and was called. Then he turned over his hole card. It was a queen. "Three ladies," he announced.

Archie Templeton grimaced. "That beats me. I only got kings up."

His opponent had raked in the pot before the all too obvious truth struck Archie. "Hold on there, governor. How can there be five queens in one deck?" He exposed his hole card which was a queen.

The sharper's face flushed. "If there's five queens in the deck," he said coldly, "you must've put one there yourself."

"Why, you blasted bounder, you!" Archie was on his feet, flaming with indignation. He didn't get any further because he was looking at a gun. The gambler had plucked it from his left breast.

"I said you put it there yourself, Limey. Want to argue about it?" The gun was aimed at Archie's throat.

The whole barroom was looking on.

The tight silence was broken by Kirk Calloway. "If there's any slug-swallowin', Mr. Cold-decker, you'll do it yourself. Drop that gun."

The man's eyes flicked toward Kirk and saw the bore of Kirk's forty-five. "Who invited you in?" he challenged.

"Drop that gun," Kirk repeated. "I saw you palm that extra card. The gent gets his money back." He cocked the hammer.

The gambler dropped his gun. He glared balefully at Kirk. "Some day I'll get you for this, mister."

"Any time," Kirk said. He nodded to an overalled railroader standing by. "Count the deck, please. Then take a look in his pockets."

29

The railroader found fifty-three cards in the deck; also an extra ace and an extra king, with matching backs, were found in the sharper's coat pocket.

"Now take back what you had when you came in, Mr. —"

"Templeton. Archie Templeton. And thank you, sir." Archie repossessed himself of his losings.

A stocky man with a badge pushed through the crowd. He was Otero's town marshal. When the situation was explained to him, he turned sternly to the gambler. "This is the third complaint against you, Macklin. So I'm givin' you just twelve hours to get outa town. If you're around after the stage leaves in the morning, I'll toss you in the jug."

Macklin got sullenly to his feet. He got as far as the door, then turned to fix a bitter stare on Kirk Calloway. "We'll meet again some day," he warned.

Kirk sat down with Archie Templeton and Archie insisted on buying drinks. "If it weren't for you, sir, I'd be stony. May I ask your name?"

"Calloway. I'm heading down the trail in the morning."

"Into New Mexico?"

"Likely. Depends on whether I catch up with four white mules."

"I remember. You asked about them when I got off the stage. Are you in the cattle business, Calloway?"

"I've punched cows some," Kirk admitted.

"If you're ever down around Las Vegas, drop in at the CLC. I represent the owners." Archie produced a card and passed it across the table.

"British outfit, huh? Well, if I ever need a job I might take you up on that."

Still under the spell of gratitude, Archie wrote a note addressed to Charlie Swift. It directed that the bearer, Kirk Calloway, be afforded every courtesy at the ranch.

Kirk put it in his wallet. "Time I'm turnin' in now. So long and good luck, Templeton."

"Cheerio," Archie said.

It was barely daylight when Kirk Calloway rode out of town. He had taken the carbine from his blanket roll and put it into the saddle scabbard. The roll itself was tied behind the cantle. It meant slow riding, for Kirk himself in full range gear weighed considerably over two hundred pounds.

He held the bay to a running walk for the first ten miles. "I don't aim to push you any, Red," he promised. There was no use of it, for he didn't know how far or where he was going.

This was the broad, hoof-beaten, wheel-rutted Santa Fe trail. In places it was half a mile wide. Kirk passed a train of burros packed with bales of freight, heading for the railroad at Otero. Or what was that new name? La Junta? A few miles farther on he met a caravan of wagons, some bullock-drawn, some horse-drawn, all covered with New Mexico dust.

He came to an adobe cabin beside the trail. In a lean-to off it was a smithy and wheel shop. A brawny, bare-torsoed Mexican was pounding white-hot iron. Evidently he made his living shoeing horses and repairing wheels for trail outfits.

Kirk drew up and dismounted. "*Buenos días, señor.*" As a people he had always had a fondness for the Mexicans. He'd never known one of them to refuse shelter, water, or information.

This one laid aside his hammer and smiled a welcome. "May I serve you, señor?"

Kirk inquired, "Did you see a wagon with four big white mules pass down this way? Week or so ago?"

The brown smile widened. "Have I not eyes, señor? Ah, *que linda!*"

Kirk had never heard mules called lovely. Then he grinned as the Mexican added, "Her eyes are like the cornflower and her hair is like the sun, señor. Yes, they have stop here while I shoe a mule."

A cloud of dust came in sight, and Kirk heard the pound of trotting hoofs. A stagecoach came rocking down the trail. It was headed southwest, toward New Mexico, and must have left Otero only a little while after Kirk Calloway.

As it rolled by, he glimpsed the face of a passenger. The gambler, Macklin.

"This white-mule outfit," Kirk prodded. "Did they mention where they were going?"

The blacksmith shrugged. "*Quién sabe, señor?* Perhaps Trinidad, perhaps Santa Fe. They do not say."

Kirk thanked him and rode on in the wake of the stage. With a speed greater than his own, it was soon out of sight.

Later he stopped at a water hole to rest the bay. A wagoneer from Santa Fe was watering there. Kirk asked his usual question.

32

"Don't recollect seein' any white mules," the wagoneer said. "But I took the Taos Pass cut-off and came down Cimarron Canyon. That way I'd miss outfits on the main trail through Las Vegas."

Kirk rode on, sometimes at a canter, more often at a running walk. Twice during the afternoon he saw herds of antelope. But no buffalo. Buffalo had been getting scarce these last several years. Always he passed wagons and pack-trains plodding toward Otero.

Would he ever catch up with the four white mules? And what would he say when he did? A rich red suffused Kirk's face. He'd sound foolish if he told them the truth. "We got to figure out a story, Red. Shucks, we don't even know her name."

He'd only seen the girl for a brief hour, back at Cottonwood Falls, Kansas. She was riding alone on the prairie and had seemed distressed and confused. Astride a calico mare, in the sunset, with her yellow hair loose in the wind, she had enchanted Kirk Calloway. One of her mules had strayed, she said. A big white mule with dappled flanks and branded spur-on-jaw. Kirk had found the mule for her. It was grazing back of a hill.

So she'd invited him to supper and he'd ridden with her to a covered wagon by the trail. Her father was there, a big, bluff, homespun fellow with a square white beard. His campfire was crackling when they rode up, and he'd thanked Kirk for finding the mule.

Kirk had only lingered with them for an hour. Long enough to warm himself by the fire. Long enough to eat a cornbread supper. Long enough to realize he'd missed something in his lonely, wandering life. Long enough to fall in love.

He hadn't known it, then. He'd said good-by without even giving his name, or asking theirs. He knew nothing about them except that they had a calico mare, four white mules, and a covered wagon, and that the tongue of that wagon was pointing west down the Santa Fe trail.

Why hadn't he asked them a few questions? Perhaps it was because of the peculiar code of reticence in men like Kirk Calloway. Reared among rough-cut rangemen, he'd learned to talk impersonally with strangers.

Two restless, dissatisfied weeks, and then he'd taken a train down the Santa Fe trail as far as rails went. He could gain on them, that way. But they were still ahead of him, the girl and the four white mules. Jogging along now he saw in the distance two high, snowy cones, exact twins, and he knew they were the Spanish Peaks. Stringing easterly from them along the state line was a chain of box mesas. She, the girl with the blue eyes and the yellow hair, was somewhere between those mesas and the setting sun.

CHAPTER
FOUR

Vogle's Scheme

In a town of gun-wearers, like Las Vegas, Adam Vogle's lack of one made him unique. Coupled with the facts that he never drank or smoked or raised his voice in a quarrel, his gunless personality made him stand out as a model citizen. A man of vision, too, people said. His faith in the town's future was inspiring. Didn't he invest every dollar he could lay hands on in local property?

A man from Santa Fe, changing stages here, dropped into the Vogle Mercantile Emporium to buy a traveling bag. "Howdy, Mr. Vogle. That was sure some bet those fellows made! How many steers was it? A thousand?"

Vogle, his solid figure neatly encased in a double-breasted broadcloth coat, nodded gravely. "Yes, it was for a thousand steers. As for myself, I never bet."

The customer grinned. "Odd or even, huh? Well, that beats me. I've heard of betting on a horse race. Or a rooster fight. But now I've heard everything."

"How could you know about it?" Vogle inquired. "You just got in from Santa Fe."

"Sure. But they know all about it up there, too. A think like that gets around, Mr. Vogle."

Vogle was later convinced of this when a couple of sheepmen from Taos came in. They were discussing the Baca-Harper bet.

A shrewd thought came to Vogle. In time people all up and down the trail would hear about this strange odd-or-even wager. It would put the name of Las Vegas on thousands of lips, and in many far places. It would make sensational publicity. Better than that, it would connect Las Vegas with the southwesterly march of empire.

Handled cleverly, it should advertise Las Vegas better than a full-page display in a Chicago paper. People north and east had heard of Santa Fe, but few of them had ever heard of Las Vegas. Now talk of this bet would imprint Las Vegas on their minds. Adam Vogle wanted a boom here. He was loaded with buildings, lots, close-in acreage. He wanted people to pour in and bid up the price. Advertising would do it. And here was an ad which wouldn't cost him a cent.

But an ad, to be effective, must be repeated and hammered home. Gossip about the bet would spread like a prairie fire, but unless fanned or re-lit it would die out.

Vogle saw a way to keep it burning. He went out and crossed to the Buena Suerte saloon and gambling-hall. He owned the building, although he had nothing to do with its operation. At the bar now was a line of drovers and gun-slung cowhands.

Two were Rafter Cross men. Adam Vogle edged to a place by them and ordered a sarsaparilla. It was the strongest thing he ever imbibed.

36

One of the Harper hands grinned at him. "Ain't yuh afraid you'll choke on that, Mr. Vogle?"

Vogle smiled amiably. "Hello, Chuck. How's everything at the Rafter Cross?"

"Slow," Chuck said. "Nothin's happened lately in our outfit, 'cept that big bet the boss made with Alfredo Baca."

Vogle nodded. "Yes, I heard about that. Listen, Chuck. Is it true Alfredo offered to make it two thousand steers, instead of only one? And that the colonel said it was a bit too steep?"

Chuck and his companion stared. They shook their heads slowly. "Somebody's been kidding you, Mr. Vogle. Our boss scared of a bet? Don't make us laugh."

"I didn't believe that part of it, myself," Vogle said. He put down his glass and went out.

A few doors down the street he entered José Herrera's cantina. Being owner of this building, too, he seemed now to make only a casual inspection. The patronage was entirely Mexican. At a table were two Linked Hearts vaqueros. Vogle stopped for a moment to chat and skillfully led them to discussion of their patron's wager with Colonel Harper.

The vaqueros expanded. They were proud of their patron, Don Alfredo. A grand *caballero*, Don Alfredo, who could win or lose a thousand steers like a snap of the fingers.

"Is it true," Vogle inquired with a bantering smile, "that the colonel wanted to make it two thousand instead of only one? But Alfredo was afraid to go that high?"

Both vaqueros were indignant. "*Caramba!* Don Alfredo, he fears nothing. He would be insult if he hears that, señor."

"I suppose you're right, Manuel," Vogle conceded. "His shirt or his ranch, it would make no difference to Alfredo."

He went out and turned toward the plaza. This was a wide place in the road, where adobe structures formed a square with a public well in the middle. The two-story Exchange Hotel was on the plaza, and Adam Vogle entered it for the purpose of spreading rumor. He must start talk to the effect that one of those two betters was more daring than the other. Whispers of it were sure to reach Baca and Harper. Each would resent any intimation that he was afraid to make a sky-limit bet.

Vogle, without showing his own hand, wanted to goad them into raising the ante. The bigger the bet, the more sensational the publicity for Las Vegas. It would probably take a year for the railroad to come. Vogle could envision it creeping closer and closer each month, suspense growing tighter as it neared the finish line. If their vanities were skillfully challenged, Baca and Harper might be induced to hike the bet again and again. Nothing would suit Adam Vogle better than for them to wager ranch against ranch, herd against herd, hoof, hide, and horn.

He turned in at the Exchange bar. Then he drew back. For at the bar he saw Charlie Swift. Charlie was in liquor; he was red-faced and talking volubly. Adam Vogle didn't like it. Charlie and his loose tongue were hazards.

Vogle went back to his store brooding. Sight of Charlie Swift reminded him of the narrow escape a few days ago. The lid had nearly blown off on account of a cowboy named Mark Lindsay. Charlie Swift should have had more sense than to hire that fellow. And right on the eve of an inspection by an English stockholder! But Charlie said he was short a stray man. He'd assured Vogle that he could get the boy away on some distant errand during the four-day tally.

Well, that particular hazard was passed now. Lindsay, according to Forgy and Dalhart, was deep under sod on the prairie. But nothing like that must ever happen again. Partners were always a risk. You couldn't trust them. Especially when they got plastered every week or so like Charlie Swift. Adam Vogle, by nature, was a lone wolf. He didn't like running with a pack.

For the first stages of his plan he'd needed them. That part of it was over now. Six thousand cows had been turned into cash, and the cash invested in Las Vegas properties. It was all held in Vogle's name. The next stage was to wait for the railroad and in the boom sell out at three to one.

Fretfully Vogle reviewed his position. It was perfect except for the existence of four confederates. He'd taken no active part in the cow-steal. When the loss was discovered, he couldn't be connected with it. He was safe except for a slip by Swift, Stites, Dalhart, or Forgy.

Decision steeled Vogle's eyes as he called a clerk. "Bring out my rig, Jose."

The rig was a two-horse buggy in which Vogle sometimes drove about collecting rents.

39

He went out to it with a package under his arm. The package was about the size and shape of a shoe box. He put it under the buggy seat and drove out of town.

A few miles down the Gallinas Creek meadow he turned west up a swale between two piñon hills. The swale narrowed, deepened, and became a canyon. At the head of it Adam Vogle got out with his package. He walked another fifty yards to a spot where he'd often been before. Strewn on the ground were hundreds of empty brass shells.

Vogle opened the package and brought out a .45 gun, two boxes of cartridges, and four cloth bull's-eye targets. He selected four piñon trees close together. Against the bole of each, breast-high, he tacked a target.

He sat down on a stump and loaded the gun. He put it in his inner breast pocket. Two targets were directly in front of him, one slightly to the right, the other slightly to the left. None of them was more than three yards away.

They might be four men with whom he was supping at a bunkhouse table.

Deliberately he drew, swung the gun in an arc as he fired four times.

Two targets showed a hole in the bull's-eye. A third was clipped in the three-ring. The fourth, his last shot, he'd missed altogether.

That wouldn't do. Many times he had come here to practice. He must keep it up until he could score four bull's-eyes.

Swiftness of draw didn't matter. There'd be the element of surprise. Who would expect the gunless Adam Vogle to pull a gun? He could even bring out the gun idly, saying he'd found it on the range and did anyone know who'd lost it? Then he could —

Again Vogle swung the gun in an arc, firing four times. This was better. One bull's-eye, two fours and a three. Still, it wasn't good enough.

He continued to reload and fire. For an hour he sat there. Empty cylinders of brass accumulated at his feet.

Finally he made four bull's-eyes.

Another salvo and he did it again.

He could do it. So why wait any longer? From the first he'd planned this. But he'd intended to wait until the sell-out and it was time to divvy up.

Yet why risk a slip in the meantime? Another incident like that close squeak with Lindsay? Why not now? Vogle went grimly back to his buggy. If he hurried, he could make the CLC bunkshack for supper tonight.

CHAPTER
FIVE

The Race for the Pass

Near sunset of February twenty-sixth, Kirk Calloway rode into El Moro, Colorado. He had come eighty miles on his journey from Otero.

At El Moro he saw a depot and a tiny engine switching freight cars. He knew that the Denver and Rio Grande had dropped a narrow-gauge track down here from Denver. It was therefore eighty miles nearer to Raton Pass, bottleneck gateway to New Mexico, than the Santa Fe. Had he wanted to, Kirk could have come this far by train. He could have stayed on his Santa Fe train to Pueblo, and there changed to the D. & R.G. narrow gauge.

But in that case he might have overridden his objective. If the white-mule outfit had chosen to file on land between Otero and El Moro, he would have missed them by circling around through Pueblo.

Inquiries had now assured him that they'd gone on.

Kirk put the bay in a livery barn for feed and a rub-down. He didn't plan staying all night here. Kirk knew a man named Dick Wooten who lived only about twenty miles farther on, and he could push on that far after supper.

As he was eating at a lunch counter near the depot, Kirk heard a train rattle in. Passengers from Denver and Pueblo alighted, and two of them came into the eating-place. They were biggish men in huge greatcoats, collars turned up against the chill evening wind. Each was a man to look at twice, forceful, with the appearance of an executive used to driving hard against obstacles. They took seats at the counter near Kirk.

One of them whispered, "Did you notice who got off that other coach, Robby?"

"Don't tell me it was General Palmer."

"Worse than that. It was McMurtrie and De Remer."

"That means a leak, Morley."

Morley nodded. He was a shrewd-eyed man in his forties, with bushy sideburns covering most of his face. "It can't be a coincidence, Robby. They must have gotten wind we were coming. I wonder how."

"Don't forget we use the same wire into Pueblo, Morley. We long ago broke their code. No doubt they've broken ours."

Morley frowned. "I see. Means we'll have to hurry."

They gulped coffee and were gone.

Kirk saw them half an hour later as he called at the livery barn for his horse. He was just mounting the bay when the two men rushed in. "We want a rig. And your best team. We might have to keep it out several days. Can you have it ready in an hour?"

Kirk didn't hear any more. He rode off down the dark street and forded the Picketwire River. A four-mile jog up its other bank brought him to the rival town of Trinidad. The place was quiet and lightless. Kirk turned up the collar of his sheepskin coat and rode on. "Hate to keep you up this late, Red, but we'll do better if we bed down at Wooten's."

The trail led him into an ascending canyon, winding between piñon slopes, narrowing with each mile. But it was better than most mountain roads, and Kirk knew why. He knew that Dick Wooten himself had built it over the pass, hacking, blasting, cutting, and filling for twenty-seven rough, steep miles.

It was nearly midnight when, just below the pass, Kirk came to a chain across the trail. This was Wooten's tollgate. A group of buildings loomed just beyond it. Wooten's house, roadside hotel, stables, and wagon sheds. Everything on feet must pay to pass here.

A Mexican boy appeared and took down the chain. Kirk tossed him a dollar and rode on to the hotel. Its windows were lighted. Kirk heard gay young voices and the strumming of guitars. "Don't you folks ever sleep?" he asked the boy.

The boy grinned. "Uncle Dick likes company," he said. "And *los jóvenes* like the *baile*."

"Sure," Kirk agreed, "young folks like to dance." He went to a stable and off-saddled. He'd only met Wooten once, on a buffalo hunt in eastern Colorado, but he'd heard of the man all his life. As who hadn't? Dick Wooten, trader, Indian fighter, rancher, pal of Kit Carson, scout for Fremont, and now proprietor of the most famous toll pass in the southwest. Naturally a man like that would attract hero-worship from Trinidad and surrounding settlements. And, just as naturally, the

44

young people hereabouts would pick Wooten's mountain hotel for their weekly frolics.

Kirk went in and registered. In the dining-room off the lobby a dance was in full swing. A knotty, bearded man in his late sixties strolled out of it and met Kirk face to face. Kirk put out a hand. "Remember me, Uncle Dick?"

Wooten didn't. But he recognized Kirk as one of his own breed and made him welcome. "Show him a room, Juan." To Kirk he added, "Soon as you've slicked back yer hair, young fellah, come down and jine in."

Kirk went up to his room. He didn't feel like dancing. He was saddle-weary and needed sleep. But he wanted to ask Wooten if four white mules had passed through the tollgate here.

He returned downstairs but couldn't, for a while, get the ear of the old frontiersman. A group of teenagers had him encircled. Others were whirling to guitar music. A Mexican *linda*, sitting alone, smiled seductively at Kirk.

"Tell us, Uncle Dick," a Trinidad boy was asking, "how come you built this wagon road over the pass?"

"Well, son," Wooten said, "it was like this. Back in 'fifty-two I driv nine thousand head o' sheep from Taos, New Mex, all the way to the gold camps of California."

"Gee! That was some drive, Uncle Dick. How long did it take you?"

"A hun'erd and seven days, son. And I found them gold miners plenty hungry fer mutton. Sold them nine thousand head o' sheep, I did, and rid back with fifty thousand dollars in my saddlebags."

"In gold?" the boy marveled.

"In gold and gold drafts, son. Then I figgered I'd better spend it some way so it'd fetch me security fer my old age. So I picked this pass. Got me a franchise from the two territorial legislatures of Colorado and New Mex. It said if I built a good wagon road over the pass, I could charge fer it. So here I am."

At the first chance Kirk put in a query of his own. Dick Wooten answered it promptly. "Yeh, I recollect 'em because you don't often see four matched white mules like that. They was a right cute gal in the outfit, too."

"How long ago was it?"

"We don't keep books on folks passin' through. But seems like it was about a week back. Hello! Didn't I hear a rig drive up?"

The door opened and two overcoated men came in. They were the pair Kirk had seen at El Moro.

Wooten's eyes lighted up. "Dern't if it ain't Mr. Robinson! Hi there, Robby." He shook hands warmly.

"And this is Ray Morley," Robinson said. "Ray's my number-one grader."

Dick Wooten clapped his hands. "Step up, everybody," he shouted to the dance floor, "and meet distinguished guests. This here's Mr. Albert Alonzo Robinson, chief engineer of the Santa Fe railroad. And this here's his top *segundo*, Mr. Ray Morley."

The young people flocked up, chattering. Robinson and Morley exchanged disturbed glances. But Wooten, with a chuckle, reassured them. "You don't need to worry none, Robby. They're Trinidad kids, and

46

Trinidad's on your side. It's kinda sore at the D. & R.G. fer pickin' El Moro as a terminal fer that branch down from Denver. So if it comes to a race, us folks are all pullin' fer the Santa Fe."

The two engineers relaxed. "In that case," Robinson said, "I'll let you in on a secret. Tomorrow the Santa Fe will start construction over Raton Pass. That is, if we can make the necessary arrangements with you, Uncle Dick. It'll wreck your toll business, but we're prepared to pay you whatever's right."

Wooten stared. "You're startin' to build on the pass in the mornin'? How the heck can you do that? Your rails end at Otero, a hun'erd miles back up the line."

Robinson smiled. He was a bold-featured man with a heavy black mustache and wavy hair roached high in front. He explained: "We don't have to build the line rail by rail, as we go. We can start grading anywhere. Raton Pass is the key point, the bottleneck; you couldn't possibly squeeze more than one railroad through it. So we begin there. In the morning."

"What with?" Wooten questioned.

"With a grading gang Lew Kingman's bringing up from Willow Springs and Cimarron. The minute we start dirt flying on that grade, the pass is ours forever. Rails and ties can catch up later."

One of the youngsters let out a cheer. Wooten smiled grimly. "Help yourself, Robby."

"We want to do right by you, Uncle Dick," Robinson said. "Whatever you think's fair. President Nickerson mentioned fifty thousand dollars."

The old Indian fighter considered the offer gravely. His response astonished everyone in the room. "No, at my age I reckon I don't need that much money all in one lump. Wouldn't know what to do with it. Tell you what, Robby — you give me and my family a lifetime pass and twenty-five dollars a month in groceries, and we'll call it square."

The deal was made on exactly those terms.

As Robinson and Wooten were shaking hands on it, a horseman galloped up outside. The rider came dashing in. "Are those Santa Fe gents here?" he asked breathlessly.

"Yes. I'm Chief Engineer Robinson. What's up?"

"I'm from Trinidad," the rider explained. "They's somethin' you oughta know. Them fellahs've rounded up a gang of men and wagons. And tools. They're on the way now."

"You mean the D. & R.G. engineers? McMurtrie and De Remer?"

"That's right. They aim to start flingin' dirt before daylight. They got wind of your game, Mr. Robinson; so they figger to beat yuh to the pass."

People had said of Albert Alonzo Robinson that he was the greatest railroad builder in America. Here was a chance to prove it. He turned gravely to the only recruits available, a score of young couples dressed for dancing. "Boys, want to go to work for the Santa Fe?"

"What doin'?" a boy asked.

"Digging. Mostly it'll be standing on a certain spot with a shovel in your hands — and not letting anyone push you off it. The job starts right now and lasts till noon, at more pay than you ever earned in your life."

The boy grinned and looked at Wooten. "Gimme a shovel, Uncle Dick."

Almost to a man the other youngsters volunteered.

Robinson noticed Kirk Calloway standing there. His eyes fixed on a .45 gun slung from Kirk's hip. "We'll need a guard, young man. Somebody to see that this crew of mine isn't disturbed. How about it?"

"I'm hired," Kirk said. "Calloway's my name."

Robinson slapped him on the back. "Good. We don't want any shooting. At the same time we're not going to let 'em push us around." He turned briskly to Wooten. "I want every team, wagon, and tool you've got, Dick."

"They're yours," Wooten agreed. "Boys, go out and throw harness on everything in the stalls. Load every pick and shovel you can find. Juan, there's a few freighters asleep upstairs. Rout 'em out. Tell 'em they're going to work. And see if you can find my buffalo gun."

He went stamping about, shouting orders. Kirk buttoned on his sheepskin coat and went out to saddle Red.

By three o'clock they were all trooping up the hill. Wagons loaded with picks, shovels, and crowbars, Robinson and Morley in a buggy, Kirk at their wheel on Red, and a crowd of chattering boys who had deserted their partners to become railroaders. Boots clicked on the flinty trail, and lanterns flickered in the dark. Wheels rumbled over the crude plank bridges which Dick Wooten had built over the tumbling canyon creek.

The gorge narrowed, and in a sheer-walled box of it Ray Morley stopped them. "This is the place. We begin right here."

He got out with a lantern and found a stake. Then he sighted a line by eye straight toward the pass. "String out along that line, boys, and begin leveling the ground."

Shivering in the cold night air, the crew began work. Dick Wooten laid aside his buffalo gun and took up a shovel.

Kirk tied Red to a pine sapling. Robinson called to him. "This way, Calloway."

The chief engineer led Kirk about ten yards downtrail from the strip being graded. "Just stand here, Calloway. You get the idea?"

Kirk grinned. "You bet I do, Mr. Robinson." He took a wide-legged stance facing down the trail and loosened his holster flap. From the darkness below came the rumble of wheels.

"There they come," Robinson said grimly. "But we got here first."

Kirk asked, "When do you figure to get rails and ties this far?"

"We've already cut in the frog at Otero," the chief said. "That's a hundred miles from here. If we lay track at a mile a day we'll be here in about four months."

"Steep climb up here. Don't you aim to tunnel through?"

"Later, yes. But first we'll just run a shoofly switchback over the pass and down into Raton, New Mexico."

"You mean Willow Springs?"

Robinson nodded. "But the railroad'll call it Raton."

"That as far as you're going?"

"No, we'll push on to Las Vegas. That will probably be our temporary terminal till we can dig up some more finances. A railroad's like a cowboy, Calloway. It's always going broke."

Kirk saw lanterns and heard voices from the darkness downtrail. The shape of a wagon loomed, its wheels crunching gravel. Behind it came other wagons all loaded with men and tools. A dozen horsemen flanked the wagons. On the lead vehicle rode two D. & R.G. engineers.

These two jumped to the ground as the head of the caravan stopped within five yards of Kirk Calloway.

Kirk faced them with his hand resting on the butt of his forty-five. Behind him he heard the shovels of Ray Morley's crew punching at the hard ground.

"Sorry, De Remer," Robinson called out. "But you're half an hour too late."

The D. & R.G. man glared at him. "You can't get away with this, Robinson. Our rails are eighty miles closer than yours."

"But can't you see we're grading?" Robinson challenged. "The pass belongs to the Santa Fe by right of prior construction."

Men were piling out of the wagons. Most of them were Mexican laborers recruited in and around El Moro. They carried picks, shovels, crowbars. A voice from the crowd yelled, "Unload that fresno, Jake. Take

51

two teams and hitch on to it. Sam, get that powder and we'll do a little blasting."

"Not on this pass, you won't," Kirk Calloway warned.

A man on a spotted pony pressed forward. He wore crossed belts and two guns. His face, in the pale lantern light, seemed vaguely familiar to Kirk.

"Who's gonna stop us?" the man growled.

"You're lookin' at him," Kirk said. "You say you got powder and want to do a little blastin'. I got some powder, too. Six shellsful."

The man swung to the ground and took a menacing step forward. But De Remer restrained him. "Hold on. We better talk this over." He turned to his fellow engineer and held a whispered conference.

It was still only a little after four in the morning. Ray Morley came up and took a stand between Kirk and Robinson. "De Remer," he yelled, "you and McMurtrie might as well turn around and go home. Only way you can get through here is to shoot your way through. You try that and you'll answer in court."

The man with two guns jeered, "You gonna let 'em bluff us? Say the word and I'll cut loose."

"Need any help, Calloway?" The voice was Dick Wooten's. The old Indian fighter appeared at his elbow with a buffalo gun. "Who said somethin' about cuttin' loose?"

Alarm overspread the faces of De Remer and McMurtrie. They led their gunman back to a fire one of the Mexican laborers had kindled by the trail. There they went into a worried huddle.

"I've seen that guy before, somewhere," Kirk muttered to Wooten.

"You mean that two-gunny?" Wooten said. "He's been hangin' around El Moro lately, lookin' for trouble. Name's Roach."

"And that spotted mare of his!" Kirk brooded. "Seems like I've seen *it* before, too. That big white patch on the left flank —" He stopped, staring into the lantern light at Roach's mount. A calico mare!

It was like the one the girl had ridden, back at Cottonwood Falls, Kansas. The one belonging to the four-white-mule outfit. But Kirk couldn't be sure. There were lots of calico mares. He hadn't noticed any brand on the girl's mount.

But the name Roach registered. "I took a job as deputy under Bat Masterson last spring, back at Dodge City," Kirk told Wooten. "This guy Roach shot up the town one night, and we made him shag his shanks farther west."

"How come," Wooten wondered, "we find him workin' for the Rio Grande?"

Ray Morley offered a simple explanation. "McMurtrie and De Remer recruited all the laborers they could pick up in El Moro. They expected to get here first. But they needed a guard, same as we did. They looked in some bar and saw a two-gunny there. So they hired him. Chances are they don't even know his name."

"Want me to start him running?" Kirk asked.

Robinson shook his head. "You mean do we want you to start shooting? Definitely no."

"I won't need to shoot. If my hunch is right, he'll be high-tailin' it outa here in five minutes." Kirk raised his voice. "Hi, Roach, where'd you get that calico mare?"

Roach, at the fire, whirled sharply. "Who wants to know?"

"A four-white-mule outfit wants to know. They lost a mare like that as they passed through El Moro."

Roach didn't answer. Leading the mare, he backed out of the firelight, and darkness swallowed him. In a few minutes Kirk heard hoofbeats retreating down the trail.

Ray Morley chuckled. He yelled at De Remer, "Looks like your main gun deserted. Give up?"

De Remer came sullenly to face them. "This isn't the only pass over the hump," he said. "We know a better one."

"That so?"

"Sure. We had this country surveyed to a gnat's eyebrow before the Santa Fe ever got west of Dodge. There's a better route up Chicken Canyon and down Dillon Canyon on the New Mex side."

"We know about that," Morley bantered. "It's seven miles longer and a lot rougher. Help yourself. We'll keep this one."

"Keep it and be damned," De Remer retorted. "We're going up Chicken Canyon. See you in Las Vegas. There'll be a D. & R.G. train waiting when you get in."

As cold gray dawn broke, the Rio Grande caravan turned and went rumbling back down the trail.

Robinson smiled broadly. "That Chicken Creek route's impractical, didn't you say, Ray?"

54

"Sure it is. And they'll soon find it out." Morley turned to Kirk and shook hands. "Thanks, Calloway. You've helped us make history."

Robinson added, "And the Santa Fe doesn't forget its friends. If you ever want a pass, just drop me a line."

Kirk stood by as guard over the graders till noon. Then reinforcements under Lew Kingman came along, and he wasn't needed any more. He said good-by to Dick Wooten and rode on over the pass.

In midafternoon he dropped into the town of Willow Springs, soon to be re-named Raton. At the livery barn there he inquired about four white mules.

"Sure," the liveryman said, "that outfit passed through four-five days ago. They stopped to buy a ridin'-pony."

"Did they say why they needed one?"

"Yep, they said the pony they'd had disappeared one night while they was camped on the Picketwire, over by El Moro. Friends of yourn, are they?"

"I saw them one time. Man and a girl? Did they mention their names?"

"Yeh, I had to give 'em a bill o' sale for the sorrel mare they bought. But I didn't keep no record of it. Seems like the name was Dunton or Duncan or somethin' like that."

"They say where they were heading?"

"Nope. They trailed southwest outa here, with the gal ridin' the sorrel."

Kirk thanked him and rode on.

CHAPTER
SIX

The Dunbars File a Claim

On that same twenty-seventh of February, ninety miles farther down the trail, Alex Dunbar forded the clear, cold riffles of Gallinas Creek. Just beyond the ford he came to a Mexican plaza — a square of adobe houses all facing inward, compactly, except for an opening on each side to permit the entrance of wagons.

Alex Dunbar drove his four white mules through one of these openings and stopped at a well in the center of the square. On one side was a tiny church. All the houses were flat-roofed and very old, their mud bricks crumbling. A sign by the well said: *Nuestra Señora de los Dolores de Las Vegas*.

"What does it mean, Christine?"

The girl beside him on the wagon seat had been studying Spanish avidly ever since leaving Iowa. She translated promptly. "Our Lady of Sorrows of the Meadows. What a pretty name, Father! But it doesn't look like the place Mark wrote us about."

"I can see dust a mile or two farther on," Alex said. "And some more houses. Maybe that's the main town." He clucked to the mules and drove on out the other side of the plaza.

Beyond here the Gallinas Valley broadened into a great level meadow. The trail, diverging from the creek, followed the meadow's edge and presently became the street of a town. Here again were flat-roofed adobes. And here, unlike at the sleeping plaza just passed, was life and commerce. More houses going up. Heaps of mud bricks sun-drying in the vacant lots. A street full of people and teams and tethered horses. Wagons loaded with green lumber for partitions. Saloons. Finally the trail widened into a plaza bigger and newer than the one back at the creek.

Christine's eyes searched the plaza walks. "I don't see Mark anywhere, Father. He said he'd meet us here."

"How could he meet us, Chris, when he didn't know what day we'd come? Chances are he left a note sayin' where we can find him." He drove on to the post office and stopped there.

Christine jumped to the ground. "I'll run in and see." As she crossed the walk, men all along the street observed her with frank admiration. Yellow-haired girls who wore pants tucked into spurred boots weren't often seen this far southwest.

She was in the post office only a few minutes. She came out with a letter and climbed to the wagon seat with it. "It's been there a month, Father."

Christine opened it eagerly, her eyes brushing through the message enclosed. Then she read the impersonal part of it aloud.

" 'The country out east of here is the best stock range you could find anywhere. But it's no good for farming except a few little strips of creek bottom. Unless you pick one of those strips, you'll go busted. This big meadow here at Vegas is all taken up. But I spotted a couple of adjoining quarter sections on Conchas Creek that are still open. They're the north half of section 33. You can look up the township and range at the land office. This spot's right where two forks of Conchas Creek come together. I blazed a cottonwood there and cut Chris's initials on it. You'd have a mile of running water and 320 acres of rich, loamy bottom land. You can't beat it in all New Mexico. Rafter Cross has a salt trough on it, but it's government land. I'll be seeing you. Mark.'"

There was a postscript. "'While I'm waiting for you to show up, I'll find me a job riding for some cow outfit around here.'"

"Sounds good, Chris," Alex Dunbar said. "You could file on one quarter and I could file on the other. We'll go out and have a look."

"Shouldn't we find Mark first, Father?"

"Mark'll keep. He'll hear we hit town and look us up. Right now let's get these mules fed and stalled."

A sign down the street advertised a livery barn. Alex drove there, a sorrel mare bought at Willow Springs following at the end of a lead rope. "They've come a long way," Alex said to the liveryman. "I want 'em treated right. Oats and bright dry hay." He looked the stalls over personally, insisting that they be bedded with fresh straw. Iowa-bred, Alex Dunbar always fed his stock before feeding himself and family.

58

He took Christine back to the plaza and engaged rooms at the Exchange Hotel. They were second floor rooms whose unplastered pine walls went only part way to the ceiling. "Not much privacy, Chris," Alex grinned, "but it'll only be for one night."

He went then to the bank and opened an account. The banker expanded when he saw the draft Alex presented. It was for twelve thousand dollars. "Glad to have you with us, Mr. Dunbar. Anything else we can do for you?"

"You can tell me where the land office is."

The banker took him outside and pointed. "Right where you see that team of blacks hitched, Mr. Dunbar." He looked approvingly at the customer's broad homespun back as Alex left him. This evidently wasn't the usual type of impoverished home-seeker. Here was a settler of substance, a solid citizen. "There'll be plenty more like that," the banker remarked to his teller, "when the railroad gets here. Money and people! And new blood. That's what we need, Frank."

Alex Dunbar hurried to the land office. "Can you show me a map?" he asked the clerk. "I want to see what land you got open out east of here. Out along Conchas Creek."

The clerk produced a plat with sections shown in squares. Privately owned land was shaded, and government land was unshaded. The courses of creeks were shown by winding blue lines.

Alex ran his finger down Conchas Creek. He saw that it headed about twenty miles east of Las Vegas and flowed generally east toward a junction with the

Canadian River. There were several forks, and Alex easily located one in the northwest quarter of a certain section 33. He made a note of the township and range.

"May I have four filing-blanks?"

The clerk gave them to him. On the back of one Alex drew a rough sketch of Conchas Creek and the sections through which it passed. Then he went back to Christine at the hotel.

Her hair still damp and curled from her bath, the girl was in bed and asleep. Alex realized for the first time how much the long trek had wearied her. Driving all day, camping by the trail night after night. There'd been blizzards and snowfalls and weeks of bitter cold. Alex looked down on her fondly and with a sense of guilt. Had he been right in bringing her out to this rough, tough country? There were months of winter ahead yet. Months of cruel hardship until they could build cabins.

Her eyes opened and she smiled, stretching her bare arms luxuriously. "I'd forgotten what a bed felt like, Dad."

"Maybe we should have waited till summer, Chris." His voice was troubled but gentle. "Or maybe we'd better stay right here at the hotel till spring."

"What? Silly talk, Dad. That's why we came early — so we can get a crop in. How can we get a crop in unless we begin plowing right away?" Her blue eyes took a mocking sternness. "Now don't you go soft on me. It's Conchas Creek or bust, bright and early in the morning."

"You're just like your ma." Alex choked a little. "That's just what your ma said, thirty years ago, when we driv into Iowa." He leaned over and kissed her forehead.

Bright and early in the morning they took the trail again. This time it was a dim range trail fording the Gallinas just east of town, crossing the broad meadow there, and then on across a grama grass prairie. Christine was again in overalls, astride her sorrel mare. Alex clucked to his four white mules, and the wagon creaked bravely toward the Conchas.

They topped the divide between the Gallinas and Conchas watersheds. Beyond, the range at this season lay brown and bleakly uninviting. No trees, no fences, no houses. Nothing but sagebrush and bunch grass and grama sod. A fair pasture country, Alex thought, but no good for farming. He could tell by Christine's face that she, too, was disappointed.

Then, three hours out of town, they saw a line of gaunt, leafless trees. The trail dipped into a narrow valley. A few cows were grazing there. The leafless trees proved to be cottonwoods. They fringed a thin, running stream. A ten-inch pipe would have carried all of it. This, according to the map, would be Conchas Creek near its head. Alex followed it downstream.

They came to a fork which doubled the flow in the creek bed. Alex looked at his sketch. This wasn't the fork. He continued on.

The valley broadened. The grass here was cured vega, knee-high except where it had been trampled by cattle. Alex Dunbar brightened. "You could mow native hay here, Chris, just the way it is."

A few more miles brought them to a fork where a grove of majestic cottonwoods covered about five acres. Here the valley was half a mile wide. One of the cottonwoods was blazed and showed the initials, *C.D.*, cut there by Mark Lindsay.

Alex jumped to the ground with a shovel. He dug a hole and his fingers sifted the soil from it. "Deep and sandy!" he exulted. He gazed out across the valley. Its level sweep seemed ideal for farming.

"It will be beautiful when spring comes!" Christine chanted.

The glow on her face brought a decision. "We're home, Chris. Let's unhitch."

They off-harnessed the mules and turned them loose to graze. Alex was pulling a tent from the wagon when Christine called him. She had wandered into the grove a little way and found a long wooden trough. Alex came and saw blocks of rock salt in it.

"Sure, Chris. Mark's note said some ranch keeps a salt box here. But it's government land. The plat says so. We'll file us a couple of quarters."

They pitched the tent and made camp by the wagon. Christine set up a folding table and stools. Alex took four filing-blanks from his pocket. "You fill out one in your name, and I'll fill out one in mine. You take the northeast quarter, and I'll take the northwest quarter. We'll make 'em out in duplicate."

When the blanks were made out and signed in duplicate, Alex took a hatchet and sharpened two stakes. Christine brought two empty tin cans from the wagon. Then they drove one stake close to the creek fork. Alex put his own filing-duplicate into a can and inverted the can over the stake.

"It's my land now," he said proudly.

He strode downcreek, taking long strides and counting them. Christine followed with the other can and the hatchet. After a thousand paces Alex knew he was on the next quarter section east of the wagon. He drove a stake on the creek bank. Christine put her own filing-duplicate into a can and inverted it over the stake.

She spread her arms and whirled in elation. "And this is *my* land!" she cried. "Do we build my house first, or yours, Dad?"

"Either way you say, child."

She put her arms around him and hugged him. His eyes dimmed a little.

"Just like your ma did that other time," he murmured, "back in Iowa."

Hand in hand they returned upstream to the wagon. There Alex Dunbar put the originals of the two filing-claims in his pocket and mounted the sorrel mare. "I hate like the dickens to leave you, Chris. But I got to file these claims at the land office. Don't worry if I'm late gettin' back."

"I'll be all right, Dad."

Alex turned the mare toward Las Vegas. As he jogged away he twisted in the saddle to call back, "If I see Mark Lindsay, I'll fetch him along out here."

At the land office that afternoon, Alex filed the claims and paid the filing-fees.

"To prove up," the clerk informed him, "you have to build a dwelling on each claim and establish residence. You have to cultivate at least forty acres on each quarter and —"

"I know the law," Alex broke in. "Where can I find a building contractor?"

"Pedro Guttierez has an office down the street. He built the house I live in."

Alex found Pedro Guttierez. "I want a three-room adobe house. Flat roof. Pine floors and partitions. One window in each room. I'll pay a bonus for fast work. Want to get my daughter in out of the weather. What about it?"

"Is it in town, señor?"

"No, it's down on the Conchas."

"Then I must charge for hauling material that far." Guttierez named a price which Alex accepted at once.

"Can you start hauling tomorrow?"

"Sí, señor. I have teams and men who are not occupied. Where shall I send them?"

Alex spread out his plat and put a finger on a certain fork of the Conchas. "Right here. Later I'll want another house half a mile farther down the creek."

The Mexican's face clouded. "I am sorry, señor. I have change my mind. At that place I will not build for you."

"Why not? I've just filed there. It's my land."

"I am sorry, señor. You must get someone else."

"But you said —"

"I did not know it was there. Señor the colonel would not like it if I build there."

64

"Señor the colonel who?"

"Colonel Harper. For twenty years his cattle have graze there. He keeps a salt box there. He has men with guns. They do not like for people to build fences and houses on their range."

Alex reddened. "Their range hell! Look, I came a thousand miles to file a quarter section of land. That's all I want. Just a quarter section for myself and another for my daughter. The government sent out circulars begging people like us to come out here. What good's the land if I can't build a cabin on it?"

Guttierez shrugged, spreading his hands in regret. "You are right, señor. Colonel Harper owns much land, and his cattle graze on a million acres that he does not own. He is an honest man. His word is like gold in the bank. If you go to his house he will feed you free and let you stay there as long as you like. But he has — what is it you say — the prejudice? He does not like plows. He does not like fences. He does not like cabins on his range. He gets very angry sometimes, señor."

Alex gave up and went to look for help elsewhere.

On Conchas Creek, Christine replenished the fire and piled a stack of wood for the night. She set up a cot in the tent and spread blankets there for her father. Her own bed, until a cabin was built, would be in the covered wagon.

She bustled about, humming contentedly. Out in the brown grass of the bottom land she could see four white mules grazing knee-deep. A cottontail rabbit scurried by. A pair of mallards flew down creek, heading for the Canadian River. There'd be game here.

Twice today the girl had seen antelope on the horizon. When the cabin was up, and the trees were in leaf, and the young corn was sprouting —

"Hello there, sister. Where's your menfolks?"

Christine turned to see a man on horseback. His small, unfriendly eyes peered from beneath the drooping brim of a sombrero. Bearskin *chaparajos* encased his legs, and on his right thigh she saw a gun.

His horse was branded +V on the hip.

"My father's in town," she said. "I'm expecting him back any minute." She knew, though, that it would be well after dark before Alex Dunbar could return from Las Vegas.

"How long you aim to camp here, sister?"

"We're not camping," Christine told him. "We've come to stay."

The man's lip curled. "Nesters, huh? You're on the wrong crik, sister. When your old man gets back, tell him I said to move on."

She took a step nearer the wagon. "Who are you?"

"I'm Jack Dillon of the Rafter Cross. This here's one of our saltin'-stations. Tell yer old man he'd better file some place else."

"We like it here," Christine said defiantly. She was edging toward the wagon.

"Listen, sister. I'm tellin' yuh fer your own good. This here's a cow country. It ain't fit fer nothin' else. Ain't enough rain to raise crops. You'd starve out. When you got hungry you'd start eatin' Rafter Cross beef. They all do. That's the only way a nester can live in this country."

66

Christine's face flamed. Before she could answer, the man had swung from his saddle and was taking long, bow-legged strides toward a stake. A tin can was inverted over the stake.

"It's fer your own good," Dillon repeated. "It'll save you a peck of grief later." He stooped, took the can off the stake and pulled a filing-paper from it. Then he struck a match and held it to the paper.

"Don't you dare!" The girl's shrill voice made him look over his shoulder. She had snatched a shotgun from the wagon and was aiming it at a spot just below the small of his back.

But the edge of the paper had already caught fire. Sight of the tiny flame infuriated Christine Dunbar, and her finger tightened on the trigger. The shotgun roared. Dillon fell screaming to the ground, writhing there.

Christine stepped quickly forward and took the forty-five gun from his belt. She broke it at the hinge, shook the shells out, threw the gun one way and the shells the other. Then she stepped back, this time aiming the shotgun at Dillon's head.

"Get up. You're not hurt."

To the man's amazement he found that he wasn't. He got to his feet, the flesh of his rear anatomy still stinging.

"We keep one barrel loaded with buckshot," Christine told him, "and the other loaded with salt. That's what hit you — a few grains of salt. Now pick up your gun and get out."

Jack Dillon saw the bore of the buckshot barrel staring at him. He saw fight and fury in blue eyes back of it. He saw a slim, tense finger curled on a trigger. "Don't shoot!" he begged in a panic. Staggering to his empty gun he picked it up. Then he climbed to his seat and was off at a gallop toward Las Vegas.

CHAPTER
SEVEN

Murder in a Ranch House

Inquiry at Wagon Mound informed Kirk Calloway that he was still several days back of the four white mules. They'd gone on down the trail — how far he had no idea. He took a room at the Mound for a sound night's sleep.

In the morning, long before the sun had topped the butte shaped amazingly like a covered wagon, and which gives the town its name, Kirk was riding southwest out of Wagon Mound. "Maybe they went all the way to California, Red. Or maybe they stopped at Vegas. I hear they got a land office there."

At an easy jog he made Las Vegas by midafternoon. It was full of men and teams and the dust of freighting wagons. Half a dozen new buildings were going up along the main street.

Kirk rode through the plaza, spotting a hotel there, and then on to a livery barn. "Looks like you folks are gettin' ready for the railroad," he remarked to the liveryman.

"We sure are, mister. They say this here's gonna be a division point. Stoppin' with us long?"

"I'm looking for some friends. Covered-wagon outfit with four white mules and —"

"They filed on some land east o' here. You mean that Dunbar outfit, I reckon."

It was all Kirk wanted to know. Except, of course, the girl's first name and the exact location of the filing. He stalled his horse and hurried to the land office.

"Yep," the land clerk informed him. "They filed on Conchas Creek about thirty miles east of here. You filing out that way, too?"

"No, thanks. I just thought I'd look 'em up."

Kirk took a room at the Exchange Hotel and freshened up. He saw an odd sheepishness on his face as he surveyed it in a mirror. He grimaced at it. "She'll think you're a goof, fellah. You ride up and say, 'Well, here I am. Remember me? I met you a thousand miles back up the trail. So I followed you to New Mexico. My name's Calloway, and I'm the world's champion long-distance masher.'"

It wouldn't do. She'd laugh at him. So he'd have to make it natural and plausible. The thing to do was get a job on some ranch around here. Breaking broncos or punching cattle. Then in the course of his duties he could happen by the Dunbar camp and explain: "Imagine meeting you here! Howdy, folks."

At suppertime he went down to the lobby desk. "Any big cow outfits around here?" he asked the clerk.

"A few, Mr. Calloway. See those two men eating supper together?" The clerk pointed to a table in the dining-room. "They're Colonel Cal Harper and Don Alfredo Baca. Two biggest cowmen in the county."

Kirk decided to tackle one of them, it didn't matter which. He rather liked the cut of both, although they were opposite types. One was evidently a Mexican *rico*. Probably had one of those big grants with a hundred-year-old title from the King of Spain. The other looked like a fire-eating Texan.

Kirk went in and took a table near them. They seemed to be having a friendly argument. At any rate they were chiding each other. From snatches Kirk caught they seemed to have made a sizable bet of some kind with the outcome still undetermined.

"Whispers have reached me, *coronel mío*," the Mexican was saying, "that you offer to double this bet but I am afraid. I, Alfredo Baca! Poof! What is a mere thousand steers? Or two? It makes no difference."

The old Texan gave him a suspicious stare. "You sure you didn't start that rumor yourself, Alfredo? Just to make me look like a piker?"

"But of course not, señor. I was wondering if it was, perhaps, the other way — that you, perhaps, try to make *me* look like the piker. Just to clear all doubt, let it be understood that I make a standing offer to double the bet."

The Texan blinked. Kirk could see that he was a proud old rooster — sensitive in a chip-on-shoulder way. A man who'd never let it be said that he was afraid of a risk.

Kirk saw him refill his whisky glass and gulp down the drink. Then the old man stared defiantly at his companion. "If the offer still stands ten seconds from now, Alfredo, you're covered."

Ten silent seconds ticked away. Then the Spanish ranchman purred: "So it is *two* thousand now, instead of only one. I take odd, you have even." He extended a hand across the table.

The Texan grimly shook it.

What, Kirk wondered, were they betting on?

Alfredo Baca dined leisurely, sipping his wine after the Latin fashion, and Kirk Calloway finished supper first. He went out into the lobby, still uncertain as to which ranchman he would tackle for a job.

As he opened his wallet to pay the check, fate made the decision. A card fell out. Kirk had forgotten all about it. The card said:

Archibald Templeton
Malden Square   London

Beneath this was written in pencil: *Representing the Crown Land and Cattle Co., Las Vegas, New Mexico, and introducing Kirk Calloway.*

In the wallet, too, was a note to the local manager. Here was a job already offered. A near-by outfit called the CLC. So why bother these two high-betting strangers?

Kirt went to bed. Early in the morning he rode toward the CLC. It was on a fork of the Gallinas, he'd learned, not far southeast of town.

A wagon trail led in that general direction. Presently Kirk came to grazing cattle branded CLC. They were in good flesh. Clearly the CLC was not overstocked.

A few miles farther on he sighted ranch buildings. When he arrived there he found a two-story barn facing a one-story bunkhouse. There were corrals and sheds

72

with a brushy creek back of them. Well apart from these stood a small, neat frame house with its gabled roof painted red. That, Kirk guessed, would be the manager's cabin. No one seemed to be about. The place had a strangely deserted look. In one corral a calf was bawling; from another came the whinnies of distressed horses.

A cow with swollen udder was circling the calf corral. To Kirk it was clear that someone had neglected the ranch chores this morning.

He knocked at the door of the main house. There was no response. Kirk went to the back door where again his knock was unanswered. This door was slightly ajar. He pushed it open and saw a deserted kitchen. "Anybody home?" he yelled.

He went down to the bunkhouse and knocked there. "Anybody home?" Again no answer.

When he opened the door he saw four men. They were seated at a table and slumped forward on it. All of them were dead.

They'd been dead at least a day or two. Possibly longer than that. A foul odor filled the room. The table had a half-eaten supper on it. There was a fifth chair, empty. On the floor by the empty chair lay four empty shells. They were six-gun shells of .45 caliber.

Five men had sat down to supper here, some days ago. It was clear to Kirk that one of them had shot the other four. Two of the dead men wore holstered guns. Two did not, but a pair of gun belts hung from a near-by bunk post. The killer, Kirk concluded, was a fast and accurate gunman. Fast enough to deliver four shots before his bunkies could spring into action.

Kirk looked the scene over carefully, noting details. Then he backed out without touching anything. He must bring a sheriff here. Mounting the bay, he loped toward Las Vegas.

He'd gone only a few miles when a Mexican boy crossed his path. The boy was on a burro and headed toward Las Vegas.

"You know the county sheriff?"

"*Sí, señor.*"

Kirk scribbled a note stating the bare facts of his findings at the ranch. "Take this to the sheriff, boy, and *ándale.*"

The boy rode on with the note, and Kirk turned back to the CLC. Two motives impelled him. The murder evidence should not be left unguarded. His experience as deputy under Bat Masterson at Dodge City had taught Kirk that much. Second, there was stock in the corrals needing attention.

When he opened the corral gates, the bawling calf ran out to its mother and a bunch of saddle ponies raced out to the creek. By strict rules Kirk knew he should have kept them imprisoned until the sheriff came. They were evidence that chores had been left undone here for perhaps two nights and days. But Kirk Calloway had a fondness for stock and couldn't bear to let these animals go longer unwatered.

In the center of the barnyard was a deep well. A rope over a pulley balanced two oaken buckets. Kirk drew water, found it cold and sweet. He off-saddled Red and watered him. Then he sat down on the well stoop and rolled a cigarette.

74

For hours Kirk waited there, restless, impatient to turn all this over to the law and be gone about his own business. Which was to cloak himself in a job and then go calling on Christine Dunbar.

It was midafternoon before he saw people approaching across the prairie. There was a buckboard and three horsemen riding at the wheel.

They came trotting up and stopped by the well. A slight, dark, well-groomed Mexican dismounted. He inquired courteously, "You are the Señor Calloway who sent me the note?"

Kirk nodded. "But I sent for the sheriff." This man he recognized as one of the two ranchers who'd taken supper last night at the hotel.

"I am Alfredo Baca," the man said, exposing a badge in the palm of his hand. "The señor has found dead men? You will lead us there, please?"

His polite dignity impressed Kirk. He led the way to the bunkhouse. The others followed. The man who had driven the buckboard was the county coroner. The others were Mexican deputies.

Baca and the coroner went in first. "*Madre de Dios!*" gasped Baca.

"Looks like Charlie Swift," the coroner exclaimed. "Him and his whole outfit."

"These men, I know them well," a deputy put in as he peered past Kirk. "They are Carlos Swift; he was the manager here. These others have the names Dalhart, Forgy, and Stites."

"It was at least two days ago," the coroner decided. "Whoever did it has that long a start."

"*Caramba!*" Alfredo Baca spread his hands in dismay. "He will be far away by now. Guillermo, did Charlie Swift have only three vaqueros?"

"I think he had one more, Don Alfredo. But I did not know him. He has not work here long."

Baca went into a huddle with the coroner. Kirk waited outside, hoping to be dismissed.

"There was stock in the corrals," he said when Baca came out. "They needed water so I turned 'em out."

Baca's nod was approving. "Let us go to the house, señor."

On the way to the manager's cabin Kirk explained that he'd just ridden in from Kansas, arriving in Las Vegas late yesterday. "I had a letter from one of the English owners, staking me to a job here."

"We must get word to these English people," Baca worried, "so they can make arrangements here. There are many cattle in this brand and now no one to watch them."

"Whose responsibility is it?" Kirk asked.

"Mine, señor. I am the sheriff, so I must appoint a custodian till the owners provide one of their own."

They entered the manager's cabin and found an office there. On the desk Baca saw two small, leather-bound record books. He examined them.

"This one, señor, is the tally book." He thumbed through it to a total on the last page. "It shows 8,084 head in the brand CLC. This does not count unweaned calves. Also it shows that an inspector from England was here only a few weeks ago. He has checked the tally and initialed the total."

"I reckon that would be Templeton, the man I met at the railhead."

Alfredo Baca thumbed through the other book. It was merely the ranch's month to month payroll. The current roster listed a manager and four stock hands. Alfredo read them aloud: "Charles Swift, Albert Forgy, Ray Stites, Ed Dalhart, Mark Lindsay."

At the last name, Alfredo's eyes met Kirk's. The same thought struck both of them. That empty chair at the bunkhouse table should have been last occupied by Mark Lindsay.

"I do not know him, señor," the sheriff said. "But we know that five men were here; now four are dead and the other has gone away."

Kirk's nod was a bit doubtful. "Sort of circumstantial. No?"

Alfredo Baca shrugged. "True, señor. Many men of bad character pass through this country. Some will kill at the least displeasure, wait only, like the drop of a hat. One such ranges only two counties south of here. He is only a boy, but he has killed many men. He kills them as casually as you would roll a cigarillo. Like that." Alfredo snapped his fingers four times. "His name is Guillermo Bonney, and some call him Billy the Kid."

"Maybe he stopped by here for supper," Kirk suggested. "Maybe somebody made a remark he didn't like, so he cut loose."

But Alfredo shook his head. "In this affair he has no guilt. I make it my business to know where this Guillermo Bonney is. For the last month he has been in Lincoln County, where two factions have a big quarrel.

Bonney is in that, up to his neck, so he has not been here. The sheriff down there has kept me informed."

"Then it looks like our man Lindsay," Kirk brooded.

"We have evidence on no one else," Alfredo said. "So I will issue a warrant for this Mark Lindsay. Let us go now, señor."

CHAPTER
EIGHT

The New Deputy

Leaving the coroner and deputies to bring the bodies in at leisure, Alfredo Baca and Kirk Calloway rode together toward Las Vegas. Alfredo was riding a long-limbed black racer which he called "Noche." "It is a strain which we breed on my rancho, señor. When you are my guest there, I will show you many fine horses."

He spurred the black into a fast single-foot, and Kirk had trouble keeping up. When they slowed to a running walk Kirk asked, "Was that a horse race you were betting on last night at supper?"

"Oh, so you heard?" Alfredo laughed and made a gesture of deprecation. "No, it is only a little game of odd or even I play with Colonel Harper. He wins if the railroad arrives on an even day of the month. It is amusing, señor."

Kirk stared at him. He'd heard of colossal wagers on one turn of the dice, but never anything like this. It must have taken generations of sporting ancestors to breed such a bet. Alfredo, noting his amazement, smiled. "What is the difference, señor? A horse runs fast and the race is soon over. But if it only crawls, like a new track across the prairie, there must still be a finish line. The longer the race, the longer the thrill."

Kirk found himself liking the man more and more. Here was a strange mixture of aristocrat, ranchero, law officer and devil-may-care sport. Here also was charm, courtesy, and a calm culture. A sheriff with neither badge nor gun in sight.

"About this CLC rancho," Alfredo murmured. "One of its owners was here recently, counting the cattle. You say you met him in Colorado?"

"Yes, on his way home to England. He's had time to get to New York and be on a ship by now."

"*Que lástima!*" worried Alfredo. "So now I must send word to the British embassy at Washington. They will send a cable to England. A long time, señor, before they can have people here to take care of the property."

"In the meantime, as sheriff, it's in your lap?"

"*Sí, señor.* I must put a deputy there to watch the cattle. If I do not, *ladrones* may drive them away."

Light faded, and it was quite dark when they turned into the main street of Las Vegas. They were passing the Buena Suerte saloon when Alfredo pulled to a stop. "*Caramba!*" he exclaimed. "Did you hear?"

"Sounded like a gunshot," Kirk said.

It had come from within the Buena Suerte. A moment later came another.

Alfredo Baca sighed and swung to the ground. "They give me no peace, señor. If you will wait only a moment, I will go in and take the man's gun from him." He tied Noche to a hitchrack.

Jack Dillon was drowning his humiliation. He'd been at it for two days now, but only in the last few minutes had it brought him any real satisfaction.

Being chased off a homestead by a girl had been a little more than he could bear. A few grains of salt embedded in the seat of his pants no longer stung him, but the sting of shame still burned. If he returned to the Rafter Cross, the other punchers there would laugh him off the ranch. There'd been nothing he could do but ride to town and get roaring drunk.

That, and recover his prestige at the expense of someone else. Opportunity for this had arrived in the person of a plump little barbed-wire salesman from Chicago. Better yet, the barbed-wire salesman was unlucky enough to be wearing a brown derby hat. He'd dropped in peaceably at the Buena Suerte for a glass of beer. Over it, he'd made the acquaintance of a stockman from Bernalillo. Could the stockman use a shipment of barbed wire?

The stockman couldn't.

But Jack Dillon, standing by, could use a barbed-wire salesman with a brown derby hat. Moreover, by chasing such an upstart clear out of New Mexico, he should win the applause of every honest cattleman. And at the same time recoup his own standing among men.

Having been chased by Christine Dunbar, Jack Dillon, at the fag end of his two-day bender, would now do a little chasing himself.

The salesman was backed up against a wall. His face was ash; his knees were water. His right arm was outstretched, holding the brown derby hat.

Plunk! Dillon, five paces away, fired another forty-five bullet through it.

"You promise?" he demanded. "You catch the next stage to hell outa here?"

"I promise." The salesman shivered. He'd been told that if he moved, or dropped the hat, the next shot would be aimed at his stomach. The hat was now a battered sieve. Dillon fired another slug through it.

"And you'll tell every barbed-wire salesman in Chicago to stay to hell outa New Mexico?"

"I will. May I go now, please?"

Upon this gentle scene intruded Alfredo Baca.

Dillon didn't see the sheriff until he'd fired one last shot through the hat. He was feeling fine now. Shame was cleansed away. Liquor flaming in his brain painted false values there. A dozen customers at the bar had observed all this, and dancing girls were peeping from the ballroom. In every eye Jack Dillon imagined fawning admiration.

Then a quiet voice. "Give me the gun, señor."

A bare hand was extended. The dark, unruffled face back of it was Alfredo Baca's.

Sober, Dillon would never have defied Baca. The sheriff had a reputation well known at the Rafter Cross. Moreover, every man there knew he was an intimate friend of Dillon's boss, Colonel Cal Harper.

But Jack Dillon wasn't sober. He heard a girl giggle. He heard a man down the bar whisper, "Watch Alfredo tame him." So all his cloudy brain could think of was saving face.

He cracked the gun barrel down on Baca's head. The sheriff buckled to the floor.

Dillon holstered his gun and swaggered toward the exit. Halfway there an iron grip closed on his wrist. A man he'd never seen before towered over him. The man twisted Dillon's arm, and a bone there cracked. And still the man kept twisting, twisting, till Dillon, with a scream of agony, was wrenched, writhing, to his knees.

Alfredo Baca came to consciousness on a couch in the private living-quarters he had built as an annex to the sheriff's office. It was a big, comfortable room, furnished at his own expense, with deep rugs and cushions, and with an oil painting of his ranch on the wall.

He opened his eyes and saw Kirk Calloway seated near him. Kirk, grinning, rolled a cigarette. "A mean hombre, that guy! Got any more of 'em around here?"

Alfredo sat up, rubbing a bump on his head. "I must go now and arrest him, señor."

"He's already celled, sheriff." Kirk gave the information in a tone of apology. "It wasn't any of my business, of course. Force of habit, I reckon. Last year I happened to be deputy to Bat Masterson, back in Dodge City, so I just couldn't help horning in."

"Ah! Señor Bat Masterson! Of him I have heard. They say he is a great sheriff."

"I had this Dillon guy on my hands," Kirk persisted, still trying to justify himself, "so I —"

"So you dragged him to the *carcel*. It is well, *amigo*. Shall we have wine?"

Alfredo brought it from a cabinet and filled glasses. "And what are your plans?" he inquired.

"I'm looking for a ranch job. Know where I can find one?"

"But of course. I myself am a ranchero. You will come out to my hacienda and be welcome. It is *Los Corazones Juntados*."

"Linked Hearts, huh. But look, Mr. Baca —"

"Call me Alfredo."

"What I mean," Kirk protested, "you don't need me out there. You've probably got a *mayordomo* who was born there, and his father and grandfather before him. And a crew of vaqueros who were born there. You don't need me, Alfredo, and you know it."

Kirk looked him in the eyes, and Alfredo smiled an assent. "You are right, my friend. I do not need you at my rancho. It is here that I need you. In the sheriff's office. I will make you my chief deputy."

"Would it throw anybody else out of a job?"

"No, señor. My other deputies will be glad. And I will tell you why. They are good *muchachos*, but they are not quick with a gun. They will not like to hunt for this man who shoots fast, four times, and kills four at a table with him."

Kirk nodded. "The CLC killer. You want me to bring him in?"

"We will both seek him, señor. You and I. I go now to prepare a warrant in duplicate. One for you and one for me."

"Naming who?"

"It will name Mark Lindsay and the charge will be suspicion of murder. Who else can we name? He lived with them there. Now they are dead and he is gone. You will excuse me, please?"

Alfredo went out and was gone about twenty minutes. When he returned: "I have prepared the warrants. Also a letter to the British embassy at Washington. It says the County of San Miguel will assume custody of English property here until the owners provide a new manager."

"Which may take a month or two," Kirk suggested.

"Perhaps even longer. Look, my friend. You need a place to live and a barn for your horse. So you will live at the CLC rancho as custodian representing myself, the sheriff. I will give you two *ayudantes*. They will make an inventory of the cattle and watch them. You will ride where you will, searching for Mark Lindsay."

Kirk saw at once that it suited his own plans perfectly. A job and a roof — within easy calling-range of Christine Dunbar. "I'll take it, sheriff."

"*Splendido!*" Alfredo beamed. "Now we will go to the hotel where you will be my guest at supper."

It was late. The Exchange Hotel dining-room, when they reached it, had emptied of all customers except one. He was a well-dressed business man of stocky build, clean-shaven, and with center-parted brown hair. Success and self-assurance were stamped on his broad, bold face.

"A friend of mine!" exclaimed Alfredo. "Let us join him."

He led Kirk to the man's table. "This is my friend, Señor Vogle; he is our leading merchant here in Las Vegas. And this, Señor Vogle, is my new chief deputy, Kirk Calloway."

Vogle looked up, affably. "A new deputy, eh? Any special job on?"

Alfredo nodded. "A matter of great concern, Señor Vogle. Four men have been killed at a ranch. The killer we have not yet found. But we will. We will find him and hang him."

"Glad to know you, Calloway." Adam Vogle extended a hand. Kirk took it, and it seemed to him the coldest flesh he had ever touched.

In the morning he rode out to the CLC with two Mexican deputies. Arturo Pacheco was fat and fifty. Manuel Torres was slim and twenty. "They are honest and will do as you say," Alfredo had assured Kirk. "But they like better to play the guitar than to fight *ladrones*." Pacheco, he said, was the best cook in the county.

They found the bunkhouse larder stocked with canned food and frijole beans. A frozen quarter of beef hung in a meat house. "We shall live well here," Pacheco promised as they took possession.

Kirk went to the manager's cabin and shaved. A clean shirt was in his blanket roll. By the time he had spruced up, Arturo called him to lunch at the bunkshack.

"Where, señor, do you hunt first for the killer?"

"On Conchas Creek," Kirk said.

Arturo, dishing up frijoles, stared at him. "But why there, señor? Conchas Creek is only a pasture of the Rafter Cross."

Kirk grinned and said nothing. They'd find out soon enough he was interested in a girl over there.

Soon he was off, warrant in pocket and gun on thigh, spurring Red northeast toward Conchas Creek. He struck it in about two hours and followed fresh wagon tracks down the bank. He passed two bunches of grazing cattle. A few were CLCs; most of them were Rafter Cross.

After rounding a dozen bends of the valley he saw two white mules. They were feeding on cured grass by the creek. He was sure they were mules he'd followed all the way from Kansas. Where were the other two?

A mile on down the valley he saw them. They were hitched to a plow. Back of them lay a strip of freshly turned earth, black in the early March sun. On foot, gripping the plow handles, reins looped about her neck, was Christine Dunbar. Her legs were encased in earth-stained denims. A sunbonnet hid her face.

Kirk stopped his horse there in the fringe of creek brush and watched her. A tight exultation, mixed with shyness, filled him. Pride, too, for her courage. And a sense of sureness in his own judgment. He'd known her only for an hour by a roadside fire. But even then he'd been sure. From that moment all other women had ceased to exist. He watched her reach the end of a furrow, turn the team, and plod back along the next one. The heavy doubletree bumped against her knees at each step. Clods all but tripped her. A lump came to

Kirk's throat. He knew now why he'd followed her across half a continent. It was to take those plow handles out of her hands and put his own there. It was to see her in a doorway, waiting for him, calling him home.

From a cottonwood grove ahead came sounds of hammering. Kirk rode on there and saw two men raising two-by-four studding on a log foundation. Lumber was stacked near by. There was a tent, a covered wagon, and a pole shelter. A fire blazed against the nip of the March air.

Kirk dismounted by it. The two men turned toward him. One, he saw, was the girl's father. The other was lame, wore a carpenter's apron, and looked like a Swede.

Kirk said, "Remember me? I met you back at Cottonwood Falls. Calloway's my name."

"Sure I remember, young man." Alex Dunbar advanced with a hearty handshake. "Glad to see you. But what are you doin' 'way out here?"

"I'm a deputy sheriff of this county. Heard you were here and so I thought I'd drop by." What a relief it was not to need to say more!

"A deputy sheriff, eh? Well, well! Make yourself at home and I'll call Chris." Alex went to the edge of the grove and cupped a hand to halloo: "Hi there, Chris! Knock off and come to camp. We got company."

A quarter of a mile away, she heard him. Kirk saw her unhook the tugs. She pulled harness from the mules and dropped it by the plow. The mules strayed off, cropping grass. The girl ran toward the grove.

She came up to them, her face suffused with pleasure as she recognized Kirk. "Why, it's you!" she gasped. "Away out here!"

"Calloway's his name, Chris," Alex said. "Hi, Olsen, come over and meet our friend, Calloway."

The lame Swede came over for a moment, murmured a greeting, then returned to his work.

"Calloway's a deputy sheriff out here, Chris," Alex explained. "Funny what a small world this is. We meet him in Kansas and he turns up out here."

He set a camp stool for Kirk. Christine snatched off her bonnet, loosened her braided flaxen hair, and sat down on a log. "Do you live in Las Vegas, Mr. Calloway?"

"Right now I'm takin' care of an orphan ranch, not far from here."

"An orphan ranch?" Alex questioned.

"The outfit got killed off," Kirk explained. "Seems like one of the hands was a bad hombre. One evenin' at supper he took a notion to shoot up everybody in sight. So he did. Drilled 'em all dead. Then he disappeared. So they gave me a warrant and told me to pick him up."

"With all this wild country, how can you ever find him?" Christine asked.

"I'll just keep ridin' till I do. How's things with you?"

"Not bad," Alex said. "I had a couple o' loads of lumber freighted out and got a man to help me throw up a cabin. Soon as we get the outside frame up I'll relieve Chris of the plowin'."

"But the plowing can't wait," the girl put in. "Because we have to have a crop in by spring."

"A toughie came by and tried to run us off." Alex chuckled. " 'Stead of that he got run off himself."

"And we lost Patch up on the Picketwire," Chris said.

"You mean that calico mare?" Kirk asked. "Well, I happened to run on to it on the way over the pass. Guy named Roach was ridin' it. I sent word to the sheriff at Trinidad and so you may get the mare back some day."

The girl's eyes lighted gratefully. "I raised Patch as a pet back in Iowa. She was just like one of the family."

"Sure." Alex grimaced. "That's why Chris never would let me brand that mare."

"You have to keep stock branded out this way," Kirk advised. "If you don't, it'll be grabbed off by somebody like Roach. I couldn't be sure it was your pony, even when I saw it."

Alex tossed another chunk on the fire. "About this killer you're out after. Any chance of him coming by here?"

"I don't think so, Mr. Dunbar. Chances are he took to the hills. All we know about him is he's trigger-happy. And fast. Fast enough to kill four men all at once."

"What did you say his name is?"

Kirk took out a warrant and looked at it. "According to this warrant, his name's Lindsay. Mark Lindsay."

Both the Dunbars stood up, staring. Shock tightened Christine's face. "Mark Lindsay! Why, that's ridiculous. Mark wouldn't —"

Kirk, confused, shifted his gaze to Alex. All the cordiality of a moment ago had left Alex. He said stiffly,

"If you're out gunnin' for Mark Lindsay, we don't want anything to do with you, young man."

"You mean you know him?"

"He was raised on the next farm to us, back in Iowa. He's a fine lad, Mark is. Some day he and Chris aim to get married."

"Isn't that just like a sheriff!" Christine said bitterly. "They're all stupid. A rowdy cowboy rides by here and tries to bully me off my own land. Does the sheriff do anything about that? No. He picks on Mark Lindsay. You protect the bullies and persecute the decent people. Good-by, Mr. Calloway. I hope I never see you again."

She walked off with her chin high, into the field, to recapture her plow team.

Kirk sat there, red-faced, staring after her.

Alex Dunbar said coldly, "If you'll excuse me, I've work to do." He turned his back and went to help the Swede.

"Listen, Mr. Dunbar. I didn't say Lindsay killed those men. I just said the warrant's got his name on it."

Alex whirled about and gave a stony stare. He pointed to a blazed tree to his left. The initials, *C.D.*, were on the blaze. "Mark put 'em there himself, Calloway. He picked this spot for Chris and then waited for her to come. Do you think he'd go out and start killin' people? If you do, you're just a plain damn fool. Good day."

Kirk climbed on his bay and rode wretchedly toward the CLC.

CHAPTER
NINE

The Clue

Pacheco served supper in the bunkhouse. "We shall live well here, *patrón*." He pushed a chair in place for Kirk. "You like the tortillas? Tomorrow I send Manuel to buy chickens. Then we will have *cazuela gallina*. You like the chicken soup? And why not? The county pays for it, no?"

They chattered about everything except the job at hand, which was to make an inventory of all CLC assets and apprehend the killer of its crew.

Yet it was the babbling tongue of Arturo Pacheco which, quite unconsciously, gave Kirk his first clue.

"Coffee, *patrón?*" Arturo poised the pot above Kirk's cup.

"Thanks," Kirk assented absently. But as the brown liquid filled the cup, his mind became suddenly alert.

It brought back a detail of the death scene here, at this very table, as discovered by the sheriff, the coroner, and himself. Four seated dead men and one empty chair. And five partly consumed suppers. There'd been a coffee cup at each plate. Four, each in front of a corpse, had been stained brown. They'd held coffee. But the fifth cup had been bright and unused.

The killer, then, was *not* a coffee drinker. His victims were, but not the killer himself.

Kirk said nothing about it to his deputies. Later he went up to the manager's cabin and to bed. For a long time he lay awake, wondering what he could make of it. At least he should be able to find out if Mark Lindsay habitually drank coffee.

Waking in the morning he remembered it was Sunday. The sheriff wasn't likely to be at his office today. He probably spent Sundays at his ranch, the Linked Hearts.

After breakfast Kirk rode to town anyway. He must begin a check-up on the character and habits of Mark Lindsay. Lindsay, by all accounts, was new in this country and had been on the CLC payroll less than a month.

Kirk put himself in Lindsay's place. What does an itinerant cowboy do when he comes to a strange range? *He does what I did myself,* Kirk reasoned. *He stops at the hotel for the first night or two, finds out about the local ranches, and then rides out to one for a job.*

The plaza was quiet as Kirk hitched in front of the Exchange Hotel. He went in and asked, "Did a puncher named Mark Lindsay stop here, 'bout a month ago?"

The clerk thumbed back through the registry book. On a page dated early in February he found the name. "Yes. He was here two days and nights."

"Eat his meals here?"

"Likely. I didn't notice."

Kirk went into the dining-room. Lindsay, he reasoned, would be a young man of more than average attractions. Otherwise he couldn't have become engaged to Christine Dunbar. Which meant that a waitress in a cowtown hotel wouldn't have overlooked him.

The one who took Kirk's order was a plump, dimpled Mexican.

"Fellow name of Lindsay stopped here a month back. Remember him?"

"*Sí señor*. For two days I have serve him. But he has not come back."

"What did he drink? Milk or coffee?"

"Coffee, señor. Two cups with every meal."

"How about suppertime?"

"For *comida* he has two cups, *también*. Always black, señor."

When Kirk went to the sheriff's office, Alfredo Baca wasn't there. "Don Alfredo," the jailer said, "is out to his rancho."

After inquiring the way, Kirk took a trail toward the Linked Hearts. It led him through piñon hills and across high grassy benches. It dipped into a canyon where a boy was herding goats. Beyond this it followed the backbone of a scrub pine ridge.

Patches of snow lay in the sheltered spots here. In one of them Kirk saw the tracks of buggy tires. The buggy team had passed recently in this same direction.

He dropped, finally, into an alfalfa-floored mountain valley. A stream centered the valley, and along it were stretches of fenced meadow. The fences were made of horizontal poles, and Kirk knew that they were meant not to keep stock in but to keep it out.

Buildings of a hacienda reared at the head of the valley. With its adobe church and clusters of flat brown dwellings it was more like a town than a ranch. The master's house was two-story, spacious, generously balconied, with bright blue shutters showing over a high patio wall.

Kirk pulled up at the patio gate. A Mexican boy dashed out and took his reins before he'd even dismounted. "*Bien venido, señor,*" he welcomed.

Then a gray-haired *mayordomo* appeared. "Your pleasure, señor?"

"Is Don Alfredo in?"

"*Sí.* You will enter, señor?"

Kirk followed him through the gate, across a garden, and into the house. "I'm Kirk Calloway."

Alfredo Baca, from a dining *sala* beyond an arch, heard Kirk's voice and came bounding in. "*Amigo!* We are honored." The warmth of his greeting all but smothered Kirk. "I was just telling them about you. My sister and her guest. You will join us at dinner, señor."

Kirk tried to decline. He didn't feel dressed for Sunday dinner in a household like this. But Alfredo took his arm and pulled him along.

He found himself in a dining-hall where the table was set for three. A uniformed *mozo* stood formally by it. Seated were a man and a lady. The man stood up as Kirk entered. With surprise Kirk recognized him as the Las Vegas merchant, Adam Vogle.

The lady was Spanish and about three years younger than Alfredo. She wasn't pretty. Her features were Alfredo's. Aristocratic and intelligent, but not in any sense beautiful. She was pale, reserved, and a little sad, Kirk thought. Certainly she lacked Alfredo's color and vitality.

"My sister, Rosita. And you know Señor Vogle."

Kirk smiled at Rosita, shook hands with Vogle. The *mozo* placed a chair for him. "Had we known you were coming," Alfredo said, "we would have waited." The others were almost finished eating. A boy now came in and placed steaming soup in front of Kirk.

After this came breast of wild turkey.

"You drove a buggy team out here?" Kirk asked Vogle.

Vogle nodded. "How did you know?"

"Saw your tire tracks on the trail."

Kirk decided to say nothing about the Mark Lindsay affair until he had Alfredo alone. They were dallying, now, waiting for him to catch up. Alfredo did most of the talking, which was generally about the bright future of New Mexico. It was Rosita who broke in on this.

"But the future is dull. Only the present is interesting. Tell us, Señor Calloway, about this murderer you hunt for. This Marcus Lindsay."

There it was. So Kirk came to his point at once. He took a warrant from his pocket and handed it to Alfredo. "It's no good, Alfredo. He didn't do it."

Alfredo arched his eyebrows. "But why do you say that, señor?"

Kirk told them about the Dunbars and about their old acquaintance in Iowa with Mark Lindsay. The girl, he said, had come out here to marry Lindsay. "Folks

96

like that," he maintained, "don't take up with a guy who goes around shootin' up bunkhouses."

Alfredo considered this gravely and fairly. "But men change," he argued. "Good boys ride west, sometimes, and become bad men. It has happened many times."

"Not this time," Kirk insisted stubbornly. "Sorry, Alfredo. If you insist on me serving that warrant, I must turn in my badge. But if you'll make out another one, a John Doe warrant for whoever did the bunkhouse massacre, I'll keep right on it till I bring him in."

An odd tension came over the room. Kirk failed to classify it or to realize its focus. Alfredo said, "As you wish, my friend. We shall make the warrant for John Doe. But you must have some other reason. Something which impresses you even more than the friendship of Mark Lindsay with an honest family. What is it, señor?"

Kirk smiled. "Okay. Here it is. There were five coffee cups at that bunkhouse supper. Four had coffee, one didn't. The killer's didn't. He doesn't drink coffee. I found out Mark Lindsay does. He takes it black at every meal."

Alfredo gave an approving nod. "That is a pretty clue, my friend. I was stupid to miss it myself. So we must look for someone else than Mark Lindsay."

The *mozo* was circling the table, poising a silver pitcher over each cup.

And Adam Vogle caught himself just in time. From long habit he almost said, "None for me, thank you." Never in his life had coffee passed his lips.

Fortunately the others weren't looking at him. Their attention was fixed on Calloway. So Vogle checked the gesture which almost waved the *mozo* away. The servant poured his cup full.

Adam Vogle drank every drop of it, black, and asked for more.

When they adjourned to the living-room Alfredo said, "If you and your guest will excuse us, Rosita, Señor Calloway and I will talk shop."

It was then clear to Kirk that Vogle had come only to see Rosita. Still, he was hardly the romantic type. On the contrary he seemed cold-blooded, calculating, mercenary. Kirk gave it only a casual thought. He wasn't in the least interested in either Vogle or Rosita.

Alfredo took Kirk into a den and offered cigars. He smiled knowingly. "We will leave them alone. What is it you say — two is the company and four is the crowd?"

Kirk grinned. "So that's the way it is!"

"Not at all," Alfredo hastily corrected. "At least not yet. This is his first call. He is our leading citizen at Las Vegas. But I am surprised when he asks permission to address my sister. I invite him to Sunday dinner, of course, and we will see what comes of it."

Kirk thought he saw already. The Bacas were rich. They were politically influential. For generations theirs had been a name to conjure with in New Mexico. A practical, ambitious business man like Vogle could make himself solid with a wife like Rosita Baca.

Quite possibly Alfredo saw it that way, too. But, being a Latin, his viewpoint was liberal in such matters. He came from a society where marriages were arranged, the proper ones being called alliances, and the others called misalliances. Among the right people,

98

the *gente de razón*, dollar signs were usually given more weight than dimples. Nor did a frank discussion of such matters seem at all out of place to Alfredo.

"For Rosita I should be glad," sighed Alfredo. "Her life has been *triste*. When she was very young she was about to be married. To a fine *caballero*. But a horse threw him and broke his neck. Since then Rosita has been sad. She has shunned society; for many years I thought she would take vows in a convent. She is twenty-five now. This Señor Vogle, he, too, is a fine *caballero*. Do you not agree, my friend?"

"Sure," Kirk said. "But about this CLC killer. I hear they got some tough hombres over at the Rafter Cross. Birds like that Dillon gunny. Could it be somebody from the Rafter Cross?"

"Colonel Harper is my very close friend," Alfredo said. "It would grieve me if one of his men is guilty. He hires many men who wear guns. He does not like homesteaders. He believes in the divine right of cattle kings and he thinks plows should stay in Kansas. Once he caught a nester skinning one of his cows and he thinks they are all like that. But he is honest, señor. His word is his bond. And he has given me his word that no Rafter Cross man is guilty of this crime."

"Then who can it be?"

"Some wandering bad man, I'm afraid, like Billy the Kid. Not Billy himself, because I know he was in Lincoln when it happened. But someone like him."

In a little while Kirk took his leave. Alfredo wanted him to stay all night, but Kirk insisted on getting back to town. A boy brought his horse, and he rode toward Las Vegas.

Adam Vogle left the Baca hacienda only an hour later. His nerves were still jumpy from the encounter with Calloway. Driving his buggy team over the ridge, he made two stern resolutions. From now on he would drink coffee whether he liked it or not. And from now on he'd be careful where he drove in a buggy.

Buggy tires leave distinct tracks. And this Calloway had a keen eye for tracks. He hadn't missed Vogle's on the trail today. Had he noticed similar tire tracks near the CLC bunkhouse? Had he been baiting Vogle?

It was clear that he'd questioned someone about the coffee habits of Mark Lindsay. Had he made the same inquiry about Vogle's? Adam Vogle kept a permanent room at the Exchange and ate all his meals there. Any of the waitresses could have told Calloway their star boarder never drank coffee.

No, Vogle concluded, Calloway wasn't as yet suspicious. If he were, he would have confided his suspicions to Alfredo. It was certain that he hadn't, because Alfredo's parting word to Vogle had been cordial. "You must come to see us again, my friend. Our house is yours."

So there was nothing to worry about.

Relaxing, Vogle topped the ridge and drove on down the rocky trail. All in all, his plans were working out well. The girl didn't dislike him. And she was rich — or would be some day. She was Alfredo Baca's only heir. Above everything else Adam Vogle wanted wealth —

and he knew three ways to get it. You could earn it, steal it, or marry it.

Vogle was after it on all three trails.

The third trail, however, hadn't occurred to him until day before yesterday. At least he hadn't thought of it in connection with Rosita Baca. He knew her well enough, for she'd often bought merchandise in his store. It was the Jack Dillon incident which had stirred Vogle to look in that direction.

Dillon had cracked a gun down on Alfredo. It wasn't fatal. But it might have been. The next time, perhaps, it would be. Sheriffs lived on borrowed time. In a town like Las Vegas they usually didn't last long. Sheriff Baca, this far, had been lucky. But he would carry his pitcher of nerve to the well once too often. If not this season, then the next. In the end he'd go down with his boots on, under the guns of some desperado. When he did, his estate would be Rosita's.

And Vogle could see even further than that. The fingers of his mind touched and played with even more delicate angles. There was the matter of a wager between Alfredo Baca and Calvin Harper. It was now doubled. Two thousand steers. By the time the railroad came, it might be doubled again. If Alfredo should lose, it would make a deep dent in his fortune.

But he wouldn't lose. Vogle would see to it that he didn't. It shouldn't be difficult. Any clever man, given time for planning, can delay a train for a day. Baca was betting on an odd day. So if the first train chanced to arrive on an odd day, Vogle need do nothing at all. But if it were scheduled to arrive on an *even* day, a bit of stealthy sabotage somewhere up the track would insure the reverse.

Alfredo Baca, of course, would never connive at anything like that. He would rather lose his last peso than stack a deck. But Alfredo would know nothing about it. No one need know but Adam Vogle. The first train would arrive on an odd day, and Alfredo would win the bet. And Adam Vogle would, eventually, get both ends of it plus Rosita. He would marry all of the Linked Hearts and part of the Rafter Cross.

That fortune he would pile on the three-fourths of the CLC he had already looted, all of which was salted away in realty waiting to be boomed by the coming of rails. Dusk enclosed him now, and in the distance Vogle could see the lights of Las Vegas. He drove on toward them, the fingers of his mind strumming these prospects as the strings of a harp. He would be the richest man in all New Mexico.

CHAPTER
TEN

Slated for Death

The Las Vegas barrooms were noisy this Sunday night as Vogle drove past them. He left his rig at the livery stable and walked to the hotel on the plaza.

He was about to go upstairs when an idea struck him. He turned into the dining-room and sat down.

A waitress asked him, "What may I bring you, Señor Vogle?"

"I'm not hungry. Had a heavy dinner out at the Linked Hearts. Just bring me a cup of coffee, Juanita."

She stared. "Coffee? But you never —"

"You're mistaken," Vogle snapped. "I often take coffee. Especially in the evening when I'm tired."

After forcing it down, he went up to his room. He had opened the door and taken a step inside before he saw the slip of paper. It lay on the floor just inside the door. Evidently it had been pushed through the crack at the sill.

Vogle picked it up idly, supposing it was a message from one of his clerks. Then a chill gripped him. Four short lines, in awkward printing, were scrawled on the paper. Vogle read:

Six knew;
Four died;
Now two know:
Usted y uno otro.

The last line most of all shocked Vogle. *You and one other!*

Calloway! His first thought was Calloway. The entire tone of the message was derisive. He felt a dismal certainty that Calloway knew.

Or was Calloway only guessing? Trying to panic him! Had certain clues found at the CLC pointed Calloway's mind toward Vogle? Was that why he'd called on the Bacas?

Vogle sat down in a fretting sweat. It might be that Charlie Swift had left a record in writing. A clear statement of the CLC coup, implicating Vogle. Swift might have done that to checkmate a double-cross. Or possibly Mark Lindsay, after learning the truth, had mailed a letter to a friend. The friend could be Calloway. Calloway's opportune arrival at the CLC pointed that way.

Then why hadn't Calloway exposed Vogle to Baca? To Vogle, there could only be one answer. He knew what he himself would do in such a situation. He would try to cut in. He'd put hooks out for a share of the loot.

It was like Vogle to judge others by himself. Calloway, he concluded, was playing cat-and-mouse. He planned to soften Vogle up and then, when selling-out time came, demand a split.

It left Vogle only one thing to do.

Early morning found him driving his buggy team south out of town. In his lap was a package about the size of a shoe box.

He turned up a swale and followed it into a piñon canyon. Vogle hitched his team and walked on a little way with the package under his arm. He came to a spot where the ground was strewn with empty brass shells.

Vogle opened his package. This time he took out only one cloth target. He tacked it to a tree and backed off ten paces. He took a gun from the package and began shooting. Deliberately. A quick draw wasn't important. It wasn't going to be that kind of a fight.

Vogle fired fifty rounds before he hit the bull's-eye. He must keep at it. He opened another box of shells and reloaded. Crack! A hole in the four-ring. Crack! This time in the three-ring. But it must be dead center. Ten paces, slow and sure. He'd keep at it if it took every shell in his store. The target was only cloth on a tree. But some day it would be Kirk Calloway.

Kirk spent that Monday with Pacheco and Torres at the CLC. He finally got them started on an inventory of chattel. Kirk tossed a notebook to Torres. "List everything. Every hoof of stock with the CLC iron on it. We'll check it against Charlie Swift's tally book."

Late in the afternoon he saddled Red. "If anything comes up, I'll be in town. Might stay there all night."

He rode to Las Vegas but failed to find Alfredo at the sheriff's office. "He is detained at his rancho," the jailer said. "But he sent you a message, señor. You are to make yourself at home in his apartment. Here is the key."

Kirk let himself into Alfredo's private quarters off the jail. The couch was the kind that could be made into a bed. There were blankets in a closet. He decided to take the place over until Alfredo returned from the Linked Hearts.

"I'll hang around town a day or two, Pancho. It'll give me a chance to find out who's who around here."

Kirk sauntered from bar to bar, sizing up the gunslung customers. Maybe the man he wanted had left the country. On the other hand the killer could be right here in Vegas. On a side street jutting off the plaza, Kirk found a row of dives he hadn't seen before. It was called "*La Calle de la Amargura*," The Road of Suffering and Bitterness. Its walks were flanked by bawdy houses, dance halls, and saloons. A pest hole, this street was, worse than anything Kirk had ever seen in Kansas. Yet, in startling contrast, an ancient adobe church stood at the end of it, looking sadly down it; and the name on it was *The Church of Our Lady of Sorrows*.

From bar to bar Kirk roved, absorbing a hum of talk.

"They're sure raisin' hell down in Lincoln County."

"No worse'n here, I'd say. Look at that CLC deal. Five up and four down."

"He can sure throw lead, that jasper can. Me, I'm keepin' outa his way. Two more of the same, Pedro."

At suppertime, a lean, white-thatched cattleman approached Kirk in the hotel lobby. "You're Alfredo's new deputy, ain't yuh? I'm Cal Harper of the Rafter Cross." He held out a hand.

Kirk grinned. "Sorry I had to jug one of your help, colonel. But he was on the prod."

Harper shrugged. "You mean Jack Dillon? That's all right. Alfredo turned him loose, soon as he sobered up. Reckon he'll behave himself from now on."

"Some people named Dunbar took up claims out your way, colonel. Right nice folks. Met 'em yet?"

Harper became suddenly cold. "I don't mix with nesters," he said stiffly. "They're all alike. Bustin' up good grama grass sod and stringin' wire for stock to get cut up on! When their crops burn up, they start butcherin' beef. Never knew one yet that wouldn't steal yuh blind."

"These Dunbars aren't that kind."

Harper's face flamed. "They're *all* that kind. Damnyankee, sod-bustin', beef-butcherin' parasites." The old cowman looked suspiciously at Kirk. "What part of the country did *you* come from, Calloway?"

"I was born in Texas," Kirk said.

Relief relaxed Harper's face. "For a minute, Calloway, I thought you was a damnyankee. I beg your pawdon, suh." He turned and walked stiffly out.

Late in the evening, Kirk strolled into the Buena Suerte. On a platform at the rear, a girl was singing. The bar was crowded. From an adjoining room came the rattle of dice and the whirr of a wheel. The singing girl smiled at Kirk and when she finished she pressed her way toward him.

"I am Carmencita. Will you buy me a drink?"

He thought she was just digging. But when he bought her a drink he learned better. "I will help you, Señor Calloway," she said earnestly.

107

"Help me do what?"

"I will help you hang him, señor." Her black eyes flashed. "The man who killed my *querido*."

"Your sweetheart? Who was he?"

"Carlos. He was killed with three others."

"You mean Charlie Swift? Okay, Carmencita. How can you help me?"

"I do not know. But all men come to this place, señor. When they drink they talk much. I, Carmencita, will listen."

"Thanks, Carmencita. Mix around and keep your ears open. If you pick up anything, let me know."

"Where can I find you, señor?"

"I live at the manager's cabin out at the CLC. If you don't see me around town, look me up out there."

"I know the place, señor. Sometimes I have visit Carlos there." She glided away.

Kirk sauntered toward the rear. Passing Dillon he nodded, but the Rafter Cross man didn't relax. His sulky eyes followed as Kirk moved on into the gaming-room beyond.

Roulette, chuckaluck, and three-card-monte were going on. Patronage was brisk, and Kirk strolled from table to table looking at faces.

One face gave him a start. This man was sitting alone at a green-clothed board, practicing with a pair of dice. Kirk couldn't tell whether he was a house dealer or a customer waiting for a game. But the face was familiar. It was darkly handsome, with deep sideburns dipping down from black, crinkly hair. The man's sleeves were rolled to the elbows. A center-creased gray hat tipped on the back of his head suggested he wasn't working for the house. Dealers on duty were usually bareheaded.

"Hello, Macklin," Kirk said. "You passed me on the stage, headin' this way. Workin' here?"

Macklin pushed his chair back and stood up. He was beltless, but Kirk saw a bulge at his left breast. Here was the sharper who had stacked cards against Archie Templeton up in Colorado.

"No. But I see *you* are." Macklin's eyes fixed on a badge on Kirk's vest.

"Stoppin' here long?" Kirk questioned.

"That any of your business?"

"Not unless we get a complaint," Kirk said. "We got a sheriff down here who's touchy that way. He's a sky-limit sport himself. He'll bet you his shirt or his ranch on one turn of a card. But he's dead on the level. You start stackin' decks around here and he'll cut loose. So watch your step."

Macklin's lips curved downward. He picked up the dice. "I'll roll you one throw, Calloway, to see which of us leaves town. Don't look like it's big enough for both of us."

Kirk shook his head, his gaze fixed on the dice. "I'm afraid they're loaded, Macklin."

"They're not," Macklin retorted. "But I got somethin' else that is."

"Okay." Kirk shifted his gaze to the breast bulge. "Start throwin' it."

"You talk big — with that badge on!"

Kirk unpinned the badge and dropped it in his pocket. Then he stood waiting, with an inviting smile.

When Macklin made no move, Kirk turned his back and walked out. Twenty minutes later he was in bed in Baca's room off the *carcel*.

In the morning Alfredo rode in from his ranch.

"I rode herd on the town last night," Kirk reported, "but didn't see anything I could throw a loop on. There's a girl at the Buena Suerte named Carmencita. She's on our side. And a cold-decker named Macklin. He's not."

"We must have patience, *amigo*. Where do you go now?"

"Out to the CLC to find out how the tally's comin' on. Be seein' you."

It was nearly noon when Kirk pulled up at the CLC bunkhouse. There was no sign of life. The mounts of his two assistants were in the corral, so he knew they weren't out counting cattle.

He found them snoring in their bunks. Kirk wakened them.

Pacheco looked up blearily, his breath heavy with wine. Kirk rebuked them sternly. "What do you think we're workin' for, a bank?"

"We are sorry, señor. But last night at Dos Robles there is a christening. This little *niña*, she is my niece. Afterward there is a fandango and much celebration."

Dos Robles was a small Mexican plaza down on the Pecos. "So you got home about five o'clock this morning?"

"We are in bed by four," Torres insisted. He pressed his head with both hands. "Never again will I take so much wine."

110

"Cook up some grub," Kirk directed. "Soon as we eat, we'll start counting cows."

He went on to the manager's cabin. Its doors were locked but when Kirk went into the bedroom he noticed he'd left a window open. The room was untidy, just as he'd left it upon getting up Sunday morning. On the bed was his own blanket roll, atop quilts and bedding which had been used by Charlie Swift.

Kirk hung up his coat. He was about to straighten the bulge of covers on the bed when some odd detail of it caught his eye. He stepped back, staring. He turned then to look at the open window. It was about ten feet from, and broadside to, the bed.

His tongue curled in his cheek, thoughtfully, as he looked again at the pillow-bulged covers rolled in disarray on the bed. Then he went outside and circled to the open window. Through it he looked in at the bed. It was high noon now, and he could easily see that no one was in it. But at night, with only starlight, it would look different. In the dimness it would appear that a man was sleeping there.

Through that roll of bedding, just about where a sleeper's shoulder blades would be, was a bullet hole.

Kirk stooped and picked up an empty shell. It was a forty-five, quite like those found by an empty chair at the bunkshack massacre.

And Kirk saw footprints. Bootprints. He followed them in the dust. They led a hundred yards to brush along the creek bank. Here were hoofprints. A horse had been tethered here. The would-be assassin had mounted and ridden away, losing his trail in the creek.

111

From that moment Kirk knew that he was a marked man. He didn't know why. Not even faintly did his mind reach out toward Adam Vogle. He knew only that a bullet, somewhere, had his name on it. Last night it had come looking for him. And having come once, it was sure to come again.

CHAPTER
ELEVEN

Fugitives' Hide-Out

High and remote in the Truchas Mountains, Stumpy Goff kept a small horse ranch. Truchas Peak reared not far back of it, in Santa Fe County. His house was an old abandoned mine cabin just across the San Miguel County line. No trail ran near the cabin, and Goff shared it only with his *segundo*, Jake Orme, and a silent, stolid Indian who cooked for them.

Sometimes a rider stopped by to sell, buy, or trade a horse. Stumpy Goff was always fair in a horse trade. He was an enormously fat man with a wooden leg and a neck as thick as his head. Usually he sat alone on the stoop of his cabin, puffing a pipe and gazing sleepily out across his rugged pastures of cedar and piñon.

Directly behind his cabin was a timbered cone, perfect in symmetry, and so steep that one wondered how the cedars clung to its slopes. Actually it was, or had been, a volcano, extinct these last thousand years or so. In it mining men had once found a vein of silver and had driven a tunnel partly through it. Acres of tailings had been dumped outside the mine entrance, so that the immediate environs of the cabin was now a waste of slag. When the miners moved out, Stumpy

113

Goff had moved in. It was a bleak, rocky country, but near-by pockets and swales gave Goff enough grass for his fifty-odd horses.

On a day late in March Goff saw a horseman emerge from the cedars down canyon. The man approached at a lope, the hoofs of his horse clattering on slag.

An old Indian appeared at Goff's side with a rifle. "Never mind, Chaco," Goff said. "It's only Jake."

Jake Orme, gray with dust, dismounted at the cabin. The Indian led the horse around to a shed against a cliff back of the cabin.

Goff asked anxiously, "Run into any grief, Jake?"

"Nope," Jake Orme reported. "All I had to do was take a room at the hotel right across the hall from Vogle's."

"You slipped that note under his door?"

Jake grinned. "It was duck soup. Right now I'm drier'n a buffalo skull, Stumpy. Let's go inside."

Goff, his peg leg clumping on the boards, followed him inside. He eased his three hundred pounds into a chair while Jake poured liquor. "Any new boarders since I left, Stumpy?"

Goff shook his head. "Nary a one, Jake. Just the same five hombres. And two of them aim to pull out in a few days."

"You got a new one headin' this way right now," Jake said.

"Who's that?"

"You remember Hank Roach?"

"Roach? Yeh. He on the run again?"

Orme nodded. "I found him holin' up at Wagon Mound. He's on the way here. Wouldn't let him ride with me account of him forkin' a hot bronc."

Stumpy's eyes slitted. "What's he runnin' from?"

"Some grief up at Trinidad. Seems like he met some guy on Raton Pass and the guy recognized this hot bronc. It ain't branded, but it's a calico mare you could spot a mile away. The guy tipped a sheriff, and the sheriff begun askin' Hank questions. One word led to another and Hank pulled a gun. He ventilated that there sheriff, so now he's on the run till it blows over. Listen; maybe that's him now."

From far down the valley came hoof sounds. Goff finished his drink and stumped outside. In a little while a man on a calico mount emerged from the cedars.

Hank Roach rode up and dismounted. "Hi, Stumpy. Want you to put me on ice fer a while. Month or two maybe, till things quiet down."

"You know my rules, Hank," the fat man warned. "Twenty dollars a day. And I don't keep rustled hosses around here."

"Suits me, Stumpy. I'm flush. Get rid of the mare, if you wanta. She's too light fer my size anyway. You can sell me another one when I pull out."

Goff called the Indian. "Unsaddle that mare, Chaco. Then lead her down on the flats and turn her loose with the first bunch of range stock you see. Hank, come on inside."

Actually, Goff's horse ranch was only a front for a strange type of hotel he operated here. His patrons were fugitive outlaws. They came and went, always paying in advance. Sometimes there'd been as many as a dozen and sometimes none at all. Goff's place had always been a secure asylum for men on the run, like Hank Roach.

"This way, Hank." Goff took a lighted lantern and went out the back door. Roach followed him fifty yards to a shed built flush against a cliff.

At the rear of the shed was a box stall. A manger in the stall was piled high with old hay. Goff pulled some of the hay aside, and his lantern exposed a dark, cavernous opening. It was the outlet of a tunnel which miners had once drilled into this steep, conical hill.

The tunnel was rock-walled and high enough for a man to walk through without stooping. Goff entered it with his lantern. He was remarkably active for a man of his weight and affliction. Roach followed him down a long, twisting stope to an oaken door in a bulkhead of logs.

Goff produced a brass key and unlocked the door. With Roach at his heels, he passed through this door, relocking it after him. And still the tunnel continued on, its grade slightly downward, curving and angling through solid rock.

Although he'd been here before, Roach shivered. "Hell of a hole. Gives me the willies."

Goff stopped. "You don't have to come in, less'n you want to. If you'd rather stretch a rope —"

"Let's go," Roach growled.

Stumpy led on, his lantern playing eerily on the walls.

More than a quarter of a mile beyond the locked bulkhead they saw a faint square of daylight ahead.

116

Arriving there, they emerged into an oval area covering about ten acres and open to the sky. Its walls were sheer and unscalable. Hank Roach looked up and saw the sun. But he knew he wouldn't see it long. Only for a few hours at midday could sunlight shine directly down into this wall of rock. The floor of it, however, was rich mountain loam washed in through the centuries by snow and rain. A growth of wild cherries, leafless now in March, covered most of it. A rim of snow was banked around two sides of the oval. Through a deep drift elling from this a footpath had been shoveled. At the top end of the oval stood a rambling cabin of logs.

"It's hell's ice box!" Roach grumbled.

"Quitcher gripin'," Goff retorted. "Where else in New Mexico can you find a hotel with hot and cold water?"

Literally it was true, for a warm spring emerging from a crevice in the wall gave a degree of mildness to the climate of the crater. Yet a bucketful from it, set aside, would soon be icy cold.

"Last time I was here," Roach muttered, "these capulins were in bloom."

"They'll be bloomin' again, coupla months from now," Stumpy assured him. He moved on toward the log cabin.

A man wearing a holstered gun appeared in its doorway. He called back to others inside. "Here comes Stumpy. Looks like he's got a new boarder."

Two other men came out. Both were gun-slung and unshaven. One of them recognized Roach. "Hi, Hank. Whatsamatter? Can't yuh keep outa trouble?"

"If I could," Roach shot back, "I wouldn't come to a deadfall like this. And neither would you, Smitty."

117

They went into a wide, square room, snugly chinked, and with double-deck bunks on three sides. On the fourth side was a hearth with a fire blazing. Cards lay scrambled on a table where three of the men had been gaming. Two other outlaws were asleep in bunks.

"Where's the kid?" Stumpy asked.

Smitty thumbed toward a kitchen. "Washin' dishes."

"Has he give you any trouble?"

"He did at first, Stumpy. Got stubborn, and Amarillo had to crack him one. Since then he's been Mary's little lamb."

The man known as Amarillo asked, "What you keepin' him for, Stumpy; a pet?"

"He's somebody's hostage," Goff said. "I dunno what for. They're payin' his board. What for's none of my business. Or yours. He can't bother you any. You got guns and he ain't. If he gets sassy, slap him down."

Smitty laughed. "It's okay by me, Stumpy. He does all the cookin' and chores and he keeps the snow shoveled off. If he wasn't here, we'd have it to do ourselves."

Goff pushed the kitchen door open and peered in. An unarmed man stood at the sink, washing pots and pans. "How they treatin' yuh, kid?"

When Mark Lindsay turned to face him, Goff was amazed at the change in him. The eyes were dull, the face listless. Upon arrival here he'd been defiant, lashing out with hands, feet, and tongue. Now he seemed completely subdued.

"What difference does it make?" There was no tone of challenge in Mark's voice. He turned spiritlessly back to the sink.

118

Goff rejoined his paying guests. "You fellahs sure made a good Injun outa that kid. But don't take any chances. Keep him locked in the grub room at nights, like I said."

"Speakin' of locks," Roach growled, "we're locked up ourselves. It's like bein' in jail."

Smitty chuckled. "That oughter make *you* feel right at home, Hank."

"Difference between this and jail," Goff reminded them, "is that here you can skin out any night you want."

They couldn't deny that. Because at each nightfall Indian Chaco came to the tunnel bulkhead with rations. Any boarder who was willing to risk facing posses again had merely to say so; the Indian would then lead him out to Goff's cabin and bring him a horse. At all other times the bulkhead door was kept locked, with the key in Goff's pocket.

Goff now left them and went back through the tunnel.

Emerging in the shed, he replaced hay over the manger and went on to his cabin. Jake Orme was there, but not the Indian.

"Chaco took that calico bronc down valley," Jake said. "I told him to get it plumb off our range before he turns it loose."

The trip through the tunnel had put an ache in Stumpy's leg. He sat down and propped it on a stool. "Hand me my pipe, Jake."

Jake complied and poured whisky for himself. "Everything all right inside?"

"Couldn't be better, Jake. That Lindsay kid's tame as a rabbit."

"Them guys savvy why we're holdin' him?"

Goff's eyes narrowed slyly. "They do not. And what they don't know won't hurt 'em, Jake."

Jake gulped his drink. "I'm not so danged sure," he admitted, "that I savvy myself. Just why *are* we holdin' him?"

"You're dumber'n I thought, Jake. Listen. Forgy and Dalhart wanted him held for a witness, in case they needed to build a fire under Vogle. But you heard the news, didn't yuh? Forgy and Dalhart are dead, now. So's Stites and Charlie Swift. The whole CLC outfit was shot dead in a bunkhouse, by one man. Only one man had a motive."

Orme nodded. "Vogle."

"Sure. Vogle did it to keep from splittin' with anybody. He figgers to sell out when the railroad comes, at boom prices, and keep it all for himself. He don't know this Lindsay kid's alive and kickin'. If we turn Lindsay loose, Vogle's cooked. He'll hang for a six-thousand-cow steal and four murders."

Jake was still a little confused. "But if we turn Lindsay loose, we're sheriff-bait outselves."

"Use your head. We don't need to turn him loose. A threat to turn him loose'll be enough to scare hell outa Vogle. When the right times comes, we'll make a date with Vogle out on the range somewhere and show him Lindsay. All Vogle can do then is eat out of our hand."

"Why don't we shake him down right now?"

"Because he hasn't cashed in yet," Goff explained patiently. "He won't cash in till the railroad gets to Vegas. You don't eat a goose, Jake, till you fatten him up."

"Then what was the idea of me pokin' that note under his door?"

"You not only got to fatten your goose, Jake, you got to cook him. Stew him over a slow fire. I want Vogle soft and tender when the time comes. So we begin right now makin' him sweat blood. We let him know somebody knows. He'll wonder who. He won't figure it was us put that note under his door. He'll think it was somebody right there in town. So he'll be scared stiff. Nothin' like a good case of the jitters to soften a guy up, Jake. Then when the time comes, we tell him everything's okay, all he has to do is divvy up."

Back in the crater, Mark Lindsay went docilely about his chores. Smitty came into the kitchen as Mark finished with his pots and pans. "We're outa firewood, kid. Shake a leg."

"Comin' up," Mark said, and went out to a woodpile.

This was a heap of cedar and pine deadfalls which the Indian had tossed in from the rim above. Mark took an ax and began chopping. He'd thought it out carefully. His only chance was to pretend being cowed. He must put them off guard. If he went around for a while like a whipped dog, they'd pay him less attention. First of all he wanted a gun. You can't snatch a gun from a man if he's watching you.

Mark chopped lustily at a log, hacking it into hearth-length chunks. The ax itself was a weapon, and he'd thought of using it. But he knew he couldn't swing an ax against five gunmen. And today had come one more. Six in all.

But he'd heard two talk of pulling out in a few days. That would leave four. If he could grab a gun from one, he might shoot it out with the other three.

There'd still be a locked oaken door in the tunnel. Could he chop through it with an ax? It was near the outer entrance and the chopping might be heard by Goff. But one thing at a time. First a gun. Then a gun fight.

After that he could wait at the bulkhead door till the Indian came with rations at nightfall. And then bang down on the Indian. After which he could go on to Goff's outside cabin and shoot his way through Goff and Orme.

Mark picked up an armload of wood and carried it in. Returning to the woodpile he resumed chopping. Occasionally he looked up at the crater's rim. More than a hundred sheer feet from here to there. Time and again he'd circled the wall, like a caged animal, looking for a place to climb. There wasn't any. He must go out through the tunnel or not at all.

As light began to fade, he went in and made supper for six hungry outlaws. Mark himself ate in the kitchen. All around him were plenty of sharp knives and quart bottles. Any of these could be used to strike with. But six armed men were too many. He must wait.

122

Tonight as he washed his pans he could hear them at cards in the other room. And drinking. Goff furnished them liquor with the rations, provided they paid extra for it. Mark tried to think of some way to drug the liquor. But he had no drug. Night after night he'd waited hopefully for them to get drunk. Sometimes they did, but it was always after they'd locked him in the grub room.

Tonight he didn't wait to be prodded in there. He went in of his own accord and stretched out on his floor pallet. Soon he heard a key turn in the lock. No knife or ax in here. Nothing to cut or chop with. They'd made sure of that.

For hours he lay sleepless, thinking about Christine Dunbar. Had her father's wagon arrived in Las Vegas? Had they taken up those Conchas Creek claims he'd recommended?

A sense of shame and failure came over Mark. He'd promised Christine he'd be waiting in Las Vegas. She'd crossed mountain and desert to join him there. What was she thinking now?

CHAPTER
TWELVE

Six Thousand Missing Cattle

Alfredo Baca and Kirk Calloway hunched in puzzlement over the latest tally of CLC cattle.

"Pacheco and Torres," Kirk muttered, "both swear it's right. And I've made a rough check myself. Two thousand head won't miss it five percent, one way or the other."

Alfredo frowned. "But here is Charlie Swift's tally book, señor. It says eight thousand. The Englishman who inspected in February checked the count. See, here are his initials."

"That," Kirk agreed, "seems to put Swift in the clear. He and his men were killed only a few days after the Englishman left. They couldn't have driven off six thousand head in that short time. What's the answer, Alfredo?"

"Those four men," Baca reminded him, "had been dead two days before we found them. In that two days no one was there to watch the ranch. Perhaps rustlers knew about this, so by night they drove off the cattle. There was not time to round up all, so two thousand were left behind."

"Could be," Kirk brooded. "Or here's another angle. Maybe rustlers went there to steal cattle. They begin

124

bunchin' 'em for a drive. But they don't want to be followed. So one man goes to the CLC bunkhouse and sits in at supper. He pulls a gun and shoots four times. Then he joins his gang and they work all night and the next day, getting the cows bunched and started off. About that time another CLC puncher, Mark Lindsay, shows up. He was used mainly as a stray man. So he could have been off huntin' strays when the killing happened. He finds his outfit dead and the cattle gone. He follows the trail alone."

Alfredo sighed. "If that is true, señor, it explains everything. He would catch up with these men and they would kill him. We must search for his body on the range."

Kirk's thoughts went gloomily to Christine Dunbar. She'd come to New Mexico expecting to be Lindsay's bride. Kirk told Baca about that. "She's still waitin' for him, Alfredo."

Lindsay, they agreed, could have followed the trail because it was fresh. He might even have arrived home before the drive was out of sight. But it was different now. Dust storms of the past weeks had covered all tracks.

"*Caramba!*" worried Alfredo. "We cannot find these *ladrones*. We cannot even find him who fired a bullet into your bed."

Kirk grinned. "He'll be payin' me another call, maybe."

"Who could it be? Have you enemies, *amigo?*"

"Couple of guys around here don't like me much. Dillon of the Rafter Cross and that gambler, Macklin."

125

Mail had just arrived on the stage, and a deputy now came in with a fat letter, officially sealed. Alfredo opened it and exclaimed, "It is from the British embassy at Washington, señor." His eyes skimmed over the contents.

"They thank us," he reported, "for taking custody of Crown Land and Cattle Company property in this county. They have sent a cable to England and received a reply. Señor Archibald Templeton, the company agent, will come back to America by the first ship. He will have authority to employ a new manager for the ranch." A flush of shame crossed Alfredo's sensitive face. "I shall be humiliated," he sighed, "when I tell Señor Templeton that six thousand of his cattle are missing."

"So let's try to locate 'em," Kirk said, "before he gets here. It's a cinch somebody saw 'em being driven out. You can't hide a herd that size in your hat."

"What do you suggest, *amigo?*"

"Suppose I ride a big circle all around the rim of this county. Say a radius of fifty miles from here. The drive crossed that circle somewhere. I'll ask at every plaza and sheep camp I come to."

"Good," agreed Alfredo. "I will give you expense money. Begin at the Rafter Cross and circle from there. I will work close in around Las Vegas. Between us, we may hear talk of these *ladrones.*"

"One other thing," Kirk suggested. "We still got two thousand head on the CLC and we don't want to lose 'em."

126

"That is true, señor. So I will send two more deputies to help Torres and Pacheco."

As an afterthought, Alfredo went to his files and brought out a batch of circulars received in the past several years from surrounding states and territories. When he spread them on a table, Kirk saw a veritable rogues' gallery of southwestern bad men. Most of them were notorious outlaws wanted for murder in Kansas, Colorado, and Texas. Each circular described a man and, in some cases, gave his photograph both frontally and in profile.

"Take these along," Alfredo said. "I have duplicates on file. As you ride the big circle, you can ask if any of these men have been seen."

"Names don't mean much," Kirk said. "They change 'em as often as they change horses." He looked the photographs over but failed to find one which resembled the gambler Macklin.

Kirk took his bay gelding to the livery barn. "Grain him good," he directed. "I'm taking off on a long ride."

The stage depot was across from the livery barn, and when Kirk emerged he saw a farm wagon in front of it. An arch of canvas had been removed, but Kirk recognized it by its team of white mules. He crossed over expecting to find Alex Dunbar.

Instead he found Christine on the walk directing the loading of freight. A stage hand was heaving sixteen spools of barbed wire into the wagon. A curious crowd stood by. This was the first barbed wire that most of them had ever seen.

Kirk tipped his hat. "Mornin', ma'am."

127

She recognized him with a studied disinterest. "Oh, it's you! You're the sheriff, aren't you, who wants to arrest Mark Lindsay?"

Kirk flushed. "No ma'am. I tore up that warrant and got me another one." He produced it and showed her the name John Doe on it. "I figure Lindsay's not the man we want."

She relaxed only a little. "That's generous of you!" He didn't miss the irony as she turned her attention again to the loader. "Don't forget that seed corn, please."

The loader began tossing sacks of seed corn into the wagon. "You-all aim to get a crop in this spring, miss?"

"Yes, my father's plowing right now. He's going to fence a forty to keep out cattle. That's why I had to come in for this freight. We ordered it before we left Iowa."

With her back to Kirk, she continued to chat with the loader about a spring crop. "I hear Swede Olsen's tossin' up a house fer yuh."

"Yes, we hope to get a roof on before the rains. Don't forget that bag of staples, please."

One of the regular stage drivers came out of the depot. He saw Kirk and grinned. "Well," he cracked, "I see you finally caught up with it."

"Caught up with what?" Kirk asked.

"That white-mule outfit. You're the gent asked me about it at Otero, ain't yuh?"

Kirk, coloring a little, didn't answer.

The driver said, "And later I found out you asked about it at every town on the trail." His eyes flicked from the white mules to Christine and then back to Kirk. "Well, looks like she's worth ketchin' up with, fellah." With a broad grin he sauntered on up the street.

Kirk became aware that Christine had turned and was staring at him. "You mean — you followed us here? All the way from Kansas?"

"No ma'am," Kirk floundered. The brick-redness of his face made him unconvincing. "I was just headin' this direction anyway. I just got to wonderin' how far you folks was goin'."

"That was nice of you, Mr. Calloway." Her eyes were friendly again. "If you'd asked us back at Cottonwood Falls, we would have told you."

"I didn't think to ask." An inspiration saved Kirk. "You see, it was like this. On the pass I saw a man on a calico mare that looked like yours. So I wanted to tell you. That's why I asked at every town on the trail." He hoped she wouldn't remember that Otero was a hundred miles the other side of the pass.

To his relief she changed the subject. "We're worried about Mark Lindsay, Mr. Calloway. He was to have met us here. Have you any idea what happened to him?"

Kirk had more than an idea. His grim conviction was that her fiancé was dead on the range somewhere, riddled by cow-thief bullets. He couldn't tell her that. Yet she was entitled to know the facts and probabilities. Perhaps he'd better tell them to her father instead of to the girl herself.

While Kirk debated this delicate point, Alfredo Baca went to lunch at the hotel on the plaza. He found two of his friends at a table together, Adam Vogle and Cal Harper. Alfredo joined them.

"Can you believe it, señores?" he exclaimed. "The English rancho is short six thousand cows."

Vogle's face registered just the right shade of amazement. "Did you say six thousand? The devil!"

"It is true, señores. My chief deputy will ride a big circle to ask if they have been seen. Maybe they went southwest to the Staked Plains or northwest to the Truchas. We do not know. But Señor Calloway will inquire in all directions. I have taken the liberty, Colonel Harper, to suggest that he stay all night at your rancho. You do not object?"

"'Course not," the old cowman said. "We'll be glad to put him up. Six thousand head, huh! That's a lot of beef."

Shortly, Adam Vogle excused himself and left the table. He hurried to the office of his store and buzzed for a clerk. "Bring me my horse. I will ride down to look at that land I spoke of yesterday."

It was a forty-acre tract which might lie in the path of the railroad. The clerk had heard Vogle discuss it. He also knew that his employer had recently discarded his buggy team for a saddle horse.

When Vogle went out to it, a forty-five gun was hidden in his coat. He was seen riding south out of town. Once out of sight, he veered east to an arroyo. This was a dry wash ten feet deep and with a smooth bed of sand.

Its high banks concealing him, Vogle rode northerly up this wash. He followed its twists for several miles and came to a trail crossing. It was the trail leading from Las Vegas to the Rafter Cross.

Vogle tied his horse a hundred yards down the arroyo from it. Due to a sharp bend in the bank, it could not be seen there from the trail. Advancing afoot up the bed, Vogle looked for a convenient and obscured ambush. He found one only ten yards from where the trail descended into the wash.

It was a flood-cut fissure in the bank with a greasewood bush in front of it. Vogle wedged himself into place there. It gave him complete command of any horseman who might cross here. He loaded the forty-five and waited.

He'd missed, that other time. Or, rather, he'd failed because Calloway had spent the night in another bed. Ever since that night Vogle had been living on needles. He was still certain that Calloway knew the guilt in the CLC crime, that Calloway was playing cat-and-mouse, baiting Vogle for a cut in the loot. Someone knew. A note poked under his room door proved it. Who else could it be but Calloway?

Vogle could never draw a free breath till Calloway was dead.

This afternoon Calloway would ride to the Rafter Cross. He would cross this arroyo just ten yards from the muzzle of Vogle's gun. The man's profile would be toward Vogle. He wouldn't be alert. At ten yards Vogle couldn't miss. He cocked the gun and waited.

In a little while he heard someone coming. Horse hoofs on the trail! They approached at a canter from the direction of Las Vegas. Calloway? An icy sweat bathed Vogle. Winging Calloway wouldn't be enough. He must kill at the first shot. Calloway had a gun himself. Even if knocked from the saddle he could, with a breath of life left, shoot it out with Vogle.

The horseman arrived at the bank and turned down the steep cut to the arroyo's bed. Vogle saw the horse's head, then the mane, the rider's knee. His finger tensed on the trigger.

But it wasn't Calloway. The lean, blizzard-bitten profile of Colonel Cal Harper came into view. Vogle relaxed, crouching in his ambush. Harper, not seeing him, rode on. Riding up the far bank, he resumed his canter toward the Rafter Cross.

For another nerve-racking hour Vogle waited. Then again he heard someone coming from the direction of Las Vegas. A creak of wheels identified it as a wagon. A team of white mules descended into the arroyo. Then a wagon with a girl driving.

And then Kirk Calloway. He was on a bay horse, riding at her wheel.

Vogle held his fire. He couldn't shoot with a witness present. The Dunbar wagon, with Calloway riding by it, passed on and out of sight.

Two hours later it arrived at the Dunbar homestead. The Swedish carpenter was putting up the roof rafters of a house. Off across the meadow Kirk saw the other two mules pulling a plow, Alex Dunbar plodding along behind.

"You will stay for supper?" Christine invited.

"I got to push on," Kirk said, "to the Rafter Cross."

He had evaded her questions about Mark Lindsay. Now he would ride out to that plow team and tell everything he knew to Alex Dunbar. Kirk preferred not to be present when and if Alex relayed the grim implications to the girl. Only two conclusions seemed possible, and Alex would grasp them at once. Either Lindsay had been killed by rustlers or was himself in league with them.

With four CLC men murdered, the fifth missing along with six thousand head of cattle, what alternate solution could there be?

"I'll just unload the wagon for you," Kirk said.

When he'd done so he rode out to the plow team. There he told Alex Dunbar everything known about the CLC crimes. "Lindsay wasn't there when those four men were shot, Mr. Dunbar. The man who did the shooting doesn't drink coffee, and Lindsay does. The warrant now reads, 'John Doe.' We figure Lindsay was off huntin' strays when it happened."

Dunbar gave him a straight look.

"Then where is he now?"

"We think he came home and saw what happened. Maybe he took off after the rustlers."

"And then?"

"Your guess is as good as mine."

The Iowan's face turned a shade grayer. His voice took a tone of pleading. "Look, Calloway. I've known Mark ever since he was a baby. He and Chris were raised together. And no finer boy ever lived. He wouldn't have anything to do with crooks. If you hear anyone say different, tell 'em it ain't so."

"I'd bet on it," Kirk said. "I never saw him in my life. But I know one thing about him and that's enough. I know your girl picked him, and she wouldn't pick the wrong kind."

Alex Dunbar's eyes were grateful, his voice husky and anxious. "You think he's dead?"

"Either that or in bad trouble. There's a thin chance they got him tied up somewhere. If they have, I'll find him. I'll bring him back to Christine."

"It'd make her awful happy," Alex said. "She'll grieve her heart out if —"

"You break it to her easy, Mr. Dunbar. Make her think everything's comin' out all right." With a dismal feeling that it wouldn't, Kirk rode on down the Conchas toward the Rafter Cross.

CHAPTER
THIRTEEN

Gun Talk

Colonel Harper's ranch buildings lay near the confluence of the Conchas and the Canadian. Kirk Calloway came upon them at dusk — flat-roofed adobes, their lamp-lighted windows gleaming through cottonwoods. Even the corrals had mud walls, with the exception of a spruce-poled roundpen for breaking horses.

Kirk rode up to the main house where Harper met him heartily at the door.

"I was expectin' you, Calloway. Alfredo told me you'd be along." He took Kirk in and poured two brandies. "I was just fixin' to go to supper, suh. Bein' a bachelor I eat at the bunkshack."

Baca, he explained, had already told him about the CLC cattle shortage. "We'll see if the boys got any ideas, Calloway."

Later, at the long cookshack table, Kirk repeated the main facts about the CLC's short tally. A dozen range-wise, gun-belted cowboys heard him through. Jack Dillon was there, and others like him. All in all, they struck Kirk as about the hardest-bitten crew he'd ever seen.

Comment took varied angles. Monte Hickock, the foreman, curled a tongue in his high-boned cheek.

"Sounds like a phony to me, Calloway. You can't drive that many cows without bein' seen."

Others said, "They sure didn't come this way."

"This guy, Lindsay. He trailed 'em, and they got him."

"Either that or he helped 'em."

"They's some wild country south of here, Calloway. Them cows'll be in Mexico by now."

"Maybe they was split up in small bunches and butchered. Have you asked at the reservations?"

"Don't be a dope, Ed. You can't butcher that many head that quick."

The discussion led nowhere. Colonel Harper took Kirk back to the main house and furnished him a bed.

He was asaddle early and riding north up the Canadian. The banks were muddy, and no large herd could have crossed without leaving sign. Every few miles was a camp or Mexican plaza of some kind. Kirk inquired at all of them. He displayed his circulars picturing wanted outlaws.

No one had seen men of those descriptions. Or any large cattle drive within the past month. Brush and mud along the river showed no trace of such a drive.

All other occasional encounters up the Mora brought the same negative response.

Near sundown Kirk saw a man on the creek bank far ahead of him. The man had a red-and-white pole which he held upright as he stood in a spread-legged stance back of it. The pose puzzled Kirk. Riding nearer, he saw other men approaching on foot from the northeast. They were on a single, accurate line and were driving stakes as they came. Far beyond them, almost out of eyesight, another man was sighting through a tripod-borne telescope.

Kirk had seen the same thing in Kansas. So he knew it was a surveyor's transit and that a line was being staked. A man on horseback was directing the crew. Stake by stake they came nearer. Kirk stopped by the man with the striped flagpole and waited for them.

"What's goin' on?"

"This," the forward flagman grinned, "is the main line of the Santa Fe railroad."

The man on horseback came up shouting, "We'll camp here for the night, men. Where's the wagon?"

The wagoneer was up the creek a little way, the flagman said, looking for a camp site.

The horseman saw Kirk and smiled. "Hello, Calloway. Remember me? Morley's my name."

Kirk recognized him. He was the engineer who'd been with Robinson on Raton Pass. "It's bedding-down time, Calloway," he said heartily. "Stay all night with us if you like."

Later, around a supper fire, Ray Morley told about the progress of the road. "We're highballing this way, cowboy. Laying track fast from La Junta down to Trinidad. And we've got some big grading crews on the pass."

"When do you figure on getting to Las Vegas?"

"Vegas? That's hard to say. The rough country back around Raton'll slow us up." Morley noted a badge on Kirk's vest. "Are you sheriffing down this way?"

"Yeh. Deputy at Las Vegas."

"What's this I hear about a big bet down there? Odd or even on the day we hit town."

Kirk confirmed it. "Last I heard it was two thousand steers. May be more by the time the first train comes in."

Morley chuckled. "I'll tell Robby about that. He'll get a kick out of it."

Kirk spent the night with the survey crew and rode on west early in the morning. As he advanced, the country roughened. In a few hours the Truchas foothills closed around him. He was still on the Mora Creek watershed and found an occasional settlement. No one had seen a cattle drive pass that way.

Beyond, the country seemed entirely deserted. It steepened toward a rugged sky line. Riding on, Kirk met no one but an old Mexican herding goats. Again the information was negative. "Any ranches up that way?" Kirk waved a hand toward the peaks of the Truchas.

"There is only Señor Goff's place," the herder said. "It is over the second ridge."

"Sheep outfit?"

"No, it is a rancho of horses. Once it has been a mine, señor."

Kirk continued on, climbing a cedar ridge, dipping into a rocky ravine. It didn't seem likely that six thousand stolen cattle would be pushed through terrain like this. But he must cover everything. He topped a second ridge and saw a wide valley with a few horses grazing. A gray, barren patch at the head of it looked like tailings from a mine. Kirk rode that way and soon

138

saw buildings of rusty, corrugated iron. They appeared to be the deserted quarters and shaft house of an old mine.

A wisp of smoke indicated life. Kirk dismounted at the main cabin. Its front door was open. Through it, Kirk saw a man of enormous girth seated, his artificial leg propped on a stool and his eyes closed in sleep.

"Howdy, neighbor."

At Kirk's hail the fat man opened his eyes. They fixed on a deputy's badge on the stranger's vest. Quickly they shifted to a room at the side. Then the fleshy, three-chinned face relaxed. "Howdy, stranger. What can I do for you?" He'd assured himself that Chaco was alert in the next room, covering this one with a rifle.

Kirk went in and sat down. "I'll only stop long enough for a cigarette. Any big cow drive pass this way, lately?"

"Nope. Ain't seen any. Why?"

Kirk explained his errand. He brought out a batch of circulars and showed them. "Ever see any of these birds?"

Stumpy Goff examined the circulars, recognizing several of his star boarders. "Nope. Ain't ever run across any of 'em. But I don't get around much, as you can see." He slapped his wooden leg. "Have a drink, sheriff?"

"No, thanks."

"I'll have a nip myself, if you don't mind," Goff said. He got up and stumped to a cabinet to pour himself liquor. It gave him a chance to close a half-open door beyond which crouched the Indian, Chaco. Chaco and

139

his rifle wouldn't be needed now, since this deputy was merely looking for lost cattle.

Seated again, Goff looked out at Kirk's horse. "Couldn't trade you outa that bay, could I, sheriff?"

"The bay suits me fine. You run broncs, do you?"

"I run 'em and trade 'em. Can't wrangle 'em myself. But I got two top riders. One of 'em's an Indian. Other's a waddy named Jake Orme. Jake gets into Vegas once in a while. Know him?"

Kirk shook his head. "I'm new there myself." He finished a cigarette and got up. "Since you can't help me any, I'll be ridin' on."

"Better stop for the night, sheriff. I'll be glad to put you up."

"No, I wanta make Pecos by sundown. How far is it from here?"

"Pecos? It's better'n twenty miles south on a rough trail. Just inside the San Miguel County line."

"That's what I thought. I've been circling San Miguel tryin' to see where six thousand cows got driven out of it." Kirk went outside and mounted.

Goff hobbled to the door and called after him, "Take a look at that three-year-old roan in the corral. If you wanta trade your bay fer him, it's a deal."

Kirk rode to the corral and saw half a dozen horses in there. The best was a young roan gelding.

"No thanks. I'll keep the one I've got." Kirk cantered away, angling south up a cedar slope.

Beyond it he struck a trail pointing south and followed it for two hours. In all that time he saw no man or house. Dusk was deepening when he saw the lights of Pecos.

The shabby plaza, sprawled between two upper forks of the Pecos River, wasn't inviting. Tin cans and empty bottles littered its street. The nearest thing to a hotel was a decrepit adobe house with a sign: *Salas*. Kirk put Red in a corral back of it. He went in, and an old Mexican woman gave him a room.

For supper she served him bean soup and tortillas. There were no other patrons. It was too early for bed. So Kirk went out to make his usual inquiries.

A lighted saloon drew his steps there. He looked in through its open door and saw a dim, dusty barroom. A reeking beer smell came from it and its only light was a hanging lamp. Two customers were in there. One, a slight, hatchet-faced man, stood at the bar alone. A Mexican bartender pushed a bottle toward him. The other customer sat at a rear table, riffling cards. The man at the bar wore crossed gun belts.

Something about his sharp-featured face alerted Kirk. He'd seen it before, somewhere.

Till he could place the man, Kirk moved on a short way down the walk. He stopped at a lighted window and brought a batch of circulars from his pocket. Thumbing through them he found the face he remembered. The two-gunny at the bar.

Walt Smith, the circular said. *Sometimes known as Smitty. Wanted in Pueblo County, Colorado, for killing an express messenger.*

Kirk looked through all the other circulars. The man riffling cards at the rear table wasn't listed.

But Smitty was, and Kirk's duty was clear. He was a sworn deputy sheriff and this was in the county of his jurisdiction. He drew his gun and walked back to the saloon.

He was advancing toward the bar when Smitty turned and saw him. "Put 'em up, Smitty." Kirk dead-centered his aim on the man's chest.

Smitty blinked, then raised his arms slowly.

"That's right," Kirk approved. "You've heard what they say? No law west of the Pecos! But you're not west of it yet. You're right on it and here's the law. Turn around. Now drop your left hand and loosen your belts."

Two things should have warned Kirk. First, Smitty didn't seem very much alarmed. Second, the bartender did. He ducked out of sight.

A gun roared from the back of the room, and a bullet fanned Kirk's face. He jumped a step back, firing three fast shots. The first toward a table at his left, the second at Smitty, the third straight up at a hanging lamp.

The lamp crashed, and the room went black. A barrage of bullets came from the rear table. Kirk dropped prone on the floor and threw another shot that way. Smitty yelled from the dark, "Get him, Amarillo."

Smitty himself fired, and a floor splinter spanked Kirk's chin. He rolled three rolls and came to his knees. Except for gun flashes, he couldn't see a thing. Kirk had only two bullets left and didn't dare reload. He must score with each of his last shots.

A flash from the floor near the bar. That would be Smitty. Smitty was down but still shooting. Kirk aimed carefully at the spot of the flash and squeezed the trigger. Then he shifted position, twisted on his knees to face the rear table, waited for a flash there.

It didn't come. From Smitty's direction came a groan, then silence. Kirk heard someone scurry out the front door. The bartender, probably. With a single bullet left in his gun Kirk faced the back table, waiting for the man there to shoot.

After a silent minute, he took a chance. He used precious seconds to unhinge his forty-five and slap five fresh shells into it. The slight click as he closed the gun should have drawn fire, but didn't. He got to his feet, cocked the gun and advanced cautiously.

After a few steps, his toe bumped a table leg. His groping hand touched the hair of a man's head. It was the man called Amarillo. He was slumped forward over the table, dead.

Hoarse voices came from the walk outside and a flicker of lanterns. Kirk caught a Spanish phrase or two. "These gringos! They are always fighting."

"Bring a light," Kirk yelled.

They came in, their lanterns swaying eerily toward a form on the floor near the bar. It was Smitty's; he'd been hit twice and was dead.

Kirk relaxed and holstered his gun. "That makes two of 'em. You got a constable around here?"

"*Sí, señor.* But he is away in Santa Fe."

"Anybody here want to earn twenty bucks?"

They were frightened. But twenty dollars was a lot of money to a Pecos peon. After some hesitation a man said, "If there is no danger, señor."

"None at all," Kirk assured him. "Just take care of these dead outlaws overnight. In the mornin', toss 'em in a wagon and haul 'em to Las Vegas."

One of the Mexicans had planned driving to Las Vegas in a day or so anyway. He accepted the commission.

"Look back of the bar," Kirk directed, "and see if you can find two empty boxes."

Two cigar boxes were found. Kirk labeled one of them *Smitty*, and the other *Amarillo*. He put everything from Smitty's pockets into one box and everything from Amarillo's into the other. He made a separate package of the outlaw guns.

"That does it, *amigo*. I'll see you in Vegas."

With his packages, Kirk returned to his room at the cantina. He wanted to make a report of this while the event was fresh. Two wanted men killed while resisting official arrest. Kirk opened a notebook and began writing. He knew Smitty's name and background, because it was all in a circular. All he knew of the other man was that Smitty had called him "Amarillo."

What, Kirk wondered, was his real name? Maybe something from his pockets would tell. Kirk opened the box labeled *Amarillo* and sorted through the articles there. Money, keys, tobacco, knife, and a heavy, gold-case watch. No letters or receipts of any kind.

Maybe the watch had initials. None were on the outside. Kirk tried to pry open the rear case. It was stubborn. Using a knife blade, he finally sprung it open.

A tiny, circular photograph was exposed. The smiling face of a girl. Kirk knew her. His thoughts had never strayed far from her since a night by a roadside in Kansas.

He gouged the picture from the watch and looked on-its other side. *With love — Christine* was written there.

This watch, Kirk knew with a shock, was Mark Lindsay's.

CHAPTER
FOURTEEN

Unexpected Enemy

Disturbing uncertainties rasped at Kirk's mind. Could Mark Lindsay be Amarillo himself? If so, it would completely explain his disappearance. He'd left Iowa long before his friends, the Dunbars, and since could have taken up with bad company.

It was possible, but Kirk couldn't accept it. He pictured Lindsay as younger than the gunman of tonight's fight. Alex Dunbar had called him a fine, clean boy. Boy or man, with a girl like Christine against his heart and trustfully on the way to join him here, he'd hardly throw in with outlaws. It was more logical to assume he'd been met and robbed by outlaws. That would explain both his disappearance and the watch in Amarillo's pocket.

It left small doubt that Lindsay was now dead. A dull dread preyed on Kirk as he realized he must take this watch to the Dunbars. He put away the evidence and went to bed.

He slept late. In the morning he found that a wagon, freighted with two outlaw bodies, had already left for Las Vegas. Kirk made a few inquiries before leaving, himself. How long had Smitty and Amarillo been in

Pecos? "They arrive only yesterday, señor," he was told. "Where from, we do not know."

Kirk took the trail for Las Vegas. He must turn in his report and consult with Sheriff Baca. He'd ridden only the north half of his circle; the south half must wait.

In a few miles he caught up with a burro-drawn spring wagon. A canvas covered whatever lay in its bed. A bearded Mexican was driving. "I'll see you at the sheriff's office," Kirk said. He spurred on.

The evidence was in a blanket roll back of his saddle. Mark Lindsay's watch. Desperately he tried to conjure up some loophole of hope. Something he could tell Christine. Something less brutal than merely handing her the watch and telling where he'd found it.

No one at Pecos had ever heard of Mark Lindsay. Lindsay's encounter with Amarillo could have been far away from there.

Kirk was halfway to Las Vegas when he saw a small bunch of range horses grazing not far from the trail. It threw his mind back to duties at the CLC. Pacheco and Torres were making an inventory of stock there. So far they had reported on cattle but not on horses. Any brand the size of the CLC would own fifty or more horses. And horses, turned loose on an unfenced range, often strayed far from home. There might be a CLC brand or two in the bunch now sighted.

Since checking them would only take a few minutes, Kirk reined Red that way. They were saddle stock, he noted, and mostly mares. He saw one with the Linked Hearts iron on her, and two with the Rafter Cross. Another, farther on, was a blocky calico. A mare. Her vaguely familiar coloring and lines made Kirk ride closer. He rode a complete circle of the calico mare and saw that she bore no brand at all.

Complete conviction came to him. This was a pony he'd seen twice before. Once in Kansas and once on Raton Pass. It was the mare stolen from Christine Dunbar and last seen in possession of a thief named Roach. It was tame and unbranded because it had been raised as a girl's pet on an Iowa farm.

Kirk shook out his lariat and tossed a loop over the pony's head. "I'm takin' you home, baby," he coaxed. "Come along."

A half-wild range mare would have balked at a lead rope. The calico didn't. She trotted docilely behind Kirk as he rode on toward Las Vegas.

When he arrived, he found Alfredo at the sheriff's office. Kirk showed him Mark Lindsay's watch. Alfredo listened gravely to his report.

"You have done well, Kirk *amigo*. But it will not be good news to your friends the Dunbars." Alfredo sighed. "They have other troubles, too. I must go there tomorrow and make peace."

"What other troubles?"

"They build their house where Colonel Harper for many years has kept salt. Cattle, when they are not grazing, gather around the salting-place. Especially they do that at the forks of Conchas Creek, where the *álamos* make fine shelter from the wind and sun. So Señor Dunbar does not like to have his homesite always filled with cattle. He asks Colonel Harper please to move his salt trough to some other place."

148

"And Harper wouldn't do it?"

Alfredo nodded sadly. "He tells Señor Dunbar that his cattle have salted there for many years, and will Señor Dunbar please go to hell. Either to hell or back to Kansas, it makes no difference. They are both the same, Colonel Harper says. So Señor Dunbar puts the salt troughs on his wagon and hauls them a mile down the creek. The next morning they are back again, right beside Señor Dunbar's new house."

"The Rafter Cross admits hauling them back?"

"*Si, señor.* Monte Hickock, the foreman, hauled them back himself. He warned Dunbar not to touch them. If Dunbar moves them, Hickock says he will shoot him full of bullets. Dunbar is mad. He wants to fight with his shotgun. But his daughter begs him not to. She persuades him to make a complaint to the sheriff."

Kirk rolled a cigarette broodingly. "Look, Alfredo. Will Harper back Hickock up on this?"

"I believe he will, Kirk. And for me it is bad. Because I must tell him he is wrong. And Colonel Harper has always been my good friend. In these matters his mind is stubborn. All his life he has fought pests of the range. Prairie dogs. Loco weed. Magpies that pick fresh brands. Coyotes that prey on new calves. Fences and plows. All things that obstruct the growth and free movement of cattle."

"But he didn't back up Dillon's play that time."

"That," Alfredo said, "was different. Dillon bullied a woman. Also he got drunk and hit me, Colonel

Harper's friend, on the head with a gun. So he rebuked Dillon, but he will not rebuke Hickock."

Kirk made a quick decision. "Do me a favor, Alfredo. Let me handle this. Harper's your lifelong friend, so keep him that way if you can. On the other hand the Dunbars are *my* friends. I mean I want 'em to be."

A flush on Kirk's face brought an understanding gleam to Alfredo's eyes. He smiled. "That I have suspected, Kirk. You did not come here by accident, no? You have followed four white mules — and a face that is *muy linda?*"

Kirk's flush deepened. "I got to ride out there anyway," he evaded, "to give them a watch and a pony." He motioned toward a calico mare tied outside. "It was rustled from the Dunbars on the way down here, up on the Picketwire. I found it running loose between here and Pecos."

It wasn't easy, however, to persuade Alfredo. Although Alfredo dreaded any altercation which would jeopardize his relations with Colonel Harper, his pride rebelled at side-stepping a duty. But in the end he agreed. "Be assured I will back you up," he promised. "If there is shooting, I will take part in it myself."

"Thanks. By the way, I only got half around that big circle. East, north, and west."

"I myself will ride the south arc," Alfredo said. "I know all the rancheros down that way, and they will help me."

A burro team from Pecos drew up outside. Alfredo summoned his jailer. "Take charge of two dead outlaws, Pancho. Take them to the coroner with this report."

150

Kirk put his bay and the calico pony in the livery barn. His next stop was a barbershop where, during a haircut and shave, the barber chattered excitedly about surveyors reported heading toward town.

"They have already crossed the Mora, señor. Soon their stakes will arrive in Las Vegas. Nor is that all. One of their agents was here yesterday. He bought land. And they say it does not please Señor Vogle."

"Vogle?" Kirk prompted. "Why doesn't he like it?"

"Señor Vogle has speculated. He has bought many stores and lots for the boom when the railroad comes. But the agent purchased right-of-way on the east side of the creek. Also he buys acreage there for a terminal." The barber laughed. "So Señor Vogle is not happy. His own land is here along the trail, which is on the west side of the valley. He has, perhaps, thought the railroad would run right through the plaza."

"He'll clean up anyway," Kirk predicted. "Lots won't skyrocket until the trains begin bringing merchants and settlers in. When they do it'll boom both sides of the creek."

Later he looked in at the Buena Suerte. The gambler Macklin wasn't there. But he had a word with the dancer, Carmencita.

"I have learn nothing yet, señor," she reported. "I have listen to much talk, but it is all about the railroad."

"Okay. Just keep your ears open." Kirk left her and went on to the hotel.

In the morning, leading the calico mare, he rode to Conchas Creek.

At the Dunbar claim he found the Swede carpenter on the roof of a new house. He was nailing on shingles. Not far away the framework of a shed had been erected. Midway between house and shed lay two troughs with chunks of rock salt in them. At least forty Rafter Cross cows were taking shelter in the grove, some licking salt, others lying down and chewing cuds by the creek.

At a distance in the field Alex Dunbar was digging postholes. Beyond him, Christine was plowing back of two mules. At the edge of the plowed land was a high stack of freshly cut black locust fence posts. Kirk marveled at the prodigious amount of work accomplished by two men and a girl.

He shouted to them. They turned and saw the white-patched pony. Christine unhooked her team and drove it toward the house. Alex dropped his digger and came running.

Good news first, Kirk decided. "Picked her up west of Vegas runnin' loose on the range. She's in fine shape. But you better slap a brand on her, Mr. Dunbar."

Christine took the pony's head in her arms. "Patch, I've missed you every minute." She kissed the animal's soft nose, then turned gratefully to Kirk. "We can't thank you enough, Mr. Calloway."

"No trouble at all, miss."

"And did you find out anything about — about Mark?"

It was hard to meet her anxious eyes and tell her the truth. To soften the blow, Kirk launched out with a theory which, though remotely possible, he didn't really believe at all.

"The way it looks now, Lindsay was out looking for strays. A long way off, maybe. Maybe while he was asleep in camp some crook came along and swiped his wallet. And his watch. Lindsay woke up, missed his wallet and watch, and began trackin' the thief."

"What," Alex demanded, "makes you think that?"

"This." Kirk handed them a gold watch. "It's got your picture in it, Miss Dunbar. I had to shoot it out with a fellah in Pecos. He's dead. The watch was in his pocket."

Kirk smiled. But he saw he wasn't fooling them at all. Christine took the watch, stared at it with pain-shocked eyes. Conviction of the worst was stamped on her father's face.

In a moment the girl walked slowly to the tent and disappeared into it.

"I knew she'd take it hard," Alex muttered. "Mark was a fine boy."

"Let's keep our chins up about him," Kirk said. "Now about that other matter. Lend me this team a little while, please."

The Iowan nodded. Kirk took the harnessed team and hitched them to the Dunbar wagon. He led the horses to the two Rafter Cross salt boxes.

As he began loading the troughs, Alex stepped up to help.

"No, don't touch 'em," Kirk said. "Hickock said for you not to, so we'll leave it just that way. If there's any trouble, he can have it with me."

153

With the troughs and salt loaded, Kirk climbed to the seat. "How far down the creek is your line?"

"About three-quarters of a mile. I piled up some rocks there."

"See you later. Get going, mules." The wagon rolled off.

Kirk drove till he came to a pile of rocks on the creek bank. A few wagon lengths beyond it he stopped and unloaded the troughs and salt.

He stood there rolling a cigarette, gazing east down the valley. Quite likely the Rafter Cross was expecting a move like this. Only they expected it to be made by Dunbar himself. Kirk was sure of it when he saw a horseman loping up valley toward him.

It was Monte Hickock, Harper's foreman. A big, barrel-chested man with high reddish cheekbones, he came charging up with a gun-weighted holster flapping on his thigh. "What's the idea?" he yelled.

"I was buildin' me a smoke," Kirk said. "Have one?" He extended the makings.

"I told that damn nester not to touch this here salt box. I told him if he did, I'd —"

"You'd shoot him full of holes," Kirk finished for him. "Well, he didn't touch it. I brought it here myself. So if you want to shoot anybody full of holes, you better start on me."

The red on the foreman's cheekbones spread to his ears. "So you're backin' his play, huh? Takin' up with sodbusters agin yer own kind!"

Kirk gave him a straight look. "I'll do the same for you, Hickock, if Dunbar drops a salt box in your front yard. I'll ask him to take it away, and if he doesn't, I'll take it away myself."

Hickock sat his saddle, glowering. "What'll you do," he jeered, "if I snake this salt box back to the creek fork, where it belongs?"

"Lots of things I could do. For instance, I could get a court order instructin' you to take it away. Then if you didn't, I could slap you in jail for contempt of court."

"Courts! That ain't the way we settle things on this range."

Kirk nodded. "So I've heard. Okay, Hickock. I don't want to break any old customs. So maybe you and I'd better shoot it out right now."

The coolness of the challenge jolted Hickock. His right hand moved an inch up his thigh, the fingers clawed. Kirk watched it. He was reluctantly ready. The matter was too trivial for gunplay. So he made one more try at talking the Rafter Cross man out of it. "It's the quickest way, shooting it out here and now. But it's not the best way, Hickock. Best way's to quit hazin' those poor, hard-workin' farm folks up at the fork. There's a million acres of open government land around here to put your salt boxes on."

"Coddlin' 'em, are yuh?" Hickock derided. "And you a Texan!"

Kirk bridled his retort. He saw another rider coming up valley at a hard pace. "Looks like your boss headin' this way. Maybe we better leave it to him."

Colonel Calvin Harper pulled savagely at his reins, drawing his mount to its haunches beside his foreman. "What's goin' on, Hickock?"

155

The foreman told him. "I was about to throw down on him," he finished, "when I saw you comin'."

"You can still do it," Kirk invited. "Nobody's holdin' you."

Harper caught his foreman's arm. "I can fix this up without any lead-throwin', Monte." He stared fiercely at Calloway. "He's new to this range, that's all. I'll ride in and ask Baca to fire him. Baca's my friend. He's got a cow ranch himself. He knows damned well you can't run cows with a pack of damnyankee, yellow-bellied nesters keepin' 'em away from salt and water. Leave this box right here till I see Baca."

He dug in with his spurs and galloped off, straight toward Las Vegas.

Hickock leered at Kirk. "Hear that? You're about to be fired. Maybe you can get a job diggin' postholes for that nester."

The foreman wheeled his horse and loped toward the Rafter Cross.

When the man was out of sight, Kirk drove the wagon back to the Dunbar camp. Christine, he saw, had harnessed the other pair of mules and was back at her plowing. A thrill of pride pulsed through him. He gloried in her strength — an unconquerable courage that took her, brokenhearted, from her tent, to put her small hands to the plow again. The work must go on. Grief, despair, nor fatigue could stop it. From sunup till sundown! Crops must be planted and a living wrested from the soil.

Kirk stepped down from the wagon and mounted Red. "I don't think you'll have any more trouble with

156

that salt box, Mr. Dunbar. These cows won't many of 'em bed down here from now on. They'll drift toward the salt."

"Thanks, Calloway." Alex Dunbar gazed shrewdly at Kirk. "One other thing. I'm a plain man and I like plain talk. I've heard a few whispers in town. Folks say you followed us out here from Kansas. Why?"

Kirk didn't answer. But, in spite of himself, his eyes turned toward a plow team out in the meadow, with a girl trudging behind it.

"Humph!" Alex muttered. "So that's the way it is! You ain't known her very long, young man."

"Long enough," Kirk murmured. Then he caught himself and grinned. "I don't aim to horn in where I don't belong, Mr. Dunbar. She's spoken for, you say. All right. I brought back her pony. And if he's alive, I'll bring back her man."

He loped away up creek.

Three hours later he dismounted in front of the sheriff's office in Las Vegas. Angry voices came from within.

First came Colonel Harper's. "You mean to stand there and tell me, Alfredo Baca, that you'd turn me down on a little thing like this? I thought you were my friend."

Next came Baca's: "I prize your friendship, señor. But I am sworn to uphold the law. You can ask any lawyer you wish. He will tell you that I cannot put a feed box in your front yard without your consent."

"We're not talkin' about *my* front yard. We're talkin' about —"

"Yes, señor. We're talking about Dunbar's. He, too, is a citizen. My oath protects him as much as you."

"You mean you won't fire this meddlin', Yankee-lovin' depitty?"

"I will not, señor."

"You'll back him up?"

"I will, señor. More than that, the courts will back *me* up. If you show contempt for those courts, I will ride to your ranch with a warrant."

A crash of profanity exploded from Harper. When it ended, his voice came low and bitterly subdued. "We're through, Baca. I want nothing more to do with you. Good day!" He stomped toward the door.

Kirk, on the walk outside, heard Alfredo call him back. "One thing for the record, señor. We have a small wager. Two thousand steers, is it not? Do I understand that you wish to back out of it?"

This more than anything else outraged Harper. "Suh," he thundered, "a Harper never backs out of a bet, once it's made. Honor forbids it. The bet stands."

"*Bien, señor,*" agreed Alfredo.

"But," the Texan raged, "I will never bet with you again. A gentleman bets only with his friends." He stormed out, brushing frigidly by Kirk Calloway.

CHAPTER
FIFTEEN

A New Angle

Alfredo took more than a week to ride the southerly half of the big circle. He was leisurely by nature, as well as too popular to pass a rancho without being cajoled into staying all night. Also, he was thorough. He covered his arc of inquiry with minute pains. He made Bernalillo and Staley and Pedro de Oro, all the mines and sheep camps and plazas along the south border of his county.

When he returned he was able to tell Kirk with assurance that no large drive of CLC cattle had passed that way.

"Nor can I find anyone who has seen Mark Lindsay. Surely he is dead, señor. I do not like to tell these things to your friends on the Conchas."

Something else was troubling Alfredo. Kirk finally pried it out of him.

"Two counties south of here," Baca explained, "a big war goes on. Many have been killed. Many more will be killed. They fight in the hills, they fight on the ranchos, they fight in the streets of the county seat."

"You mean down in Lincoln County," Kirk prompted. "Cattle war, is it?"

"Partly it is a range war but mostly it is political. There are two factions; and one bullet, señor, breeds another. Only last week, on the first day of April, five men took ambush in a corral back of McSwain's store in Lincoln. One of them was Billy the Kid. When Sheriff Guillermo Brady went to arrest them, he was shot dead. Then there was much more shooting, and the law can do nothing."

"That's bad," Kirk admitted. "But what's it got to do with us?"

"Government troops," Alfredo explained, "are being sent in to stop the war. There is even talk that the president at Washington will discharge our governor and appoint a new one — a general of the army, to keep order. So do you not understand my concern, *amigo?* I am a sheriff of New Mexico and we of New Mexico are a proud people. It is disgrace if a sheriff cannot keep order and must be helped by troops. Already the sheriff of Lincoln County is dead, but disgrace is worse than death. It must not happen here."

Kirk saw it then. His pride was at stake. There'd been killings in this county, too. Notably the quadruple murder at the CLC, with the killer still uncaught. Guerilla bands and fugitive outlaws from Lincoln County could easily drift in, with cavalry in pursuit. Alfredo's sensitive mind flinched at such a prospect. Stepping aside in favor of troops, an apparent failure, would be the supreme humiliation.

During days that followed word came of other battles in the neighboring county. The young outlaw known as Billy the Kid featured in all of them. At Las Vegas,

160

Alfredo Baca built new cells in his jail and doubled his force of deputies. He gave Kirk a list of known Lincoln County gunmen. "If any of them come here," he announced grimly, "we will arrest them on sight."

Kirk spent about half of his time out at the CLC. He was still nominally the custodian there, waiting for a representative of the British owners to take over. There'd been no further losses. Pacheco and Torres were riding close herd on the remaining two thousand head of cattle.

For weeks Kirk kept away from the Dunbars. He couldn't bear to face Christine and admit no trace of her fiancé. His own last rash promise to Alex mocked Kirk. "I brought back her pony; and if he's alive I'll bring back her man." If! Only a tortured reasoning could summon hope for Lindsay now.

Twice during the spring Kirk sent Pacheco to see if the Dunbars needed any help. The report was comforting both times. There'd been no more trouble with the Rafter Cross. Alex had fenced a forty and was planting it in corn. They had moved into the house, and Christine had bought herself a milch cow. A shed had been thrown up, and a cord of stove wood was stacked by it. "*Caramba!*" Pacheco marveled. "They work like burros!"

In Las Vegas, Kirk kept an alert eye for invading outlaws and listened to talk at the bars. Most of it was about the railroad. The survey stakes were already in town. Grading and trestle construction were in progress at various places up the line. The track itself, however, was still crawling slowly southwest from La Junta, Colorado.

Occasionally Kirk heard mention of the Baca-Harper wager. Everyone knew it was for two thousand steers, and everyone conceded, now, that it would never be for more. For a feud was on between Harper and the sheriff. These two never took lunch together any more at the hotel, nor met for a drink at the Buena Suerte. When they passed on the street, it was with cool, formal nods. They would stick rigorously to a bet already made, but, being enemies, would never bet again.

Often Kirk saw the gambler, Macklin, at the Buena Suerte. At cards or dice the man was taking on all comers, but there'd been no complaints. He specialized in two-handed stud and consistently won. He'd taken a room at the Exchange and apparently had no thought of moving on.

"I do not trust him," Carmencita whispered to Kirk one night. He had stopped at the bar for a word with her, as usual. "But the other *baileras* like him, señor. They think he is handsome and he buys them much wine."

"Keep your eyes and ears open, Carmencita."

It was a day later when a stage from Colorado pulled in and discharged Archie Templeton of London. The little Englishman hurried straight to the sheriff's office. He found Kirk and Alfredo there.

An embarrassed flush crossed Baca's face. "We have expected you, señor. It is with shame we confess that we do not find your cattle."

162

Archie sat down with a grimace. "Rum luck, what? But I've known the bad news for a long time. Had no more than got home when they shipped me right back." He sighed. "Six thousand head short! My word!"

"You'll take over personally, señor?"

"I'm to live on the ranch till things get settled. But I don't know the cattle business. Will you find me an experienced manager? A permanent one, I mean. What about Calloway here?" He turned to Kirk. "I met you at La Junta, remember?"

Kirk smiled. "I remember."

"Señor Calloway," Baca said quickly, "is now my chief deputy. I need him very much. Why not operate like this, señor? You live at the ranch as executive and let the men who are there now, all honest *muchachos*, do the practical work. If you need advice on decisions, you can always ask myself or Kirk Calloway."

"Righto," Archie agreed. "It won't be for long. Only till the railroad gets here. My instructions are to sell out when the rails come. Might get a fatter price then." He smiled ruefully. "You see, after losing six thousand cows, my stockholders have concluded there's too much hazard in this business."

"We will help you in every way," Alfredo promised.

"Any chance getting those cattle back?" Archie asked. "I can't see how they disappeared so quickly. I counted eight thousand myself, and a week later we heard three-fourths of them were gone."

"You counted them personally?" Kirk questioned.

"Absolutely."

"How did you count 'em? Did Charlie Swift round 'em up and drive 'em through a gate? Or string 'em out in some way so you could get a good tally?"

"Oh no. He had them in four bunches. Two thousand in each bunch."

"You saw all four bunches on the same day?"

"No, we took a day to check each herd." Archie explained in detail the procedure of his February tally.

As he finished, a light dawned in Kirk's eyes. He could see that Alfredo was having the same inspiration.

"*Madre de Dios!*" exclaimed Alfredo. "What fools we have been! The cows were stolen long before you arrived, Señor Templeton. That is why we cannot find them. This Charlie Swift! He showed you two thousand head four times."

Archie was confounded when they explained it to him. "Right under my nose, what? Oh Lord! I'll never dare show it in London again."

"Swift and his outfit," Kirk suggested, "began as long as a year ago, maybe sellin' off five hundred head at a time. A small drive like that could go for beef to a reservation and no one think anything about it. Time you got there he had just two thousand head left, so he showed 'em four times."

"But what," Archie wondered, "did he do with the money?"

"That," Alfredo said, "is what we must find out. Six thousand cattle would bring much money. Perhaps it is hidden somewhere. But you have just arrived on the stage, señor. You need to be refreshed. We will take you to lunch."

At the hotel dining-room they found Colonel Harper lunching grimly alone. Two months ago Alfredo would have gone convivially to his table. But now they weren't speaking. So Alfredo led his party to a table on the other side of the room. One man, Adam Vogle, was already seated there.

Vogle smiled a greeting to the sheriff. He masked his nervousness at Kirk's presence. Alfredo presented Archie Templeton.

"What do you think?" Alfredo chattered. "We know now why we cannot find six thousand cows." He explained the deception practiced by Swift on Archie.

Vogle kept a corner of his eye on Kirk Calloway. He was still sure that Kirk knew or suspected his own guilt. Certainly someone did, and who else could it be but Calloway?

To test Kirk's reaction, Vogle came out with a theory. "It explains something else, too, sheriff," he suggested. "It explains the disappearance of the cowboy, Lindsay."

"*Cómo?*" Alfredo asked with brisk interest.

"Everything we hear," Vogle reminded him, "indicates that Lindsay was on the level. Do you agree?"

"I agree, señor. The Dunbars vouch for him."

"If he was a crook," Vogle resumed, "we would think he killed his four partners to make off with money received from the cattle sale. But he was honest. So it was not that way."

"Go ahead," Alfredo prompted.

"For myself," offered Vogle, "I think the cattle were sold by Swift before Lindsay went to work there. We know he'd only been there a month and was used as a stray man. He was sent after strays so he wouldn't be present at the fake tally for Mr. Templeton, here. But some way he found out about it. At supper at the bunkhouse he accused them. They went for their guns. Lindsay was too fast for them. After killing them he was afraid. He'd shot in self-defense but couldn't prove it. So he got on his horse and rode away."

Alfredo was impressed. "*Caramba!* I believe you have it, Señor Vogle."

Kirk's mind balked only at the speed angle. Lindsay might beat one man to the draw but hardly four at the same time. On the other hand, someone *had* been quick enough to do that very thing. Mark Lindsay, by practice, might have become a chain-lightning gun thrower. Kirk was himself. Lots of honest men were. In this country it was a proper and valued art.

Certainly Vogle's theory was more plausible than any other yet advanced. Also it was the only hopeful idea of them all. It was the only one which left Lindsay both alive and guiltless. It made him merely a fugitive frightened away by four unavoidable killings.

Kirk spent most of the next day taking Archie out to the CLC, orienting him, and presenting him to the crew there. The Britisher assumed his new obligations with zest. In town he had bought himself boots, *chaparajos*, and a five-gallon hat. Yet he was humble about it. "What I don't know about this'd fill a book. But I'll catch on, Calloway." In his favor was the racial genius of Englishmen for adapting themselves to far-flung pioneering ventures.

"You can trust Pacheco and Torres," Kirk said. He helped carry Archie's luggage into the bedroom at the manager's cabin.

Sight of the bed there reminded him of a bullet fired through the window. He told Archie about it.

"Just to play safe, you better sleep at the bunkhouse the first few nights. Long enough for that drygulcher to find out you're living here and not me. He won't bother you any. I'm the guy he's after."

"Who is he?" Archie asked.

"You got me there. Might be a gambler named Macklin. Or a Rafter Cross puncher named Dillon. Take your choice."

"Righto." Archie took it in stride.

Late in the afternoon, Kirk rode to the Dunbar homestead. Each time he went there the transformation amazed him. Forty acres of meadow were now fenced and planted. House and shed were finished, and Kirk found Alex building a pole corral. Four mules, two ponies, and a milch cow were grazing near by. Cottonwoods were leafing, and wild plum was abloom along the creek.

"Hi, neighbor," Kirk greeted. "It begins to look like a layout."

Alex stopped work and took him into the house. Christine was hanging window curtains that she'd made from flour sacks.

"We thought you'd forgotten us," she said. "How do you like our wilderness home?" She took him proudly through all four rooms.

Stove and beds had been shipped by freight wagon from Iowa. Almost everything else was homemade or homespun, tables and chairs built on the spot by Alex and the Swede, cushions and hangings provided by some magic of Christine's. She'd wrapped tissue paper around tin cans to make vases and filled them with plum blossoms. "You are our first guest, Mr. Calloway. So you must stay to supper."

He waited until after supper before giving them the latest slant on Mark Lindsay. The Dunbars listened eagerly, firelight painting a soft glow on the girl's face.

"It's the first real hope we've had for him," Kirk admitted. "This much we know for sure. The crew was crooked. They'd been looting the ranch long before Lindsay went to work there. They sent him after strays to get him out of the way while they fooled an inspector. If he got hep to it, it was his life or theirs."

A gleam came to Alex Dunbar's eyes, and he nodded grimly. "Sure, I'd've done the same myself. He had to shoot or get shot."

"After outgunnin' 'em, maybe he was afraid to stick around. Anyway, the sheriff figures it like that. So we'll advertise in the Denver and Santa Fe papers. We'll say he's got a clean bill here and can come back anytime he likes."

Christine was quiet all the rest of the evening. Her thoughts were far away, no doubt with Mark Lindsay wherever he might be hiding. Perhaps in Arizona or old Mexico. *I'm out of it*, Kirk admitted. *I never had a chance.* Covertly and wistfully he watched her from a corner of his eye, while Alex talked about his crop and

168

a huge corn crib he planned to build. It was the first time Kirk had ever seen her in a dress. He watched every glint of the firelight on the coiled braids of her hair. Grueling labor from sun to sun had failed to jade her charm.

As he was leaving, Kirk remembered a frolic scheduled for a week from Friday night in town.

He mentioned it, carefully addressing Alex instead of Christine. "Why don't you bring her in, Mr. Dunbar? It's a big *baile* at the Exchange Hotel. You could stay all night there and —"

For a moment Christine's eyes sparkled — then she broke in: "Perhaps I'd better not."

Kirk knew she was thinking of Lindsay. He went out to his horse and rode home.

CHAPTER
SIXTEEN

A Bid for Freedom

Because Christine wasn't going to the dance, Kirk didn't plan on going himself. For ten days he divided his time between advising Archie at the CLC and helping Alfredo keep peace in Las Vegas.

When Friday week came, he'd completely forgotten about the frolic. That evening he took supper at the CLC, returning after dark to Las Vegas. He kept a permanent room at the hotel there now.

He was putting Red in the livery barn when he saw two white mules in near-by stalls. So the Dunbars were in town! Looking toward the plaza Kirk saw the hotel blazing with lights. When he arrived he found half the county assembled there. In the dining-room off one side of the lobby, a Mexican orchestra made melody for whirling couples. The opposite side of the lobby gave on to the barroom. Men being four to one, the bar was densely lined with an overflow from the dance floor. Alex Dunbar sat relaxed in the lobby, reading a stock journal.

He looked up and saw Kirk. "I talked her into comin', Calloway." He smiled. "She sure needs it. She ain't had any fun since we left Iowa. So I kept naggin' at her till finally she gave in."

Looking into the dining-room Kirk saw Christine surrounded by a dozen men. Ranch hands, most of them, all in their spangled best.

"If I was as young as you," Alex chided, "I'd be in there myself."

Kirk was in dusty chaps and flannels. He took the steps three at a time and was soon changing in his room. He scrubbed and preened his hair. What did she think of him, asking her to a dance and then not showing up!

But when he got down there, it seemed she hadn't missed him at all. She was waltzing in the arms of a tall, well-dressed man whose back was to Kirk. Over the man's shoulder she saw Kirk and smiled. Then at the next whirl he saw her partner's face. Macklin! Why would she pick a two-timer like Macklin? But she wouldn't, of course, know anything about him. He was just a good-looking, well-mannered man who'd asked her to dance.

They disappeared in a swarm of other couples. Kirk saw the square, solid figure of Adam Vogle. He was guiding a high-combed Spanish girl around, not too expertly; in a moment Kirk saw that she was Rosita Baca.

His eyes searched for Alfredo. Being a convivial spirit, Alfredo wouldn't miss an affair like this. To his surprise, Kirk saw that Alfredo had a violin tucked under his chin and was leading the orchestra. A versatile *caballero*, this sheriff of San Miguel!

When the music stopped, Kirk elbowed his way to Christine. He was just in time to hear Macklin say, "One more, please?"

"My turn," Kirk cut in.

"That," the gambler said, "is up to the lady."

She looked from one to the other, then laughed and put her arm in Kirk's. Her excuse was, "He owes me an apology, Mr. Macklin, so I must give him a chance to make it."

Kirk led her across the room. "I didn't think you were coming, or I'd have been here with bells on." He stopped at the orchestra platform and presented her to Alfredo Baca.

Alfredo bowed gallantly. "I kiss your hand, señorita. My friend Kirk has talked much of you and he has made me think you are beautiful. So now I am disappointed. Not in your loveliness, but in the poverty of his language. You are like the moonlight in Mexico. You are stars in the Rio Grande. You are like the music of waterfalls when they whisper in the spring. If my friend has not already told you these things, I am ashamed."

Christine was delighted with him. Now he was signaling to someone, calling them over. In a moment he was introducing her to his sister and to Adam Vogle.

"You must come to see us," Rosita said warmly, "at the Rancho Corazones."

Alfredo waved his bow, and the orchestra began a soft song of old Mexico, singing as they strummed guitars. Kirk danced away with Christine. "He's charming," she murmured. "How can he talk like that and still be a bachelor?"

Kirk was aware of Macklin watching them. His impulse was to warn her against Macklin. But it

172

wouldn't sound right. She might think he was jealous. In any case, it would be presumptuous. He himself was a rank outsider, the same as Macklin. She belonged to Mark Lindsay.

Macklin and others would be rushing up, he knew, the minute the dance was over. He made that prediction gloomily to Christine.

She stopped suddenly and said, "They've already danced my feet off. Can't we escape? I'd like a little fresh air."

He guided her out through the lobby to the hotel's front porch. A veranda with benches, to the left, was deserted. As they sat down on a bench, windows back of them were open, but the shades were drawn. It was on the barroom side of the building, and they could hear a hum of talk from the bar.

Macklin, trailing the girl for another dance, saw them take seats out there. A relaxed contentment on her face told him there was no use. Calloway, for the moment at least, couldn't be displaced. So Macklin went into the barroom and bought a drink.

On more counts than one he wanted to get even with Kirk Calloway. The humiliation at La Junta still rankled. And Calloway's vigilance here at Las Vegas had crabbed his usual game. He hadn't dared shoot it out with Calloway. But now, quite suddenly, he saw another way to strike at the deputy. If he could make the Dunbar girl distrust Calloway, it would burn worse than a bullet. It was simple and entirely within the law. Talk was free. They couldn't jail you for expressing an opinion in a barroom.

173

A couple of Rafter Cross men were at a booth table against the front wall. A window above them was open, its shade drawn. Macklin carried his drink over and joined the two men. "Heard anything more on that CLC stray man?" he asked. "The guy that disappeared?"

"Nope. Have you?"

They discussed it in subdued tones. Macklin was well aware that Christine Dunbar, on a bench directly beyond the partition, could hear only a hum of talk and clink of glasses. But if he raised his voice, she would hear plainly.

"Mystery, you say? Call it that if you want. To me it's open and shut. Calloway meets a girl back in Kansas. He falls like a ton o' bricks. So he follows her to New Mexico. Only to find she's already took. She's engaged to a CLC stray man. So Calloway rides off lookin' for said stray man. He comes back with the guy's watch. Claims he found it on a dead man. But did he? Don't make me laugh! With this Lindsay knocked off he's got a clear field now, ain't he? Add it up."

Christine stood up. She turned with a stare of shocked resentment toward the shaded window. Kirk said, "You heard? You don't believe it, do you?"

"Of course not. It's just — malicious gossip."

Kirk got to his feet, seething. "I'll choke it down his throat."

"Why don't you just ignore it?" Then she added shakily, "But I'm not feeling very well. If you'll excuse me, I think I'll go to my room."

174

She went into the lobby before Kirk could say anything more. He followed her to the foot of the stairs there. She turned with a pale smile and held out her hand. "You don't mind, do you? I guess I'm just tired and upset."

"He did it apurpose!" Kirk blurted furiously. "He knew you could hear him."

"But it was so stupid. Why don't you forget it? Good night, Mr. Calloway." She ran up the steps and out of sight.

No, she didn't believe it. But a seed of poison once planted could easily sprout. It would nag at her mind. It would lurk there like an ugly shadow, as weeks and months passed and Mark Lindsay failed to return. Kirk knew she didn't believe it — now. But always it was a possibility. That Kirk had eliminated a rival to clear the field for himself! She would never really believe it. But even to think about it would be barrier enough.

When she was out of sight, the rage in Kirk erupted. Blood flooded his face, and his fingers itched for Macklin's throat. He stormed into the barroom, gunless. Macklin would be unarmed, too, because guns had been banned from the dance floor.

Macklin was still seated at the booth table. Kirk caught him by the collar and jerked him to the middle of the floor. "You're a skunk-livered liar, Macklin!" His first punch was only a tap on the chin, just enough to put the man on guard. He crossed it with a right which sent the gambler reeling.

Kirk jumped after him, lashing out. Macklin ducked this one and came up with a smash that rocked Kirk to his heels. It drew blood from his lip, but he didn't feel it. He bored in, swinging, driving his man to a wall. A path cleared as a dozen men stood by, breathless and neutral. For a minute the two stood toe to toe, trading punches. From beyond the lobby came soft music. But here one could hear only the solid, thudding impacts of knuckles on flesh. An uppercut jolted Kirk. His own next swing sent Macklin crashing against the wall.

The man slumped to the floor there and for a moment seemed down for good. Kirk stood back a few paces, breathing heavily, still boiling with fury.

All at once Macklin was up and diving toward him. No one saw where he got the knife. It was in his hand as he struck, slashing Kirk's throat. Blood spurted there, but again Kirk didn't know it. He caught the knife wrist, twisted it till a bone cracked. An insane lust filled him. Never before had he wanted to kill with his bare hands.

Macklin went to his knees. Kirk yanked him upright and swung hard at his mouth. Teeth caved, and Kirk felt the cut of them on his knuckles. He kept boring in, slashing, smashing. When Macklin reached down for the knife he'd dropped, Kirk kicked savagely and again sent him sprawling against a wall. The gambler's right wrist was twisted and helpless, his face convulsed with agony. "Stop!" he pleaded. He lay in a heap there, sobbing, blinded by blood and pain.

Words choked from Kirk. "If you're in town at daylight, Macklin, I'll do it again."

He walked out of the bar and up to his room. A mirror there showed redness at his face and throat.

Dizziness came, and his knees went weak on him. A tap at his door. A voice, "I'd better patch you up, Calloway." A doctor had followed him up here. Kirk sank wearily on the bed.

It was midmorning before he was able to go out. Then, with his cuts taped and bandaged, Kirk buckled on a gun and went out looking for Macklin. The furnace in him still seethed. He'd meant just what he said about doing it again.

"Mr. Macklin checked out just before daylight," the hotel clerk said.

To make certain, Kirk looked in at the Buena Suerte. The man wasn't there. Kirk went to the livery barn to check on a horse the gambler was known to keep there. It was gone.

So were two white mules.

Kirk went back to the hotel. "What about Mr. and Miss Dunbar?"

"They checked out too."

"Did they leave a message?"

"No message, Mr. Calloway."

In the crater of a cold volcano, Mark Lindsay at last got the chance for which he had patiently waited.

Only four outlaw boarders were holing up in the place. Their numbers had varied from time to time, from as high as ten down to the present minimum. All the while Mark Lindsay had made himself seem spineless and defeated. Stir-crazy, the inmates called him. But he'd only been waiting to get them off guard.

Waiting for the chance that was his this warm June afternoon.

Three of them were outside soaking up fresh air. The other was in the cabin nodding over a quart bottle. He wore a gun, as did the three outside. Mark was unarmed, of course, and had been meek as a sheep for weeks.

The man at the table had had a few too many. It wasn't hard for Mark, sweeping out the room, to get behind him. He cracked down with the broom handle. It knocked the man's face to the table and Mark snatched his gun. With this he struck again, for keeps. The man didn't even groan.

For a long time Mark had been saving strings and tie cords from the provision packages. He dug them from the bottom of a kitchen drawer. In a few minutes the unconscious outlaw was bound, hand and foot. Mark wadded a rag into his mouth and dragged him to the windowless closet where he himself had been immured by night. He bolted him in there. Peering from the front room he saw the other three sauntering about the crater.

Maybe they'd all come in together. If so he'd have to depend on surprise. With that advantage he might out-gun all three. But it was a hazard to be avoided. So Mark opened the door boldly and called out, "Donlin, Ace wants you a minute."

Ace was the man already on ice.

Donlin strolled toward the house. Maybe Ace wanted to dice a few throws. He stepped inside and asked, "Where the hell is he?"

178

"In the kitchen mixing one."

As Donlin moved toward the kitchen, Mark crashed a gun on his head. Five minutes later Donlin was bound, gagged, and keeping Ace company in a bolted closet.

That left two to go.

But now Mark had two guns. He cocked them, stood with them just inside the door, waiting.

He heard them coming. Rocky Packard came in first, Chick Armour a step behind him. "Where's everybody?" Rocky gaped at the empty room.

"They're where you're going," Mark said. "Put 'em up." They turned and saw two cocked guns aimed heart-high.

"I'd just as soon not drill you," Mark said. "Don't make me do it."

Rocky Packard, with a twisted grin, raised his arms. "He's no skin off'n our knuckles, Chick. He's Stumpy's pet, not ourn."

Chick Armour had different ideas. As he clawed for his gun, Mark shot him through the heart. Chick, with his gun half out, buckled to the floor. He was a long-wanted killer, and this was his day to die.

Rocky Packard, with a frozen grin, saw him fall. "I'm not buyin' any of that, kid. It's your drop."

Mark took his gun and made him lie face down. There was no use gagging him. Yells couldn't be heard at Goff's cabin outside the hill. Mark even removed the gags from Ace and from Donlin. He left all three men locked in the closet.

The rest should be comparatively easy. At sundown the Indian was due at the tunnel door with rations. Throwing down on Chaco would leave only Goff and Jake Orme to fight at the outside cabin. Mark hid two of his guns and put two in his belt. He went out and walked across the ten-acre bed of the crater, heading for the tunnel.

This was a day when Indian Chaco was busy with one of his routine chores. Once a week Chaco had to toss pine and cedar chunks down into the crater from the rim above. It took lots of firewood to serve the chilly camp down here.

Chaco was peering into the crater as Mark Lindsay, double-gunned, crossed its bed toward the tunnel. A sound something like a shot had drawn Chaco to the rim. He had a rifle. He was never without it. Stumpy Goff called him the best sharpshooter in all New Mexico.

The Indian drew a careful bead on Lindsay. Careful, because his master would be displeased if the man were killed. Lindsay dead was worth nothing. Lindsay alive was worth a fortune.

So the bullet which Chaco sped from above was aimed only at the target's left forearm. Lindsay fell with blood drenching his sleeve. Chaco slid down the steep outside slope to warn Goff and Orme.

CHAPTER
SEVENTEEN

Goff Shows His Cards

Stumpy Goff's worst headache, after frustrating Mark's attempted escape, was the pacification of his paying guests. Two of them, Donlin and Ace, screamed for Mark's scalp. The third, Rocky Packard, not having been hurt himself, and possessing a sardonic sense of humor, was willing to shrug it off. "We had it comin'," he admitted, "gettin' careless like that. If I'd been him, I'd of done the same myself."

Goff finally smoothed the situation over by letting them split a cash stake found on the dead man, Chick Armour. It was proceeds from Chick's last raid in Colorado. Chaco set the broken bone in Lindsay's left arm and furnished him with a sling. Other outlaws arrived for a season of hiding in the crater, in numbers to counterbalance the sullenness of Ace and Donlin.

But Stumpy Goff was still troubled. What had happened once could happen again. Next time his hostage might be killed. At best Mark Lindsay was in a cage of tigers, and tigers scratch. Unless Goff kept Lindsay alive, he could never dictate terms to a man in Las Vegas named Adam Vogle.

Goff brooded about it for a month, while Lindsay's arm slowly mended. Finally he made a decision. He must revise the time schedule of his plans. He'd intended to wait until Vogle cashed in, before demanding a split. But that wouldn't be till the railroad came, and railroads aren't built in a day. By then Goff might have no living witness with which to bring pressure. So he decided to expose Lindsay to Vogle at once.

How? In the flesh? He didn't want to bring Vogle here and he didn't dare take Lindsay to Las Vegas.

An idea hit Goff, and he went stumping through the tunnel into the crater.

Mark Lindsay, his left arm in a sling, sat dejectedly in the cabin. He looked old sitting there, long-haired and bearded. Half a dozen gunmen were lounging about. "I wanta see this kid alone," Goff said. The others strolled outside.

The peg-legged man eased his bulk into a chair facing Lindsay. "Look, kid. When you first come here, you were stewin' about some girl homesteader on the Conchas. You said she'd fret about you not showin' up. Maybe she'd think you were dead. Or maybe she'd figure you got into trouble and had to run out. In either case she'd be purty sick."

Mark listened, alert and suspicious. What was he leading up to? It was sure to be a trick of some kind. But the statements just made were quite true. From the first Mark had worried more about Christine's peace of mind than his own physical peril.

"That's right," he conceded cautiously. "So what about it?"

"I can't see any reason," Goff said, "for lettin' her fret any longer. So if you wanta, you can write her a message. I'll see it's delivered. You can say you're alive and in good shape. You can say you expect to go back to her some day, but you can't right now. And if you wanta, you can tell her why. Tell her anything you wanta except where you are. And you mustn't mention my name. Here." Goff pushed pen, ink, and paper toward his prisoner.

Mark could hardly believe his ears. Reason told him that Goff would never in the world deliver a message to Christine. Yet there was nothing to lose by writing one. If Goff tore it up, the situation would be no worse than now.

"You're stringing me along, Goff. What for I don't know."

Stumpy shrugged his big round shoulders. "Suit yourself, kid."

In the end Mark wrote the message. When he'd signed it, Goff read it through carefully. "It's too long, kid. And too much guff." He scratched out half a dozen sentences. "Copy it like it is now, and I'll see she gets it."

"Like hell you will!"

But Mark copied and signed it, omitting the censored portions. The vital things were still there. It still informed Christine that Mark Lindsay was alive and well; it said he was a prisoner, and it told sketchily why he was being held. Nothing in it incriminated Goff personally, or revealed the hide-out.

Goff took it. "It'll make her feel better," he said with an oily grin.

"*If* she gets it," Mark amended.

The fat man went out through the tunnel to his cabin. "Chaco, keep your rifle loaded and your eye peeled. Jake and I are going to Las Vegas."

"What for?" asked Jake Orme.

Goff winked. "To buy some saddles. We run a horse ranch, don't we?"

Jake hooked up a spring wagon and they drove to Las Vegas. It was sundown when they arrived there. Jake drove through the plaza and on into the trail street beyond it. "Stop here, Jake." Goff lowered his three hundred pounds to the walk in front of Vogle's store.

He entered just as the place was about to close for the day.

"Your pleasure?" a clerk asked him.

"I need some saddles. It's a special order, bud. Lemme see the boss."

The clerk called Adam Vogle. Vogle came out of his office, completely off guard. He had never before seen this human elephant with a peg leg.

"Saddles, did you say?"

Goff dropped an eyelid, lowered his voice. "Yeh, but it was just an earful for your clerk. Somethin' else I wanta talk about, Vogle."

"Yes?" Vogle was still unalarmed.

"You got my message?"

"What message?"

Goff's answer came in a derisive whisper: "'Six knew; four died; now two know; you and me.'"

An icicle of fear stabbed Vogle. "You!" he gasped. "You sent that note?"

Goff jeered: "How would I know if I didn't send it? Watch yourself, Vogle. Your clerk's starin'. Don't stand there like a scared ghost. Just meet me tonight, and I'll tell you all about it."

"Tell me about what?"

"A deal I'm offerin'. It's got too many angles to talk about here. Meet me tonight at ten."

A murky scheming flickered in Vogle's eyes. "All right. I can meet you south of town at the Gallinas Creek bridge. At ten, did you say?"

"At ten sharp, Vogle, but not under any dark bridge. You're too good with a gun. Good enough to kill four men in a bunkshack. So we'll meet where I say."

Vogle winced. "Where?"

"In public. In a crowded barroom. You won't gun me with fifty people around. At ten, I'll be at the back table over at the Buena Suerte. Show up there and we'll talk turkey."

"I know people there," Vogle protested. "I can't afford to be seen with you."

"Why not? You sell saddles. I buy 'em. Lots of folks know I run a horse ranch. Your clerk heard me ask about saddles. Man of my build has to have his saddles made to order. So we meet in a barroom to talk it over. Folks'll hear us talk loud about saddles. They won't hear us talk soft about Charlie Swift."

Goff clumped out of the store. Vogle, he knew, would be too frightened not to show up at the Buena Suerte.

At ten o'clock, the usual crowd thronged the Buena Suerte. Cowhands at the bar stood elbow to elbow. From the gambling-room came the quick, sharp calls of the dealers. From the dance floor came chatter and song. Carmencita did her nightly number and then moved from table to table, bantering with the customers. At a rear table she saw the town's leading merchant, Adam Vogle. It mildly surprised Carmencita because Vogle, she knew, did not gamble or drink. He owned the building, but came only to collect the rent.

She perched for a moment on the arm of his chair. "You liked my song, Señor Vogle?"

"Sure," Vogle said in a harassed voice. "But run along, Carmencita. I'm busy with a customer."

She saw that the customer was an obese stranger with a wooden leg. The skin of his neck hung in folds. An oily smile creased his face, but his small eyes were mirthless. "About them saddles," he was saying. "Five of 'em can be standard. But the one for me's got to be made to order. I don't ride much, Mr. Vogle, but when I do —"

It bored Carmencita, and she skipped on to the next table.

Loud talk from the bar and music from the dance floor gave Goff, from there on, all the privacy he'd hoped for. Privacy plus security. However much Vogle might want to, he wouldn't dare kill in a crowd like this.

"Take a look at this," Goff whispered. He passed Vogle a handwritten letter signed by Mark Lindsay, and dated today.

Vogle read:

Dearest Chris:

Don't worry about me. I'm alive and well. I'll come to you soon as I can.

Here's what happened. I took a job at the CLC. It had two thousand cows. But it was supposed to have eight thousand. Before I got there the crew had sold off sixty thousand dollars' worth and turned the money over to a man in town named Vogle. Vogle bought town property with it. He was to sell out at boom prices, when the railroad comes, and split with the CLC crew. I found out about it, and the crew knocked me cold. They took me a long way off and locked me up. Their idea was to use me as a witness in case Vogle pulls a double cross. Later they were found dead, and it's a cinch Vogle did it. When I get out of here, I'll see him hanged. The man holding me won't let me say any more.

Love,
Mark Lindsay

The shock stunned Vogle. Then Goff's sly whisper jarred him to attention. "You can see it's written in the same hand that dated and signed it." Stumpy Goff took the letter and tore off the signature. This he handed to Vogle. "You can keep that much of it. The rest we're through with."

Goff struck a match and lighted his pipe. While the match still blazed, he ignited the letter. It burned to an ash between his stubby fingers.

"The signature's all you need, Vogle. Compare it with the hotel register here in Las Vegas. Lindsay stopped there for two nights when he first hit town. Later he signed the CLC payroll. Plenty of ways you can check that signature. It proves he's still alive."

Vogle took a handkerchief and mopped sweat from his face. He looked fearfully about the room. It was filled with bar talk and dance music. No one seemed to pay them any attention.

"If you got Lindsay somewhere," Vogle said with a half-choked defiance, "you'd never dare turn him loose."

The fat man leered. "Why not? Difference between you and me, Vogle, is that *you* got too much property to run out on. Me, I ain't got nothin' but horses and I could take them with me. I could leave Lindsay right where he is and fade to Arizona. From there I could write the sheriff here and tell him where Lindsay is. He gets rescued, and you swing, Vogle."

Vogle sat through a long, panic-charged silence. Then: "What do you want?"

"Just leave things as they lie, Vogle, like you planned on. Wait till the rails come. Then cash in and slip me half. You do that, and I'll finish off Lindsay."

An alternative occurred to Vogle. Goff saw it swimming in his eyes. "Don't try it," he warned.

"Don't try what?"

188

"Selling out now and skipping to California or somewhere. I'll be watching you. First deal you make, I toss Lindsay to the sheriff. Besides, sixty thousand ain't enough. We want two hundred thousand, half for you, half for me. We'll get it when the rails boom Vegas."

Vogle moistened his lips, threw a furtive glance over his shoulder. Then he leaned forward with a nervous whisper. "Be careful! That was Deputy Calloway just came in." He'd seen Kirk enter and take a place at the front of the bar. Kirk was too far away to hear anything, but the very sight of him made Vogle jumpy.

Yet he knew now that he'd overestimated Calloway. He'd been sure that Calloway had slipped that cryptic note under the door. He'd been stupid enough to go gunning for Calloway. And all the while his real baiter was with this four-chinned horse rancher, Goff.

"I've shown you my cards," Goff whispered. "If you think I'm bluffin', I'll show you the joker himself. Lindsay in the flesh!"

The card terminology should have reminded Vogle of his other angle of profit, the big bet between Harper and Baca. But just now his mind was too harassed to think of it.

One thing was fairly clear to Vogle. Goff would keep Mark Lindsay alive until the payoff. Mark was Goff's hole card, and Goff couldn't collect without him.

"Five bucks it gets here on a even day, Sam." This from a cowboy at the bar. "You're covered, Pete," Sam said.

It started a ripple of talk about the Baca-Harper bet, and brought certain dark angles of his own schemings back to Vogle. To profit from the bet, Vogle must insure Baca's winning of it. He must force the first train to arrive on an *odd* day. If the schedule called for an *even* day, he must arrange a bit of sabotage up the line.

That part of it had worried Vogle. To tear up a strip of track, he'd need help. What about this man Goff?

"You say you run a horse ranch? Got a crew there?"

"I got men and guns when I need 'em," Goff admitted.

"There's a small job I may want done just before the first train comes in. An even chance I will and an even chance I won't. Could I use your crew?"

Goff's eyes slitted. "If it's a drygulchin' you want done, no."

"Nothing like that. Just an hour of hard work, at night, miles away from anybody."

"What kind of work?"

"I'll tell you when the time comes. May not need it at all."

"Talk straight, Vogle."

Vogle talked straight, explaining that if Goff would help him in this small matter, he, in turn, would submit to the major demand by Goff.

Kirk Calloway, at the top of the bar, hadn't noticed them at all. The room was full. He was crowded in between a Rafter Cross man and a stage driver. The scene was normal for the Buena Suerte at this busy hour.

All at once Kirk became aware of perfumed lips at his ear. He heard Carmencita whisper, "Do not look around, señor. They may be watching me. I go off duty now. Follow me to my house."

190

Without turning, Kirk looked at her image in the bar mirror. "What's up, Carmencita?"

"I cannot say, here. How many they are, I do not know. They may have many ears and eyes. One I see burn a paper. It makes me curious, and I listen. My house is the first one beyond the *acequia*. Follow me in ten minutes."

Then she was gone.

Kirk finished his drink. Then he turned and looked both ways along the bar. The usual patrons. Stock hands, gamblers, girls, clerks, salesmen, a stranger or two. In booths across the room were tables, most of them occupied. One at the rear was empty. A barboy was picking up two unfinished drinks there. Dancing couples whirled just beyond an arch.

In ten minutes by the bar clock, Kirk went out the front door. The street was dark except for glows from saloon windows. He turned left toward a plank bridge where an irrigation ditch from Gallinas Creek crossed this street. The first house beyond it, she had said.

Cottonwoods were in full leaf now. They deepened the gloom as Kirk hurried that way. Stores and saloons petered out, and he came to a line of adobe dwellings. These grew progressively shabbier toward the end of the street. He crossed the *acequia* bridge. The first house beyond it was little more than a *jacal* of mud bricks.

A candle gleamed from its open window. Kirk saw Carmencita's face there. She beckoned. He opened the door and went in.

"I am afraid, señor," she whispered. "It is about Mark Lindsay. He is alive. Of that I am certain, because —"

Two shots roared at the open window. Carmencita screamed. A bullet burned through Kirk. The girl sagged to the floor and Kirk pitched face down across her body.

Above them, the candle flickered eerily. Vogle's head and arm now came entirely through the window. He aimed obliquely downward, squeezing the trigger four more times. With cold precision he emptied his gun into Kirk Calloway.

CHAPTER
EIGHTEEN

Between Life and Death

Far up the line the Santa Fe track came surging southwest. Picks and shovels flashed in the prairie sun, swung by the brawny arms of a thousand Irishmen and Swedes and Mexican laborers. There was little or no machinery. Hand power hacked its way through the cuts, and mule-drawn slips and scrapers pushed dirt into the fills. Mauls banged on spikes to a chorus of lusty song. On came the ties and on came the rails and the fishplates. A mile today and another tomorrow. From the blacksmith tent came a constant anvil serenade.

Or maybe two miles tomorrow. Everyone was trying to beat Pete Criley's record made back at Larned, Kansas, from where ninety-nine miles of track had been laid in sixty-nine days.

A new trail, and yet the old one was still there, dust-clouded, deep-rutted, and on it the bullock teams and burro caravans still plodded by.

An eastbound bullock team came along, and its driver stopped for a few minutes to gaze at the track layers and to swab the alkali from his face. Westbound came another, and its driver stopped, too, hub to hub with the other whacker.

"Hi, Pete."

"Howdy, Zeke. Got any makin's?"

A tobacco pouch was passed from wagon to wagon.

While the bulls rested, the two drivers gazed sadly at the track layers. "Looks like we'll be out of a job purty soon, Zeke."

"Sure does, Pete. Every trip I make gets shorter. Ain't no use haulin' further'n the trains come."

"How'd yuh leave things in Santa Fe, Zeke?" asked the westbound whacker.

"Kinda quiet, Pete. But they was a ruckus at Vegas as I come through."

"Another shootin', was it?"

"Yep. Seems like some gent took a shine fer a Mex gal. And seems like some other gent didn't like it. He caught 'em in her shack long about midnight, and he filled 'em both full o' lead."

"You don't say! Killed 'em both, did he?"

"He killed the gal, dead center. But I hearn the man's still breathin'. They dug enough slugs outa him to load a buffalo gun with. Paralyzed him, they say. He can't talk none. They're feedin' him dope. Expectin' him to kick off any minute."

The westbound whacker nodded. "That's the way it goes, Zeke. Me, I never fool around with no Mex gal. Not in no dark o' the moon, Zeke. See yuh next trip. Giddap."

The bullock teams moved on in opposite directions.

And on, creeping without rest through sand and sage, went the iron track.

194

At Las Vegas, Alfredo Baca stood sorrowfully by the bed of Kirk Calloway. It was three weeks after the shooting at Carmencita's. Twice during that time, for brief intervals, Kirk had regained consciousness. Each time his faintly whispered words had puzzled Alfredo.

"What did he mean, Don Eusebio?"

Eusebio Sanchez, leading local physician, had been in constant attendance. A wing of his house had been made into a ward, and Alfredo had commanded him to spare no effort or expense. Already Dr. Sanchez, in addition to probing out five bullets, had performed a delicate spinal operation. Only by a generous use of drugs had the patient been kept alive.

"What he means I do not know," Sanchez murmured. "But we have heard him plainly. 'Lindsay lives' were his words both times."

"But that," protested Alfredo, "does not make sense. Why would Lindsay shoot him?"

"He does not say Lindsay shoots him. He says only that Lindsay, whom people think dead, still lives."

Alfredo's eyes narrowed shrewdly. "Perhaps Carmencita tells him that, Don Eusebio. Someone does not wish them to know, so he shoots them both."

The doctor's nod was noncommittal. Many times he had treated knife wounds and gun wounds inflicted by a jealous lover. So to Sanchez the popular theory around town seemed more logical. Carmencita had been a bewitching young woman, and Calloway had often been seen whispering with her at the Buena Suerte. What more natural than for him to follow her home at night and for some admirer of her own race to object?

"You are the sheriff, Don Alfredo. I am only the doctor."

Alfredo gazed down compassionately at his friend and deputy. "When he is strong enough, Eusebio, I would like him moved to my hacienda. I have many servants to attend him there. My sister Rosita can be his nurse."

"The road is rough," Sanchez objected. "He cannot stand the jolting of a wagon."

"Not now. But later, let us hope. I will have a special couch made for my carriage. We will drive very slow. *Niños* will walk ahead to pick up every rock."

Sanchez leaned alertly over the bed. He had noted a flicker of Kirk's eyelids and a slight movement of the lips. "He is conscious again. Listen, señor."

Faintly they heard Kirk murmur, "He's alive. She told me. Tell Christine."

Alfredo dropped to his knees by him. "Señor Lindsay is alive? Yes! But where?"

"She didn't say." That was all. Kirk relapsed into a semi-coma.

For another month he hovered between life and death. Then, gradually, the crisis passed. Bit by bit he grew stronger. His recovery would be slow, Sanchez said. "But he has the toughness of a buffalo," he told Alfredo. "If you use caution, you may take him to your hacienda."

Later, Kirk could not remember the ride out there. They'd given him an anaesthetic so that he would feel no pain from the jolting. Of this there was a minimum, for Alfredo himself drove the carriage, and they moved like a snail through the piñon hills. Arriving, Kirk was taken tenderly from his improvised ambulance and carried to a guest room. He came to consciousness in bed there, with Alfredo and Rosita on either side of him.

Don Eusebio was there, too, and gave stern orders. "Today you will not talk with him. Already he has told us what he knows. We will feed him now. Then he must sleep."

The gray-haired *mayordomo* came in with a hot *cazuela gallina* and fed Kirk with a spoon. Then Sanchez gave him a sedative. When the patient fell asleep he said, "It will be a long time. Perhaps all winter, my friends. Send for me if he does not improve."

Mid-October found Kirk still flat on his back. Every moment pained him. But his head was clear now, and he could talk freely. He could even have visitors, Don Eusebio said. "It will be good for him, Alfredo. Tell him all that has happened. It is an antidote for boredom."

So Alfredo sat by his guest's bedside and brought him up to date. "At the sheriff's office we miss you, Kirk. We have much work there. Far and near we ride searching for Mark Lindsay."

"And no trace of him?" Kirk asked.

"Not anywhere," Alfredo admitted sadly. "We know only what Carmencita said. That somewhere he is alive."

"Any new grief come up?"

Alfredo shrugged. "Just the usual. But south of here, in Lincoln County, there have been great battles. The faction of McSwain suffered much loss in the month of July. They were besieged in McSwain's house, at Lincoln, by government troops. A company of infantry, another of cavalry, another of artillery with Gatling guns and a twelve-pounder."

"Was Billy the Kid there?"

Alfredo nodded. "He was besieged with McSwain and all the others. The other faction set fire to the house and those inside had to fight both bullets and flame. All were killed — except one. Billy the Kid, by some miracle, escaped. And now the McSwain sympathizers rally around him, and the war still goes on."

"How's the railroad coming?"

Alfredo brightened. "It comes nearer each day, *amigo*. On September fifteenth its trains began running into Trinidad. The track is now climbing the pass. Ahead of it there is much grading and building of bridges. Soon it will be in New Mexico."

"Anything else?"

"Only politics," Alfredo said. "President Hayes has appointed a new governor to the territory of New Mexico. He is a general named Lew Wallace, and on the first of this month he was inaugurated at Santa Fe. The politicians there do not like it. He is not of their crowd."

"Why was he appointed?"

"Because of the scandals and fighting in Lincoln County. He has orders to make peace. Already he has arranged to meet Billy the Kid, in person, at Lincoln and make a truce between the factions. This new governor has great courage, señor. Also he is a man of learning who writes books."

A knock at the door, and Rosita came in to reprove her brother. "You talk him to death, Alfredo. I am his nurse and I will not permit."

Kirk dozed for a short while. When he opened his eyes they were both still there. Then old Santiago, the *mayordomo*, came in to announce a caller downstairs.

"For you, señorita. It is Señor Vogle."

Rosita colored slightly and excused herself. Kirk looked questioningly at Alfredo.

Alfredo shook his head, smiling. "She has not said yes, yet. Neither has she said no. But I think it will be arranged, Kirk *amigo*. Señor Vogle is a fine *caballero*."

Over the piñon hills came a calico pony. The girl who rode it wore farm homespun and her face, under the coiled yellow braids, had a flush of purpose. Christine Dunbar had never liked sidesaddles, and she didn't use one now. That she was paying a call at the most fashionable hacienda in the county didn't bother her at all. This was strictly business. She must hear from Kirk Calloway's own lips this story about Mark Lindsay.

Mark was still alive, rumor said. The source of it, they said, was Calloway himself. Or rather it was a dance hall girl to whom Calloway had paid a midnight visit. Severely Christine assured herself that she wasn't in the least interested in that part of it. If Calloway liked that kind of women, it was no concern of hers.

199

But he *must* tell her how and why he knew Mark Lindsay was alive.

Christine guided the mare down into an alfalfa valley and up this to a mansion of brown mud bricks. She slid from the saddle like a boy and walked, spurs clinking, to the patio gate. It opened, and a *mozo* bowed her in.

"I'm told that Mr. Calloway can receive visitors. May I see him?"

The *mozo* took her to Santiago. Santiago took her to Rosita. Rosita greeted her graciously, escorted her up to Kirk Calloway.

"Christine!" Kirk's eyes lighted when she appeared at his bedside.

"We hear you're feeling better, Mr. Calloway. Father and I were terribly shocked about your — accident." Her voice was reserved and formal. She didn't sit down. Rosita had slipped quietly from the room.

"He brought you out?"

"Father? No, I came alone. I just want to find out what you know about Mark."

"A girl named Carmencita," Kirk said, "told me he's alive. That's all I know. About that time, someone began shooting."

"How could the girl know?"

"She heard talk at the Buena Suerte. A customer burned a paper, and it made her curious. So she listened."

"What paper?"

"I don't know. Sit down, won't you, Christine?"

"It's a long way back to town," she evaded. "I can't stay. Do you really believe the girl knew?"

"I'm sure she did. Somebody didn't want her to tell, so he gunned us."

"But if Mark's alive, why doesn't he come back?"

"It's anybody's guess," Kirk said. "Maybe he's being held prisoner somewhere. Why, I don't know."

"I hope I haven't bothered you," Christine said. "Thank you for sending word about Mark. Father will be glad to hear you're improved. Good-by, Mr. Calloway."

"Don't go, please."

"I must. I've a long way to go." She had an air of harassed reserve that Kirk couldn't fathom. Before he could protest again, she'd given him a quick, impersonal smile and was gone.

Rosita met her at the foot of the stairs. "You must stay all night with us, señorita. I will show you to your room."

"It's nice of you," Christine said. "But Father's waiting for me in town." She went outside where a boy brought her pony. Rosita followed, stood at her stirrup as she mounted.

"He *is* going to get well, isn't he?" Without meaning to, Christine looked up at a certain shutter of the second floor.

A wise understanding came to Rosita. "I am certain he will, señorita, now that *you* have been to see him."

The emphasis startled Christine. "I? Why should that matter?"

The Spanish girl smiled. "You pretend you do not know? But you do, of course. We are women, you and I, and so we know these things."

"What things?"

"That he loves you."

Christine reddened. "Kirk Calloway? Of course he doesn't."

"But he does! I am not only a woman, señorita, I am also his nurse. I sit by his bed when he speaks of you. I see it on his face, I hear it in his voice, I read it in his eyes."

"Then why did he —" Christine checked herself, biting her lip.

"Do not have concern," Rosita said, "about Carmencita. She was only his spy, his eyes and his ears at the Buena Suerte. One night she learned something she was afraid to tell at the bar. So she whispered for him to follow her home. When he did, she was killed. She gave her life, and Señor Calloway almost gave his own, to find the truth about Mark Lindsay."

Shame flooded Christine. She looked up again at the shutters of Kirk's room. How stupid and rude she'd been! Could she go back up there? No — she had no face for it now.

But she did lean from her saddle and kiss Rosita Baca. "Thanks," she murmured, "for taking such good care of him. Good-by." She spurred the calico mare and loped away toward Las Vegas.

Fall faded into winter, and still Kirk lay helpless in the house of the Bacas. Alfredo himself was gone most of the time, sheriffing vigorously about the county. Christine Dunbar did not return to the hacienda, but Alfredo, one day, brought word of her.

"I passed by her homestead," he told Kirk. "With her father she has been harvesting corn. And such a crop! *Caramba!* Never have I seen such corn. They are from Iowa where the tall corn grows, so they do the same thing here. How, you say? In the summer they plowed a ditch from the Conchas and they let water run down the furrows. It makes the corn grow more tall than a man on horseback. So now they get sixty bushels the acre. Three thousand bushels in all, Kirk *amigo*. They have built a great crib for it. I shall tell the governor, when I see him in Santa Fe, so that he will be proud of our New Mexico."

"You mean you're going to the capital," Kirk asked, "to see this General What's-his-name?"

Alfredo's face clouded. "*Eí*, he has sent for me to come there. 'Bring me,' he says, 'the sheriff of San Miguel.' He is a man of stern discipline. Perhaps he has heard of our outlaws here. That he does not like. He has power to remove sheriffs and appoint new ones. Or if sheriffs fail, he can send soldiers to do their work. If that happens to me, my friend, I am ashamed forever."

"Brighten up, Alfredo. Maybe he just wants to get the low-down on things around here. What's the latest on the railroad?"

"Have you not heard? Its tracks reached the state line on November first. The tunnel is not finished. But a shoofly switch has been built over the pass. And only yesterday the first engine ran over it down into New Mexico."

Kirk gave a feeble cheer. "Las Vegas, here we come!"

CHAPTER
NINETEEN

Sodbuster Rescue

Riding over Glorietta Pass to the capital, Alfredo Baca was oppressed by gloomy forebodings. What did the governor want with him? Was he to be rebuked for failure to suppress outlawry in San Miguel County? Was he to be supplanted by troops?

Having kept up with recent affairs, Alfredo could well guess the governor's mood. He knew that General Wallace was at loggerheads with most of the high-up territorial politicos. The general had intervened in Lincoln County and had personally convened, at a truce tryst, with Billy the Kid there. He had offered amnesty for both sides if the Kid would guarantee cessation of the war. The Kid had given his word, and the governor had returned to Santa Fe believing the matter settled.

Yet only a short while later the Kid had broken out in another orgy of killings. He was now a hunted fugitive hiding somewhere between the Pecos and the Canadian. Of this the enemies of General Wallace were making political capital. They accused him of appeasing, with an unrealistic faith, the nation's most notorious outlaw. All of which should put the general in rather a grim temper. Alfredo had never met him. He knew only that Lew Wallace was a rare mixture of soldier, idealist, and scholar.

Alfredo rode his black racer, Noche, down the Camino Real and into the ancient plaza at Santa Fe. He was well known there. Passing *caballeros* waved salutations, and ladies smiled from their carriages. Alfredo dismounted at the Fonda, tossed his reins to a boy, hurried in, and took a room for the night. In it he freshened himself for his audience with the governor.

Crossing the lobby on his way out, his eye caught a familiar silhouette. A darkly handsome man was drinking alone at the bar, while his free hand practiced with dice there.

Alfredo appraised him narrowly, noting two front gold teeth. Macklin! Evidently the man had replaced the front teeth smashed out by Calloway at Las Vegas. So it was to Santa Fe the gambler had come after being run out of the neighboring county! Suspicion pulsed through Alfredo. Perhaps this Macklin had slipped back to Las Vegas, for a single dark night last summer, for the purpose of killing Kirk Calloway. Certainly he had a motive. All six of the bullets could have been meant for Calloway, a stray one finding the breast of Carmencita.

Alfredo went on out into the plaza. He must speak to the local sheriff about Macklin. Now he crossed to the Palace of Governors, to keep his appointment there. More than three hundred feet long by a third as wide, the old palace took up an entire side of the plaza. At one end of it was the post office and at the other end the *calabozo*. The main part of it, with its lengthy

205

façade of columns and arches, was in effect the executive mansion. Alfredo knew that General Wallace kept both his official office and his private study there. A study in which, people said, he worked late every night zealously completing a book.

Alfredo passed through a wide portal into a spacious foyer supported by unhewn pine logs. To a secretary he presented his credentials. The secretary summoned a *mozo.* "Conduct Don Alfredo to the governor."

The *mozo*, in formal livery, ushered Alfredo to the door of a small study. He opened it, stood at attention, and sang out: "Excellency, comes now Don Alfredo Baca, the sheriff of San Miguel."

The room Alfredo entered was cold, with the severity of a cloister. The walls, as well as a corner fireplace, were adobe-plastered. The floor was bare except for one small Navajo rug. There was a brassbound chest, two high-backed chairs, and a desk. The desk was littered with handwritten manuscript. Back of it sat a man with tired eyes and a flowing black beard. He had shaggy eyebrows and a long straight nose. The ends of a wide bow tie disappeared under his broadcloth vest. A quill pen was in his hand, and he finished writing a line before looking up.

Then — "You are Alfredo Baca? Sit down, please."

"I am honored, General." Alfredo sat down.

To his relief Lew Wallace made no mention of the Lincoln County war. Instead he talked about the railroad.

"Its coming means much to New Mexico, Mr. Baca. And the present construction contract, I happen to

206

know, goes only to your town of Las Vegas. There operation will stop for a considerable time, while the line consolidates its gains and re-finances."

"Yes, Excellency."

"Which means you'll be end of rails for a certain indefinite period. You'll be the gateway to all the vast resources of our territory. The first trains will bring a legion of settlers, speculators, opportunists, pioneers good and bad, and dump them on your depot platform at Las Vegas. I want you to promise me two things, Mr. Baca."

"Your will is mine, General."

"First, I want every law-abiding immigrant treated with courtesy and encouragement. We need them. We need new blood here. There must be no hazing of sincere homesteaders. Whether they be rich or poor, whatever their race, creed, or color, if they are honest we welcome them to New Mexico. I do not believe in the divine rights of kings, Mr. Baca."

Alfredo smiled. "Cattle kings, General?"

"Put it that way if you like. Those who come with plows may be ill-advised — perhaps our climate is too dry for their purpose. That is for them to find out. Our part is to give them the right hand of Christian fellowship, for this is a Christian land." As he talked, Lew Wallace gathered up the manuscript sheets scattered on his desk, stacking them neatly before him. On the top sheet Alfredo glimpsed a bold title: *Ben Hur; Book VI*.

"These shall be so treated in my county, General."

"My other request is this, sheriff. The railroad itself must be treated with every courtesy. It has enemies here. Men who for speculative or political reasons want it to go this way or that, and men who do not want it to come at all. But we have granted it a charter and must respect it. In your county there must be no interference or sabotage or scandal which might reflect on the honor of New Mexico. This applies both to the railroad and to the citizens it brings us."

"I promise, General."

Lew Wallace stood up. His formal handshake dismissed Alfredo.

Alfredo left the palace, loyally enlisted to the service of his governor. His next stop was at the *calabozo*, where his friend, the sheriff of Santa Fe County, greeted him warmly.

"There is a man here named Macklin. Once we ran him out of Las Vegas. Has he given you any trouble?"

"Not yet, Alfredo. We heard he had a fight with one of your deputies just before he came here. He has lived at the Fonda ever since."

"Could he have slipped away one night last summer for a quick shooting at Las Vegas?"

"That I cannot say. An alibi that far back is hard to check. Here there have been no complaints against him. Only once have we had to question him."

"When was that?"

"Only a few nights ago, Alfredo. He was seen drinking at a bar with a wanted man named Rocky Packard. Packard disappeared before we could pick him up. Macklin was still at the bar. We questioned him. He said Packard was a stranger of whom he knew nothing. Maybe that is true, maybe not."

Alfredo shrugged. "Macklin is of no interest to me," he said, "as long as he stays out of my county. If you hear of him heading back that way, will you let me know?"

"By all means, Alfredo."

As he crossed the plaza on the way back to the Fonda, Alfredo noted rolling black clouds overhead. The air was getting cold. A blizzard, he felt, was in the brewing. To get home ahead of it, he must make an early start in the morning.

The blizzard struck with fury a day later, ripping down from the Dakotas to the Rio Grande. Its central path was the Texas Panhandle, but its western edge caught the plains of New Mexico. The Linked Hearts ranch suffered, but not so much as Colonel Harper's Rafter Cross. Alfredo's cattle had the shelter of cedar and piñon hills. And they were only on the edge of the storm.

The Rafter Cross brand, out on the bare prairies along the Canadian, was lashed into forlorn, hump-backed huddles. There was no sheltering vegetation except fringes of cottonwood along the streams, and these, in midwinter, were without leaf. In two days of wind and sleet they became gaunt, icicled frameworks. Then came snow and still more snow. Huge drifts of it trapped the cattle of Calvin Harper, marooning them without food in great bawling, shivering, driftbound herds.

Harper might have weathered it if it hadn't been for a severe heelfly scourge in August. This scourge the Linked Hearts, up in the Glorietta Hills, had escaped. So Baca's cattle had gone into the winter fat. But winter had caught the Rafter Cross stuff in poor flesh due to stings in the hoof which had kept the cattle running, tails out, nervously aflight through much of the fall season. When the heelfly bites, the steer runs for the nearest creek. He stands in water for relief, when he should be out feeding.

It had left the Rafter Cross in no shape to weather a norther like this one. Calvin Harper was an old-time Texas cowman. Always he had treated cattle like nature treats buffalo. You turn them loose to graze; you round them up for hides and beef. Hay and grain were for horses; not for cows. Never in his life had Colonel Harper put up any winter feed for his cattle.

The only remedy he had, in a situation like this, was to scrape the snow and ice off cactus plants and set fire to them. This Monte Hickock and his crew did desperately for a week. Fire burns the spines off, and starved cattle close in on the toasted cactus pulp. The Rafter Cross had done this before, in other winters. Their stock knew what smoke rising out of snow meant. Always they floundered toward it, jostling and horning each other to get at the feed.

But the Rafter Cross had fifteen thousand head, and there wasn't enough cactus. And the strongest ones always got to it first. The weak cattle, that really needed it, stood hunched in the drifts waiting to die.

210

The hard fight to save them got Harper down himself. An old leg injury flared up, shooting pains through him, and drove him from the saddle. All he could do was sit in the house, fretting impotently, while his crew rode the range tailing up weaklings and burning cactus.

Monte Hickock came in with a frozen nose and with ice festooning his eyebrows. "It ain't no use, boss," he reported. "You might as well write the springers off right now. The he-stuff'll maybe pull through. They'll be skin and bones but they'll live till a thaw. You can't hardly kill a steer. Same goes for the dry cows. But the springers, they're goners. You can count 'em dead right now."

By springers he meant cows due to drop calves in the spring. Being heavy with calf they were less active at foraging, at pawing through ice to grass or at horning away competition at a cactus burn. Also each springer had another life to feed in addition to its own.

Harper pulled glumly at his mustache. "How many springers we got, Monte?"

"Around three thousand." Hickock spread his frostbitten hands over the stove, then added with a grimace, "And it's gonna be dang cold skinnin' them three thousand carcasses. Ain't time and men fer it, nohow. Most of 'em'll spoil."

"You got a man through to Las Vegas?"

"Sure, boss. But all the hay they got in the feed stores there ain't any more'n enough fer the horse-stuff in this county. Anyway you couldn't haul it out here."

Someone knocked, and Harper supposed it was another of his hands coming to thaw out. But when Hickock opened the door, the man who stood there was Alex Dunbar.

Alex stepped inside, chilled to the bone, but no chillier than the stare Harper impaled him with. Ever since last spring Harper had frigidly ignored the Conchas Creek homesteader. Sight of him now brought back bitter memories; it was in a quarrel over this man that the colonel had lost his best friend, Alfredo Baca.

Starved out, probably, Harper thought. *Starved or frozen out! I told him it would be that way, the damnyankee sodbuster.*

But aloud the colonel didn't say that. He was a Texan, and this man, for the moment, was under his own roof. "Set and warm," he said stiffly. "If it's grubstake you want, you can go help yourself at the cookshack."

"No, thanks; we're pretty snug," Alex said. "But I noticed some of your cows, Harper. They're in bad shape. Why don't you send over and get some corn and fodder? I got three thousand bushels cribbed, and forty acres fodder in the shock. You could pay me whatever you think it's worth."

Cal Harper stared at him, shocked stupid. "Three thousand bushels! It ain't possible!"

"Take a look in my cribs."

Monte Hickock nodded. "Yeh, boss, he's got it all right. I rid by there when they was harvestin'."

Alex said, "I reckon your cows don't know how to eat corn. But if you'll chop up some cornstalks and put

212

'em in a trough, and then sprinkle a few ears o' corn over it, they'll eat some of the corn by mistake and get used to it. After that they'll go for it big."

Harper reddened to his ears. He hated this man. He hated all damnyankee nesters. But as much as he hated Dunbar, he loved stock more. And from far out on the range came a mournful chorus, the plaintive bawling of starved cows.

Ten ears a day to each of his three thousand springers would carry them through to a thaw. It would save not only the cows but the coming calf crop. It wasn't the money involved which weighed most with Harper. He was a stockman. He couldn't bear to see cows drop dead. Letting them die, if it could be avoided, was to Calvin Harper the unforgivable crime.

"I'll pay top market price," he said to Alex. And to Hickock: "Monte, call in the boys and hitch up every wagon on the place."

Three days later it was still snowing. But through the fluttering flakes, now, came fewer bawlings of distress. Here and there, on the Rafter Cross range, circles of red gleamed through the curtain of white. Each circle was a bunch of cows grouped around a trough. Each trough held fodder with ears of corn mixed through it. Day and night the wagons hauled. Alex Dunbar contributed his own wagon and his four white mules. He, too, loved stock and couldn't bear to see it die. That much, when the chips were down, he had in common with Calvin Harper.

Soon the cattle learned to eat corn alone. It gave strength and life. The fodder stalks, now, could be scattered anywhere on the snow. Three thousand head on the hoof, and as many yet unborn, were saved for the Rafter Cross.

When the sun finally came out, and the snow began melting, Colonel Harper rode to the Dunbar homestead. He handed a check to Alex Dunbar. Then he rode on to Las Vegas.

Alfredo Baca was at the sheriff's office. It surprised him when the gaunt figure of Cal Harper loomed in the doorway.

"Alfredo," Harper muttered, "maybe I —" He stumbled on what came next. Never before had Cal Harper taken water. But Alfredo could see something strangely humble about him. And something wistful in the man's eyes which brightened Alfredo's.

"Yes, Colonel?"

"Mebbe I was wrong, Alfredo. I mean about that Dunbar outfit. I reckon they got as much right around here as we have. So why don't you and I — I mean — dammit, if you'll step over to the plaza I'll buy you a drink, Alfredo."

For Alfredo it was almost too much. He came forward joyfully. For a moment he was all Latin, and his arm went around the colonel's neck. "*Amigo de mi alma*, I have missed you so much!" Words failed him. He hooked his arm in Harper's and the two hurried to the Exchange bar.

"What'll you have, Alfredo?"

Alfredo much preferred wine. But this was an occasion. "The same as my friend the colonel," he said jubilantly to the bartender.

214

So two whiskies were set out.

"Your health, Alfredo."

"To our friendship, my colonel, and may it never be blighted again!"

Then it was Alfredo's time to buy. Reconciliation warmed with each sip. It brought them to a glow which made Alfredo propose: "And just to prove I love you, my colonel, I will bet you another thousand steers."

Harper nodded. That he could understand. One may bet with his friend. And with a friend you cannot lose, for what is your friend's is yours.

"Done, Alfredo. Only this time let's make it cows instead of steers."

"*Seguramente, amigo.* I take the odd, you the even. Now it is two thousand steers and one thousand cows, is it not?"

"Right, Alfredo. And we won't have so long to wait, now. They tell me that there track's comin' right along."

Again they were happy, these two. So they made a night of it. As a rule Alfredo was a temperate man. He was not what his people call a *tomador*, a taker. But this was a celebration with every barrier down. So he permitted himself to get drunk with Colonel Harper.

215

CHAPTER
TWENTY

Fateful Deadline

On a day late in February came word that the Santa Fe had run its first passenger train as far as Otero Station, Colfax County, New Mexico. A cheer went up at Las Vegas. For Otero Station was fifteen miles this side of Raton. It was well this side of the pass and down on the plains again. Track laying, barring bad weather, would now come apace.

Las Vegas was roaring and ready. Snow from the big storm had melted, except for patches here and there. Lumber rolled in from the hills, and a new line of buildings sprang up along the staked right-of-way. These soon took the name of New Town. It roughly paralleled Old Town, where the plaza lay, and where the bullock trail to Santa Fe passed by the Buena Suerte and the big, booming store of Adam Vogle.

The railroad itself was freighting in lumber, by team, to have a depot and at least a bare minimum of terminal facilities ready to receive the first train. No construction contract had been let beyond Las Vegas. Here, definitely, would be the next stopping-place in a march of empire.

West of the Gallinas River lay the Old Town plaza, and east of the river ran the staked line of the railroad.

The gap between them was about three-quarters of a mile, and this space was now rapidly building up with shack restaurants, tents, and saloons. Lot prices in both sections were already up, but Adam Vogle did not sell. The maximum, he knew, wouldn't be reached until hordes of cash-flush Easterners came swarming on the first trains. Only a maximum of profit could satisfy Vogle. It was more than ever necessary now, since he must split with a man named Goff.

Day by day the track came nearer. It crossed the great Maxwell Grant, punched on southwest into Mora County. Its advance city of tents, housing its army of laborers, moved on to Wagon Mound. Culverts and timber trestles were in place even ahead of that. Construction trains, backing like crabs, pushed flat cars laden with rails and ties to the ever-advancing end of track.

But track, from the angle of the Baca-Harper bet, didn't count. The line would straggle into Las Vegas, the grade on one day, the ties on another, and the rails on still another. So one thing was definitely settled. Everyone in town knew it. It was even advertised in the local paper. The wager would be decided only when the first public and officially scheduled passenger train arrived opposite a certain cottonwood tree in Las Vegas. The tree happened to be approximately on a line between the Exchange Hotel, in Old Town, and the brand new Close and Patterson dance hall, in New Town.

The question was, would that train arrive on an odd or an even day of the month?

Alfredo Baca, with all his virtues, had one weakness. He enjoyed that peculiar type of adulation which frontier communities give to the nonchalant, sky-limit chance-taker. He lived in a world where the piker, the tinhorn, the penny-better, was at the very bottom of the social scale. To be the extreme opposite was to be great in the eyes of men.

Of his physical courage Alfredo was not vain. Of his casual calmness at the turn of a card, with a fortune at stake, he was. It was much the same with Colonel Calvin Harper. "*Que caballeros!*" men whispered whenever these two passed. And they liked it.

"It's a bit stiff, isn't it?" Adam Vogle suggested slyly to Alfredo. "Maybe you ought to call it off."

Alfredo bridled. "I call off a bet? *Nunca, señor.*"

"*You* wouldn't, of course," Vogle said quickly. "But I was thinking of Harper. His cattle didn't do any too well last winter. Maybe he figures he can't afford it, and is just too proud to say so."

An astute psychologist, Adam Vogle! The effect, he knew, would be exactly the opposite of his apparent intention.

That night at the Buena Suerte Alfredo said to his friend Calvin Harper, "Your cattle did not do so well last winter, *coronel mío*. If you think we have wagered too many, you may fix the number at whatever you like."

Up went the colonel's feathers. He was stung to the quick. "Whadda you think I am, Alfredo, a piker?" He glared from under shaggy brows. "Huh! You can afford it and I can't! Is that it? Why, you cocky little bantam!"

218

He snorted and fumed as one may only snort and fume at a bosom friend. "Only thing about that bet I don't like, Alfredo, is that sometimes I get mixed up. I forget whether it's two thousand steers and one thousand cows, or two thousand cows and a thousand steers. Why not make it two of each? Then we won't get mixed up any more."

Alfredo shrugged. "*Cómo no?*" he agreed. "Two of each. Will you have another drink, señor?"

Word of it spread quickly through the town. A thousand cows had been added to the bet. *Que caballeros!*

A committee was already arranging a big celebration for the day of the first train. No one knew when it would be, but it was certain to be early in the summer. So the committee scheduled a rodeo. A band was recruited. Two elaborate balls were advertised for the night for whatever day the first train arrived — one at the Exchange Hotel in Old Town, one at Close and Patterson's in New.

The committee spared no effort. This, they predicted, would be the biggest jamboree ever held in New Mexico. Las Vegas was guaranteed to be wide open, fiesta-mad, and crowded with everyone who could arrive by wheel or saddle. Then the committee chairman came up with an inspiration. He announced that a feature of the celebration would be the public payment of a bet between Cal Harper and Alfredo Baca.

On the very depot platform, as the first train pulled in, the loser would hand to the winner a bill of sale for the chattel wagered.

"Why not?" consented Calvin Harper.

"*Cómo no?*" echoed Alfredo Baca.

There was no holding of stakes, nor a single scrap of writing to confirm the wager. Just the word of two Western gentlemen. Each knew the other, and that his word was his bond.

Early in May, at the Baca hacienda, Kirk Calloway made his first trip downstairs. He was still weak. He wasn't yet ready to climb a saddle. He'd lost thirty pounds and wore the pallor of a man long abed. But his spirit was restless. He wanted to get out and go.

"Look, Alfredo. I've imposed on you folks long enough. Take me to Vegas and I'll get me a room there."

His host wouldn't hear of it. "Your visit has honored us," he insisted. "Besides, Don Eusebio would not permit."

From the music room came strains of an organ. It was Sunday afternoon, and Adam Vogle was calling as usual. At dinner a few minutes ago, Vogle had congratulated Kirk on his recovery.

Alfredo held a match to Kirk's cigarette. He proceeded, then, to bring his guest up to date on events at Las Vegas. "You will not know the place, Kirk. It is two towns now, but they will soon be one. The stores and the bars overflow. Everyone is excited. They wait for the railroad like a ranchero waits for his harvest."

"When will it get there, Alfredo?"

"Late in June, we think, or early in July." Alfredo told him about the big celebration planned, making no mention of his own wager.

220

Kirk became aware of a sudden silence from the music room. The organ had stopped, and for minutes not even a whisper came from Rosita and her guest.

Alfredo checked his chatter in the middle of a word, his eyes staring past Kirk. Kirk turned and saw Vogle and Rosita. They were hand in hand; the girl's cheeks were brightly pink.

Vogle gave a self-conscious grin. "Tell them, Rosita."

"We are happy, my brother," Rosita announced in Spanish. "You approve?"

Alfredo bounded forward, kissed her cheek, wrung Vogle's hand warmly. "But of course! This I have been expecting." He added with a chuckle, "Why did you wait so long?"

"I wasn't a very good salesman." Vogle grinned. "But it's all settled now." He looked a little smug about it, Kirk thought.

Alfredo clapped his hands. "Santiago! Bring wine. We must drink to the bride and groom."

As the wine was served, Kirk looked narrowly at Rosita. She said she was happy. But was she? What could she have in common with this money-grubbing gringo merchant? From the first he'd struck Kirk as entirely out of her world. Had she consented mainly to please her brother?

"And where," Alfredo chattered, "will you go on the *luna de miel?*"

"The honeymoon?" Vogle smiled. "There are only three directions you can go from here. Mexico City, California, or New York. I offered Rosita her choice."

"So we shall go to New York," Rosita said. "To New York and Washington."

"A wise choice, sister," Alfredo applauded. "A carriage honeymoon is not good. And only to the East can you go by train."

"And the date?" Kirk inquired.

"That's all settled, too." Vogle beamed. "We'll get married exactly one week after the trains start coming to Las Vegas."

"To your happiness!" Alfredo raised his glass.

"Funny thing!" Kirk murmured a few minutes later. "The way everything depends on when the railroad gets here. It's the deadline on Alfredo's bet. And now the same goes for Rosy's weddin'."

Adam Vogle nodded. His mind closed shrewdly on a thought he did not speak. Yes, the coming of the railroad would determine and date both of those outcomes. But there was another — and of this they did not know. The fate of a pawn named Mark Lindsay waited that same deadline. His purpose as a hostage would be finished when settlement was made with Goff. And Goff, after the payoff, must, for his own protection, destroy Lindsay.

A wedding, a fortune, a life — all of these three would be won or lost on the same day of decision.

CHAPTER
TWENTY-ONE

Feverish Excitement

By late May Kirk was taking mild exercise outside. On his first sortie to the stable he found his bay horse in a stall there. His saddle hung on a rack. Alfredo had brought them from town.

"Won't be long now, Red." He stroked the bay's nose.

It was mid-June before Dr. Eusebio Sanchez let Kirk ride into Las Vegas. As he left, the hacienda was in a fever of preparations. A crew of seamstresses were there, busy with Rosita's trousseau. "It is no place for men." Alfredo sighed. He rode to town with Kirk Calloway.

The change there amazed Kirk. Scores of unpainted board fronts had been erected east of the creek. Almost as many more had been wedged in among the older, mud-plastered buildings near the plaza. Shanties, tents, and trail wagons filled all the space between. He saw a depot with the painted name, *Las Vegas*, hardly dry yet. Back of it was a bandstand. Holiday spirit ran high, and an atmosphere of ribald suspense.

"It's gone loco!" Kirk marveled. "You'd think the track was here already."

Many old friends hailed him. "Hi, Calloway. Did they dig all them slugs outa yuh? Hi, Alfredo."

The chairman of the celebration committee came up. "Have you heard, Alfredo? The track has crossed the Mora River. It is in our own county now."

"Yippee!" a man yelled. "And foggin' this way fast!"

They rode eight blocks from New Town to the plaza and Kirk took a room at the Exchange. Later he dropped in for a little while at the Buena Suerte. It was packed with trade, but orderly. Monte Hickock was there. The Rafter Cross foreman grinned sheepishly at Kirk. Apparently he held no grudge. Kirk bought him a drink.

"How you comin', Calloway? Last I heard they was minin' lead in your guts."

"The guy shot a little too low." Kirk grinned.

"Ever figger out who it was?"

"Never did."

Another Rafter Cross man chimed in. "It wasn't Billy the Kid. He wouldn't do a sloppy job like that."

Leaning against the bar, his last experience here recurred vividly to Kirk. Carmencita whispering in his ear. She'd been breathless, acquiver with some definite conviction. Not just a hunch, but a positive conviction. "Lindsay lives," she'd told him at her cabin.

If he'd been alive then he could be alive even now. Had Christine Dunbar, Kirk wondered, given up hope?

In the morning he rode out to the CLC. Archie Templeton, he found, had gone back to England. The brand had been sold late last fall, so the ranch had suffered no loss from the big midwinter storm. The land itself would soon be put on the market. Kirk found only Pacheco installed there as caretaker watching over a few odds and ends of chattel.

He rested overnight with Pacheco and the next day rode on to Conchas Creek. Where he had left a struggling homestead, he found now a prosperous farm. A second cabin had been built down the creek, to prove up on Christine's personal filing. At the upper place, where the creek forked, the fenced meadow now covered eighty acres. Half of it was in oats, half in barley. A ditch from the creek fed water to the plantings, which were lush green and knee high.

Christine was at her father's cabin. When Kirk knocked, she opened the door with a glow of glad welcome.

"Kirk Calloway! It's grand to see you up again." She was in a cook apron, her sleeves rolled above the elbows. Cupping her hands she called happily, "Dad! Who do you think's here?"

Off in the creek brush, chopping sounds stopped. Alex came in with a lusty greeting. "I'm setting a plate for you, Kirk." Christine hurried back to the kitchen. Her warmth puzzled Kirk. When she'd called at the Linked Hearts she'd been cool and distant.

He couldn't know that Rosita, with her parting confidence to Christine, had changed all that.

After dinner Kirk steered the talk to Mark Lindsay. It brought gloom to Christine's face. "Poor Mark!" she sighed. And by her tone he knew she'd given up hope.

Kirk spent the rest of his visit in a stubborn effort at reassurance. "He's being held somewhere, Christine. Why do I think so? Because if Carmencita hadn't been brimful of some secret about him, she wouldn't have been shot."

"If you could only be right!"

"I am. I feel it in my bones. Remember what I said one time? I said I'd bring that boy back. It still goes."

"You've been a wonderful friend, Kirk."

When he left they followed to his stirrup. "You folks'll be in town, won't you, for the big celebration?"

"Sure," Alex promised. "You mean when the first train comes in? Sure we'll be there. We wouldn't miss it. I'll fetch Chris in, and we'll stay all night at the hotel."

A warm, provocative light in Christine's eyes made Kirk bold. "They're havin' a *baile* there, that night. What about lettin' me take you?"

She smiled. "That will be nice, Kirk. I'll look forward to it."

It made him feel good all over. He loped to the CLC and rested overnight. In the morning he rode into Las Vegas. At the hotel there he buckled on his gun belt and reported to the sheriff's office.

Alfredo raised his eyebrows when he saw Kirk's gun and badge. "Take it easy," he protested. "You are in no shape for duty yet."

"Who says so?" Kirk retorted. "I'm fit as a fiddle. You've coddled me long enough, Alfredo."

His friend shrugged. "If you insist. You are still my chief deputy, of course. But no hard riding, Kirk. If there is an arrest to be made, I will make it myself."

Kirk strolled about town, mingling with the crowds. To his delight he ran into Ray Morley, construction engineer for the Santa Fe.

226

Morley slapped him on the back. "We heard you were shot up, Calloway. Good to see you around again."

"How's your railroad coming?"

"She'll be comin' 'round the mountain." Morley chuckled. "Look!" He pointed up the Gallinas Valley. "See that dust? It's a grading crew. The track layers are pushing right behind 'em. We'll be driving spikes right here in town within two weeks."

The imminence of the graders brought excitement to a pitch. The contagion of it infected everyone, most of all. Colonel Calvin Harper and Sheriff Alfredo Baca. Kirk was present, late in the evening, when the wager between those irrepressible plungers reached its final maximum.

The two had been fraternizing all day, twitting each other over drinks, each trying to outdo the other in an extreme of insouciant *sang-froid*, each secretly basking in a public adulation.

"You see I was right, *coronel mío*." Alfredo glowed. "What makes the cup sweet is the slow sip, the long and teasing fulfillment. It is like the lover's kiss. This we have tasted, now, for more than a year."

The stakes had been upped, a few evenings ago, to three thousand steers and three thousand cows.

"When you lose all them cattle," Harper bantered, "you won't need so much grass any more. You'll be payin' taxes on more land than you can graze."

"That is true," Alfredo admitted. "Only perhaps it is you who will have more land than cattle. Does it not disturb you, my friend?"

Harper gulped his liquor, glanced down the bar where customers listened with bated breath. "So why not fix that, Alfredo?" he proposed. "All things come in threes, the sayin' goes. So let's toss in three thousand acres of land. Then we'll close the pot for good."

"A worthy ideal" echoed Alfredo. "It is done." He extended a hand to bind it. "Three thousand steers, three thousand cows, three thousand acres."

Harper nodded. "Odd or even, Alfredo."

"*Exactamente*," Alfredo said. "I have the odd, you have the even."

On those ultimate stakes the wager was bound irrevocably. Beyond that it did not increase.

News of it swept through the town. Adam Vogle heard and smiled smugly. Baca would win. Vogle himself would see to that. Baca was a sheriff and this was New Mexico, where sheriffs died young. Everything Baca owned would some day be Rosita's. And Rosita, exactly a week after the railroad came, would be the bride of Adam Vogle.

CHAPTER
TWENTY-TWO

Ace in the Hole

If track construction had counted, the outcome would have been settled on July first. For on that day the last spike was driven in Las Vegas. One is an odd number, and Alfredo had the odd end of the bet.

But track completion didn't count. Neither did any of the puffing little work trains which for several days now had been dumping materials in the new yards at Las Vegas. Only when the first public passenger train chugged in, officially scheduled, would the issue be decided.

Half of San Miguel County was there, cheering, when the last rail was laid and the last fishplate bolted. High officials of the Santa Fe were in town for this, the completion of the first full division into New Mexico. There, too, were many dignitaries from the capital. This was a proud day for the Santa Fe and for all New Mexico.

A score of prominent citizens took off by stage for Trinidad, to return as a triumphant escort on the first train and to decorate it with bunting. Those who remained in Las Vegas waited, wondered, itched to know the outcome. Crowds milled about the depot.

229

When would the first train be scheduled? Not today and probably not even tomorrow. Construction was one thing; operation was another. Any new operation would be decided by the high command, back in Topeka, Kansas.

Rumor spread that an announcement would be posted on the depot. A thousand Las Vegans thronged there, watching for it.

Just before sundown it was posted. July fourth being a national holiday, it said, and the latest extension of the Santa Fe being of historical significance, the pioneer passenger train was scheduled into End of Track, at Las Vegas, on July 4, 1879.

A cheer. Then a hush. Neighbor looked at neighbor, most of them grimacing with a slight disappointment. For as between Calvin Harper and Alfredo Baca, Baca was generally the more popular. This announcement, definitely, settled the bet in Harper's favor. Four is an even number, and Harper had the even end of the bet.

Gringo cattle folk swarmed off to congratulate Harper. Others went sadly to console Baca. Three thousand steers, three thousand cows, three thousand acres! *Que mala suerte* for Alfredo!

Alfredo was at the Exchange Bar when he heard about it. He took it, as any *caballero* must, standing up.

"It is of small importance." He smiled. "You will join me, gentlemen?" He insisted on buying for everyone present. Magnificent either in victory or defeat was Alfredo Baca.

The tall, grizzled figure of Cal Harper loomed in the entrance. His blizzard-scarred eyes should have held triumph, but didn't; instead an odd look of hurt was there. He came forward almost sheepishly. "Well, Alfredo, looks like I got all the luck."

That was all he could say. Other things he wanted to say, but didn't dare. Winning lacked the relish he'd expected. Had it been possible he would have called the bet off or at least he might suggest easing up on the stakes. But Cal Harper knew better than that. He knew his friend's pride. He could not insult Alfredo Baca.

Alfredo said brightly, "I congratulate you, *coronel mío*. Manuel, your best for my friend, Colonel Harper."

Shortly Alfredo went out and found a lawyer. He directed the lawyer to prepare a deed for three thousand acres of land, in Harper's favor, and a bill of sale for six thousand head of cattle. "Date them July fourth. I will present them to Señor Harper at the celebration."

The lawyer didn't like it. He knew the Baca estate and its limitations. It wasn't as large as most people thought. Alfredo had been born a *rico*, but he'd spent freely all his life. Payment of this bet would leave him only the home hacienda, a small herd and a few narrow alfalfa meadows. "Isn't there any way out of this, Alfredo?"

Alfredo looked at him coldly. "Out of it, señor? You suggest I keep a few miserable cows in order to lose what is worth much more?"

"Worth more?"

"Certainly. My honor, señor."

Details of the first operation were soon abroad in town. The train would leave Trinidad early in the morning of July fourth and arrive at Las Vegas shortly after noon. The celebration committee launched into frenzied preparations. Placards went up in every bar. Feature events could be advertised to the exact hour, now. An all-day rodeo, with prizes, guaranteeing the best riding-talent in the territory. Band concerts, speeches by the bigwigs. A fandango at the Exchange Hotel and another one in New Town. Take your choice. And above all, the payment of a record wager to Colonel Harper by that prince of *caballeros*, Don Alfredo Baca.

While Las Vegas was whooping it up, on that night of July first, Adam Vogle rode quietly out of town. He guided his horse northwest, making sure he wasn't followed.

He was riding to an arranged tryst with Stumpy Goff.

Vogle dreaded it. But it was vital for two reasons.

First, he had insisted on seeing Lindsay in the flesh. Only if Lindsay was alive as a potential witness could Goff have any hold whatever on Vogle. Exposure of a dated handwriting a year ago proved only that the hostage had been living then. It did not insure that he was living now.

In a few days Vogle would be selling out his Las Vegas realty, to eager incoming speculators, for something like two hundred thousand dollars. Half he must give to Goff — but only if Goff could show his hole card, Mark Lindsay. If not, then Vogle could laugh at Goff and take all.

232

But there was another stake, and one which he wasn't obliged to share with Goff. The equity of a husband in the estate of Rosita Baca. That estate, if Baca won a bet from Harper, would be large. If Baca lost, it would be small. Therefore the first train *must* arrive here on July fifth — a day late. It could be arranged. And Goff, as a price for Vogle's submission to the major extortion, had agreed to co-operate.

Tonight he must give final instructions on that score. Also with his own eyes he must see Lindsay.

The meeting-place, by Goff's insistence, would not be where Lindsay was regularly confined. Where that was, Vogle didn't know. Nor did it matter.

The night was moonless, and Vogle almost missed a landmark. It was a double piñon at the outlet of a steep, narrow ravine. Vogle turned up the ravine at a walk. In the darkness he could barely see ten feet ahead. A coyote yelped and sent a shiver through him. The entire expedition frightened Vogle. But Goff had no reason to harm him. Profit for Goff could come only through Vogle.

The horse stumbled. Rocks and roots studded the trail. Vogle dismounted; leading his horse he groped blindly forward. He cursed the railroad for scheduling an even day of arrival. Had it been an odd day, arrangements for sabotage wouldn't be necessary.

He forced his mind to more pleasant things. To his wedding, in less than ten days now, with Rosita Baca. A luxurious train trip to New York. The opera, shops along Fifth Avenue, and grand hotels. They would delight Rosita. More than ever she'd think him a fine *caballero*.

The ravine took a bend. Rounding it, Vogle saw a light far ahead. It could be a campfire or a lamp at a cabin window.

Goff's voice startled him from the dark. "That you, Vogle?"

Vogle could barely make him out. The fat man was on the seat of a spring wagon. His team was drawn up under a cedar. "Who else would it be?" Vogle answered.

"You all alone?"

"Would I be fool enough to let anyone else in on this? Sure I'm alone, Goff."

Goff said harshly, "Well, I'm not. I got an Indian with a rifle. He's the best shot in New Mexico. You can't see him, but he's not ten yards away. The rifle's got a bead on you, Vogle. If you pull any tricks, he cuts loose."

"Where's Lindsay?"

"Follow me." The spring wagon creaked off up the ravine. Vogle followed. They advanced directly toward the glow of light ahead.

A square, squat shape loomed in the dark, and they stopped by it. Vogle saw that it was a small rock cabin and guessed that it had once been used as a line camp by some ranch. A sheep ranch, by the smell of it. On the near side was a foot-square opening, more of an air vent than a window. Candlelight glowed from it.

"Take a look," Goff invited.

Vogle dismounted and moved nervously to the open vent. Peering through it he saw Mark Lindsay. Lindsay sat on a keg, his pale profile toward Vogle. Goff had shaved him and cut his hair, so that Vogle would more easily recognize him. The prisoner's feet were free but his hands were tied back of him.

Vogle had seen him once or twice, during Lindsay's brief employment at the CLC. This was that same stray man, all right. Alive and eager to testify, he made a hole card that Vogle couldn't beat.

Sullenly Vogle retreated to Goff's wagon. Somewhere close by a moccasined foot crushed gravel. Vogle couldn't see the Indian, but he sensed a rifle aimed at his head.

"Want to talk to him?" Goff challenged.

Vogle shook his head. There was nothing to be gained by exposing himself to Mark Lindsay.

"Then let's get outa earshot." Goff drove a little way down the ravine and Vogle trailed after him.

They stopped beyond hearing from the cabin. "You've seen my hand," the fat man said. "And you've heard my proposition. When the boom hits Vegas, sell out and slip me half. If you do, I'll finish off Lindsay. If you don't, I'll turn him loose."

"You win," Vogle said, "but there's one small condition. An hour's work by three of your men on the night of the third."

Goff nodded. He understood that Vogle wanted a train delayed, but he'd been given no details of the plan. "What's the play, Vogle?"

"About fifteen miles before it gets to Vegas," Vogle explained, "the railroad track goes through a deep clay cut. It's just wide enough for the track to go through,

235

and it's got steep banks. I want those banks blasted with enough mine powder to slide a hundred tons of dirt over the track."

"Can three men do that?"

"Easy. One to stand guard and two to dig the powder holes."

"You don't want a wreck. Just a delay."

"Right. I want to delay a train one day."

Goff didn't like it. "It'd be simpler," he argued, "just to blow out a trestle. No diggin', that way."

"We can't tell how long it would take to repair a trestle," Vogle explained. "The railroad would have to bring in new timbers. If it took two days, or four, I'd be right where I started."

"I getcha. You want Baca to win his bet. Why?"

"That's *my* business. Take it or leave it, Goff."

"How do you know it won't take two or four days to clear dirt off the track?"

"Because the repair crew won't need any timbers or material. All they'll need is men with shovels and what few slip teams they can crowd into the cut."

"How long would that take?"

"Not less than twelve hours or more than thirty-six. I've figured it close, Goff. Now listen. All you do on the night of the third is plant the charges. You don't light the fuses. Two of your men can hightail it. The other man hangs around with a fast horse. He waits till about noon on the fourth. When he sees the smoke of a train, he lights the fuses and fans outa there."

Goff caught the idea. It would take the railroad a few hours to assemble men and teams. Chances of clearing the track before midnight would be nil. They'd finish some time the next day, and the train would go on into Las Vegas — arriving on the fifth, an odd day of the month.

"If that's all you want done," the fat man agreed, "it's a deal."

Vogle rehearsed him in the details. Then he gave his horse the reins and let it feel its way down ravine toward home.

When he was out of sight and hearing, Goff whistled for Chaco. The two of them took Mark Lindsay back to the crater.

CHAPTER
TWENTY-THREE

The Sheriff's Midnight Ride

All through the second and third of July, the county of San Miguel streamed into Las Vegas. Hotels and rooming houses overflowed. Crack riders from as far away as Socorro arrived to compete in the rodeo, and many of them had to spread their bedrolls in vacant lots or on the plaza. Peon families from the Rio Grande Valley slept in their wagons. Saddle horses stood wither to wither at every hitchrack.

In midsummer heat, the town reeked with dust and sweaty leather. Hundreds of stock hands sounded off with yells and song, racing around the plaza with skyward-aimed shots. Alfredo Baca and his deputies mingled among them, tolerantly hospitable and yet permitting no gross rupture of the peace.

"Our first trainful of visitors," he announced at every bar, "must not think us barbarians. Fun is something else. Have all you want, *amigos*."

Many speculators from up the line came in by stage and wagon, trying to beat the boom. A man from Denver bought the lease on the Buena Suerte, paying a fat price. Then he asked Adam Vogle for a figure on the building itself.

"Thirty thousand," Vogle said.

"Too much."

"You won't think so," Vogle smiled, "after the first few trains come in. You'll be lucky if I don't hike the ante."

That was late on the afternoon of the third. Vogle saw Kirk Calloway saunter into his store and went to wait on him personally.

"How's the bridegroom?" Kirk grinned.

"Impatient," Vogle admitted. "May I serve you?"

"Yep. Best silk shirt in the house."

"Dolling up for a dance date?" Vogle chaffed. He produced an offering of soft blue silk.

"I'll take it," Kirk said. "Now let's see some fancy boots."

When he was equipped with finery calculated to make an impression on Christine Dunbar at tomorrow night's frolic, Kirk got a shave and a haircut. He stopped at the Exchange dining-room for supper, then went up to put the purchases away in his room.

Yells and gunshots came from the plaza outside. Alfredo would need his full crew tonight, keeping order. Tired from policing the town all yesterday and today, Kirk stretched on his bed for an hour's rest.

He awoke with a guilty start. He'd slept three hours. This was the big night, and he shouldn't be letting Alfredo down. Hurriedly Kirk buckled on his gun belt and went out.

He made his way through milling crowds and found Alfredo in his private quarters off the sheriff's office. Alfredo had a disturbed look and was reading a letter.

"Have you seen Macklin, Kirk?"

"You mean that riffler I ran outa town a year ago?"

Baca nodded. "He's back. It says so in this letter from my *muy amigo*, the sheriff of Santa Fe. It came on the afternoon stage, but I have been too occupied to read it till now."

"What's the low-down?"

"When I was in Santa Fe last winter, I saw him at the Fonda there. So I spoke to the sheriff about him. I asked the sheriff to let me know if Macklin ever heads back this way. So now, with the big excitement here, Macklin comes."

"So the sheriff tipped you. Well, it's a free town. Reckon there's nothin' we can do about it, long as he behaves himself."

"But the letter," Alfredo worried, "tells me something else. It says Macklin was heard boasting at a bar, there in Santa Fe. It says he comes to Las Vegas to clean up on a sure thing."

"What sure thing?"

"That we do not know. Perhaps with loaded dice, perhaps with the trick deck, or with a shell game. With those, in the great crowds here, he might win much money. The crowds are our guests, Kirk, and I do not like to have them cheated."

"Sure," Kirk agreed. "I'd like another poke at that guy, anyway. Let's go pick him up."

"Only if we find him cheating," Alfredo assented. He put on his sombrero and they went out together.

"I'll cover the dives along the track," Kirk suggested.

"And I will cover Old Town," said Alfredo.

240

He left Kirk and began looking into saloons and cantinas along the trail street. When he went into the Buena Suerte, he saw Macklin.

The gambler was neither dicing nor playing cards. He stood at the bar with a well-known and respectable teamster from Wagon Mound. The two were discussing something in low tones. The teamster wore a puzzled expression. Macklin had a holstered gun, but so did half the men in the room.

Macklin's well-featured profile was toward Alfredo. He saw the man smile at his companion amiably, and the smile exposed two front gold teeth. There didn't seem to be anything questionable about his present deportment.

In a moment Alfredo saw him beckon to the bartender. Pedro came, expecting an order for another round. Instead Macklin, with some whispered instruction, passed money across the bar. The teamster also passed money to Pedro. Then Macklin strolled off toward the roulette room.

Alfredo stepped up and got Pedro's ear. "They make a bet, Pedro? They ask you to hold stakes?"

"*Sí*, Don Alfredo. This Macklin gets three to one odds. But even then he is a fool, señor. He cannot possibly win."

"Has he made other bets?"

Pedro nodded. "Four times already I have held stakes for him. And always he gets the odds. *Que tonto!* He bets that you will win from Colonel Harper. But already you have lost to Colonel Harper. Is it not so, Don Alfredo?"

A tension gripped Alfredo. It was true he had already lost. Official announcement had been made by the railroad. And the railroad, of course, could not be detained or corrupted. The train might be an hour late, or two, or three, but never a full day.

"Is this Macklin so stupid," Pedro grinned, "that he does not know what happens tomorrow? What good will odds of three to one do him, since he is sure to lose?"

"A brandy, Pedro."

Over it, Alfredo brooded fretfully. He recalled the wording of the letter. Macklin was here to clean up on a *sure thing*.

The sheriff's sensitive nostrils quivered. Fraud was in the air. It smelled to high heaven. Somebody was stacking a deck. Was Macklin working on his own or did he represent some huge gambling-ring? Was there a scheme afoot to wreck the train? What a scandal for New Mexico!

Whether he himself won or lost a bet was, to Alfredo Baca, relatively unimportant. If he won it must be a fair win, and not by the stacking of a deck. People might even whisper that he'd had a hand in it himself. *Vergüenza!* A shadow of shame like that would crucify Alfredo.

He remembered his promise to the governor. The railroad must be treated with respect, courtesy, and honor. There must be no scandal or corruption!

Stiffly Alfredo Baca marched his slim, slight figure into the gaming-room. He found Macklin in a booth

242

there. The man was promoting a bet similar to the one just made with a teamster.

"You are under arrest, señor."

Macklin looked up, startled. His eyes swept over Baca for a gun. Seeing none, he smiled insolently. "What for?" he demanded.

"On suspicion of fraud. You will follow me, señor." Alfredo turned his back and took three steps. Macklin did not follow.

Alfredo whirled to face him. "You do not hear well, señor?"

"Where's your warrant?" Macklin was on his feet, now. His right thumb was hooked in his belt, near the butt of his gun.

"This is my warrant." Alfredo extended his left hand with a badge exposed in the open palm.

What jolted Macklin was not the badge but the eye-baffling speed with which this cocky little Mexican had produced it. Could his other hand produce a gun equally fast? There was a slight bulge at Alfredo's right coat pocket.

"I offered you the courtesy, señor, of permitting you to follow me. That courtesy you declined. So you will now walk ahead."

"Where to?"

"To the *carcel*, señor."

"And if I don't?"

"If you do not, I will kill you," said Alfredo.

All the while he contemptuously ignored Macklin's holstered gun. He looked neither at the gun nor at the man's gun hand, but stared straight into his flickering eyes. The cool assurance of it unnerved Macklin. Fear froze his draw.

"*Ándele!*" commanded Alfredo.

And Macklin walked. Fully armed he walked out through the barroom. Apparently unarmed, Sheriff Baca strolled after him. No customer at the bar sensed an arrest.

Keeping back of him, stride for stride, Alfredo followed him to the jail.

"In here, señor." He ushered Macklin into his private quarters there.

Once inside, the man tried to bluster. "Put up or shut up, sheriff. If you think you can make this stick, you're —"

"Your gun," Alfredo cut in. "Put it on the desk."

His cold stare impaled Macklin. Then, sullenly, the gambler drew his forty-five and dropped it on the desk.

"And now your knife."

With a shrug, Macklin put a long, sharp throwing-knife beside the gun.

"Now you may sit down," Alfredo invited, "and we will wait for my deputy, Señor Calloway."

Macklin stared. "Calloway? What's he got to do with it?"

"He is out looking for you, señor."

"What for?"

Alfredo smiled. "Have you forgotten? Once you lied about him so that a girl would hear. It was to make her think he had killed her *querido*. So he thrashed you. As a *caballero* he could do nothing else. When your teeth were out and you lay screaming on the floor, he said he would finish the job if you did not keep away from Las Vegas."

Macklin tried to sneer. "Yeh, he talked big. So what?"

Alfredo looked at the wall clock. Its hands read a quarter before midnight. Then he called in a Mexican deputy. "Pancho, find Señor Calloway. He is in New Town looking for this man, Macklin. Tell Señor Calloway to report here at exactly midnight. Not sooner, not later."

Pancho hurried off toward New Town. Alfredo, ignoring Macklin, lighted a cigarillo.

"So that's it!" Macklin charged. "You got nothin' on me. This pinch was a bluff. You just suckered me in here, disarmed me, so that Calloway can come in with a gun and beat me up."

"I make no threat," Alfredo corrected. "I say only that Señor Calloway comes here — in just fourteen minutes."

"Yeh — to bend a gun over my head."

"Whatever he does, señor, I am sure he will not need a gun. He did not need one that other time, remember?"

A growing pallor on Macklin's face told that he remembered only too well. His tone took a faint whine. "You dasn't let him, Baca. You're a sheriff. It ain't legal, and you know it."

"Whatever he does to you, I will not see it. As Calloway comes in, I will go out. He will have you all to himself."

Four minutes ticked by. Macklin got up nervously and took a step toward the door.

Alfredo said quietly, "You will sit down, señor."

Macklin sat down. "You said I was under arrest," he blurted. "Either I am or I ain't. If I ain't, you gotta let me go. If I am, you gotta put me in a cell."

Alfredo nodded. "If you were in a cell," he murmured, "you would be safe from Señor Calloway."

Macklin squirmed. "All right. Put me in one."

"That I will do," Alfredo promised, "the minute you answer one small question. Tomorrow a train comes. Yet you bet that it will not. In Santa Fe you make boasts that you have a sure thing."

A murky relief came to Macklin's eyes. He had the look of a man who expects a major indictment and suddenly finds himself charged only with a misdemeanor. "No law against betting. You do it yourself."

"But not with a stacked deck. Nor by wrecking a train so that it will not arrive in Las Vegas."

"It ain't gonna be wrecked —" The denial slipped out before Macklin could check it. He withdrew into a cage of silence.

"Not a wreck?" Alfredo probed. "Then perhaps a few rails will be dislodged, or a bridge blown up, so that the train will be late. If you tell me this, I will put you in a cell, señor."

"And if I don't?"

"I will leave you to Señor Calloway. He is very angry. He does not like the lie you spoke before a lady." Alfredo sighed. "But I hope he will not kill you, señor." The clock said seven minutes till twelve.

"I don't know a thing," Macklin swore. Sweat stood in beads on his face as another minute crawled by.

"Please yourself." Alfredo shrugged.

Two minutes later the sharp clicks of riding-boots could be heard coming down the walk. They came briskly to the jail door. "That," suggested Alfredo, "will be Calloway." He stood up. "I leave as he enters, unless —"

"How can I tell you if I don't know?"

"But you *do* know. You make bets and you call it a sure thing."

Pancho poked his head in. "Señor Calloway is here, Don Alfredo."

The clock said 11:59. "Tell him to enter in exactly one minute, Pancho."

Macklin said desperately, "All I know is bar gossip. A guy named Rocky Packard had a bun on, in Santa Fe. I happened to be there. Ain't no law against hearin' bar talk, is there?"

"Calloway will enter in half a minute. Talk fast, señor."

The gambler blurted it out. "There's a deep cut fifteen mile up the track. Somebody's gonna blow it tonight. I don't know who. It's supposed to pile enough dirt on the track to make the train a day late."

Alfredo crossed to a door giving directly to the cell block corridor. "You will come this way," he said. Fires of fury burned in his eyes.

Macklin skipped through the door. Alfredo opened a cell, waved him into it and locked the cell. He stepped back into his own quarters just as Kirk Calloway entered from the forward hall.

"What's all the mystery, Alfredo? Anything up?"

"*Bastante*," the sheriff answered grimly. "Bring me a rifle, Pancho. And my horse."

"Bring mine too, Pancho." Kirk read fight on Baca's face. He had no idea what it was about. But if Alfredo Baca was riding at midnight, with a rifle, Kirk Calloway didn't mean to be left behind. He'd failed to find Macklin in New Town. Macklin, he concluded, wasn't important now. Bigger game was afoot.

Pancho brought two saddled horses each with a carbine in scabbard. Alfredo swung to the back of Noche, his black racer, and was off up the street at a gallop. Kirk, on Red, caught up with him.

"Where we headed, Alfredo?"

"To avert a scandal, señor. We ride to preserve the good name of myself, of Las Vegas, and of all New Mexico."

CHAPTER
TWENTY-FOUR

"Viva el Santa Fe!"

They streaked out of town, Alfredo simmering with indignation. Bit by bit Kirk got it out of him. Unknown persons were plotting to block the track in a cut up the line. They must be stopped at all cost. "*Madre de Dios! It is cheating. It is loading the dice. I am mortified, Kirk. If I permit this to happen, never can I meet the eyes of honest men.*" Alfredo dug in with his spurs and raced on.

They followed the new track, starlight glinting on its brave little fifty-six-pound rails. There was no right-of-way fence. Here and there was a shallow borrow pit from which fills had been made; and occasionally there was a cut through some rise of ground. But generally the roadbed, with its ladder of ties and rails, was laid flush on the virgin prairie.

Behind them the revelry in Las Vegas faded. Now could be heard only their own hoofbeats drumming on sod. At a trestle they made a slight detour to cross an arroyo. Kirk looked at his watch. They'd been riding twenty minutes and must have come about six miles.

"I know the place," Alfredo said. "It is a deep cut through a piñon hump where the graders worked long before the track arrived. Powder placed there would slide many tons of earth across the rails."

Kirk, stirrup to stirrup with him, gave a sardonic laugh. "You're a funny guy, Alfredo. Here you are riding hell-bent into a fight just to keep yourself from getting rich."

"No," Alfredo corrected. "It is to keep myself from getting poor. To be shamed before men is the greatest poverty of all."

"For *you* it would be," Kirk conceded. "Okay. So let's shoot ourselves out of a jackpot." He pulled his carbine from its scabbard and pumped in a shell.

They loped on up the track, the bay blowing hard in an effort to keep abreast of Noche. The track curved to miss a tall, cedared butte. Alfredo pointed to its top. "My grandfather hid up there one time," he said. "Indians were hunting for him. This was Mexico, then, and his fiestas were not ours."

"Like the Fourth of July." Kirk grinned. "That's what it's been for exactly forty minutes, Alfredo."

A hump in the terrain, densely studded with piñons, loomed ahead. Alfredo slowed to a canter. "*Cuidado*, Kirk. This is the place." In the dim night light they could see the track disappear into a cut.

Harsh scraping sounds came from the cut. It was like the clinks and thuds of shovel and pick.

"We better tie up right here, Alfredo."

They dismounted and tethered the horses to a piñon. Each with a carbine in hand, they advanced afoot.

A voice challenged, "Hey there, where you goin'?"

250

Alfredo answered boldly, "I am Alfredo Baca, the sheriff of San Miguel."

A six-gun boomed from the piñons, and its slug breezed by Kirk's ear. He and Alfredo dropped flat.

Again they heard a voice in the gloom ahead, this time yelling to someone in the cut. "Hi, you fellahs. Better quitcher diggin' and start shootin'."

Kirk heard feet scrambling out of the cut. He crawled to a piñon and lay back of it, elbows on the ground, alert to shoot at the first visible target. To his left Alfredo whispered, "How many?"

"Maybe two, maybe ten," Kirk said. He fired a decoy shot to test them out.

Three answering shots came from the gloom ahead.

Aiming at the sound, Kirk pumped five back at them. Then came a single crack from Alfredo's carbine.

"Only three of them, Alfredo. Shall we take 'em?"

"*Cómo no?*" agreed Alfredo. He got to his feet. "When they shoot again, we advance."

Kirk reloaded and stood at Alfredo's elbow. Piñon boughs overhead shut out starlight and kept them from being seen. Alfredo tossed a handful of gravel off to his right. Instantly a volley of forty-five bullets answered from the trees ahead.

Kirk and Alfredo closed in, pumping a shot with every step. This time there was no response. Kirk thought he heard running feet. He was sure of it a moment later when he heard horses gallop away.

At the top of the cut they found one man. A rifle slug had drilled through his head, and he was dead. Alfredo held the flare of a match near his face. "His name is

Donlin," he told Kirk. "Many warrants are out for him, but sheriffs could never learn where he hides."

The dead saboteur had a flat, sallow face; its pallor suggested a long term out of sunlight, as though he'd been in a hospital or a prison.

At the rim of the cut lay two bulging sacks. Kirk looked into them. "Black powder," he reported.

Alfredo had already slipped halfway down the cut bank. There he found the digging-tools of two men. A row of blast holes had been dug in the bank, spaced about ten feet apart. A powder charge set off in each would have sent an avalanche of dirt sliding across the track.

"We were just in time, Kirk."

"Right, Alfredo. Just in time to keep you from winning that bet with Harper. Any use chasing those guys?"

"Not in the dark, Kirk. And they will know how to cover their tracks. Look to see if they took the dead man's horse."

They hadn't. Kirk found a saddled horse tethered back in the piñons. With a lighted match he examined the brand. It wasn't a local brand and had been made long ago, when the horse was a colt. The horse might have been stolen, or it could have changed hands by bill of sale many times since a colt. So there wasn't much chance of tracing its background through a brand.

He led the saddled horse to Alfredo.

"I will remain here on guard," Alfredo said. "It is not likely those men will come back, but I will take no chance. You will ride fast to Las Vegas and send

252

deputies here to relieve me. Then I will follow with this dead man and his horse."

Kirk protested, but it was no use. "I am the sheriff," Alfredo insisted. "It is my personal responsibility. As soon as we destroy this powder, you will go."

They carried the two powder bags into the piñons and emptied them, scattering the powder thinly over a wide area of ground. Even if the saboteurs returned in force, they could not recover it. Nor was it likely that they could find another supply close by.

"As soon as you get relief on the way, Kirk," Alfredo ordered, "go to bed. Rest for the celebration tomorrow. And be fresh for your lady at the *baile*. It is my command."

Again Kirk failed to talk him out of it. He rode away, leaving Alfredo alone on guard. The slim little sheriff made a militant figure as he stood there in the starlight with his rifle, stubbornly vigilant, guarding not only a railroad but his own precious honor.

The bay was tired. Kirk had to take it easy getting back. The first streaks of dawn were showing as he rode into the livery barn at Las Vegas. He tossed his reins to the night man and hurried out to get recruits.

At the jail he aroused Pancho. Pancho was devoted to Alfredo. When he heard about his chief's lone vigil up the line, he quickly enlisted half a dozen of his friends. Kirk crossed to a barroom. All the bars in Las Vegas had been open all night. In this one Kirk found a group of Rafter Cross men. "Somebody tried to stack the cards against your boss," he told them. "But Alfredo

253

stymied them. What a guy!" Hearing the details, the Rafter Cross men raced for their horses.

As they headed up track in a cloud of dust, Kirk was assured that Alfredo would get prompt and efficient relief.

He himself went to his room and to bed. His bones ached. A fast thirty-mile ride, plus a gun fight, had taken its toll. Almost immediately he was sleeping like the dead.

Shouts and shots awakened him. He sat up, blinking. It was an hour past noon on the Fourth of July. This was the big day, the climax long awaited in Las Vegas. All of San Miguel County was just outside Kirk's window, celebrating, sounding off, tense for the arrival of an historic train.

Kirk hustled downstairs and wolfed a plate of ham and eggs. Then he rushed out into the crowd like a boy at a picnic. Cowboys were circling the plaza, firing into the air. Ranch girls and gaily bedecked señoritas paraded arm in arm. Huge placards announced a rodeo already in progress up the Gallinas Creek meadow. Graders and construction men overflowed the bars and streets.

Kirk threaded through them. He stopped at the jail only long enough to be assured that Alfredo had been relieved at the cut and was back in town. Just where, Kirk could easily guess. Brassy music came from the bandstand in New Town. Most of the crowd would be there to see the train come in. There, too, would be Alfredo Baca, sprucely punctual to pay his wager to Calvin Harper.

254

What about Christine Dunbar? Kirk, pushing his way toward the depot, searched the crowds for her. He seemed to see everyone else. There were Adam Vogle and Rosita Baca. Just beyond, looming tall in his holiday frock coat, stood Colonel Harper. Moments later Kirk glimpsed Alfredo Baca. The sheriff was on the depot platform, chatting with the railroad agent. The agent had his watch out and was gazing intently up the track.

For minutes more the band blared forth, giving tone and melody to the tumult of the crowds.

Then a hush. An expectant tension!

The shrill cry of a Mexican boy broke it. "*Viene!*"

"It comes!" A thousand throats echoed it. From far up Gallinas Valley came a toot. Every eye strained that way.

The first train was rolling into town.

Its smoke curled lazily down the vegas. Soon Kirk could hear the labored punching of its pistons, the grind of its wheels. Then he could hear no more in the cheer that arose around him.

"*Viva el Santa Fe!*" It came in a mighty exultant chant from the most hospitable people on earth, that strange mingling of Latin and Rebel and Yankee which inhabits New Mexico. Today they were all one race, roaring a warmth of welcome to this one small caravan of engine and coaches. Even the chubbiest *muchacho* of them all knew what it meant. It was the end of the old bullock trail and a new milestone in the march of empire.

The top-heavy little engine, pulling its chain of rattling, open-vestibuled coaches, came chugging in. With a hiss of steam it stopped just beyond the depot. Bunting of red, white, and blue draped every coach.

Then the band blared again, and a thousand forty-five rounds belched skyward. Passengers were tumbling out of the coaches, including the local booster expedition which had gone up the line to decorate the train, as well as the first echelon of home-seekers and sharp-eyed speculators alert for profit.

Las Vegas, at the moment, paid them little attention. The cheers were for the railroad itself. For Conductor Charlie Brooks, smiling proudly at the steps of the first coach, and for Dan Daley, climbing down from his engine in overalls and long-visored cap.

Kirk turned toward the bandstand, saw Colonel Harper standing just in front of it, his arms folded, an expression akin to embarrassment on his blistered old face. Suddenly the band and the cheering broke off. In the hush, every eye fixed on Alfredo Baca.

A path cleared for Alfredo as he left the platform and walked toward his friend, Calvin Harper.

Every ear strained to hear him say:

"The day is even, *muy amigo mío.*"

"So it is, Alfredo."

"So I owe you a small settlement. I felicitate your good luck, señor." Alfredo brought papers from his pocket and handed them to Harper. Everyone knew what they were. A deed and a bill of sale. Alfredo Baca was now poorer by three thousand acres, three thousand steers, and three thousand cows.

256

Kirk watched Colonel Harper's face. On it he saw a pained reluctance. He sensed that Cal Harper, if he dared, would have renounced these winnings or at least would have made them lighter. But that, of course, would be an insult to Alfredo Baca. Alfredo was a proud *caballero*. One does not offer charity to the likes of Alfredo.

Harper took the papers and put them in the inside pocket of his holiday frock coat. "Alfredo," he said, "anybody can be a good winner. But it takes you to be a good loser. I heard about last night. You could have stayed out of it, and the train wouldn't 've showed up till tomorrow. I mean —" The colonel flushed. He gulped and went on: "Oh, dammit to hell, Alfredo, let's go have a drink."

Arm in arm, the two strode off toward the Old Town plaza.

Again came cheers, and Kirk went brushing through the crowd looking for Christine. When he failed to find her, it occurred to him that she and her father might be watching the rodeo stunts down the meadow.

Kirk wanted to see them himself. So he hurried to the livery barn in Old Town.

He was leading his bay from a stall when a big-boned roan in the next one caught his eye. It was not one of the horses usually kept here. Yet Kirk had a feeling that he'd seen the animal before.

The liveryman saw him looking at it. "It's the horse the sheriff brought in this morning. There was a dead man roped to the saddle. You was in that scrap, too, wasn't you, Calloway?"

Kirk nodded absently. In the darkness last night he'd been unable to distinguish the color or lines of the horse. Now he could. Here was a big young roan with a white star above the eyes. Where had he seen it before? Kirk looked into the roan's mouth. It was four years old.

Then he remembered. A year ago he'd seen a three-year-old roan with these markings. This was the same horse. Last night it had been ridden by one of the would-be saboteurs.

The fat man with the wooden leg! Recollection hit Kirk with a jolt. He'd been riding a circle around the rim of the county. A horse ranch in the hills! And now that he thought of it, there'd been something not too convincing about that horse ranch.

Kirk backed out of the stall and rolled a cigarette. Vaguely he recalled seeing the fat man with the wooden leg on one subsequent occasion. When? It was on Kirk's last day of duty here, before someone had filled him with lead and laid him up for nearly a year.

The day of the night that Carmencita, at the Buena Suerte bar, had learned a secret! A secret which her last breath had whispered to Kirk Calloway — "Señor Lindsay lives!"

Three strings! Could he tie them? The fat man with a none-too-convincing horse ranch. The fat man who came to town on a day Carmencita learned a secret about Mark Lindsay. The fat man who owned a horse ridden last night by an outlaw saboteur. The fat man who lived in an old mining shack.

Could this be the fourth string? An old abandoned mine, Kirk brooded, would have tunnels and stopes. If a prisoner could be immured anywhere for a long time, it would be there.

His mind kept playing on the four strings. One by itself was nothing. Or two. But together they made a cord. Or might make one. Mark Lindsay! Was there a chance in a thousand he was being held in an old mine?

Lindsay was Christine's fiancé. Kirk had never seen him. And tonight he, Kirk, had a dance date with Christine. Twice he'd promised her he'd bring Lindsay home. Twice he'd failed. How would he feel holding her in his arms tonight, with Lindsay rotting in some underground prison?

It wasn't likely. But it would nag at him till he was sure. What would Alfredo Baca do, in a case like this? He'd ride straight for Goff's ranch. To Alfredo it would be a point of honor. He'd proved it last night. Could Kirk do less now?

He snatched up his saddle, with the carbine still in the scabbard, and tossed it on the bay. When he'd tightened the cinch, he wrote a note.

Christine:
Just got a new tip on Mark Lindsay. So I'm riding it down. Sorry to miss the baile.
Yours, Kirk C.

He folded the note and gave it to the liveryman. "Take it to Miss Dunbar at the hotel, will you?"

Minutes later Kirk, with a blanket roll tied back of his saddle, was loping northwest toward the Truchas Hills.

CHAPTER
TWENTY-FIVE

The Rescue

It was still daylight when he hit the rough country at the head of the Gallinas. Kirk left the trail there and spurred to the summit of a hogback. He couldn't be far, now, from Stumpy Goff's place. Nor far from the common corner of three counties, San Miguel, Mora, and Santa Fe. He must reconnoiter cautiously. After the affair last night, riding boldly up to the horse ranch would only invite bullets.

Piñons grew on the hogback, and Kirk used them as a screen as he rode westerly up the ridge. He came finally to a bare bald and from there he could see every rugged outline ahead. Truchas Peak towered among lesser mountains. In the foreground was a truncated cone of unusual symmetry and with steep, cedared slopes. It was barely three miles away. At the near foot of it Kirk made out a cluster of sheet-iron roofs. They looked like old mining buildings, and he remembered them. It was the place Stumpy Goff used for the headquarters of a horse ranch.

Light was fading. Kirk led his bay down into a deep woody pocket and found water there. Since he was certain to be out overnight, he had put two rations of coffee and bacon in his blanket roll. Now, sure that the hogback would screen his smoke from Goff, he made a fire. Then he made a bed of cedar needles and spread his blankets. Stalking Goff by night didn't appeal to him. In the morning he could at least see his way through the woods. He'd need daylight to look the layout over. So Kirk, after a slim supper, rolled himself in blankets by the fire.

At dawn he was off again, still planless. He rode up the ravine a mile or so, then angled up to high ground. The mine ranch, visible from there, showed no life except a few corraled horses. Tailings from the mine had destroyed all vegetation near it, making it hard to approach.

Kirk dismounted and led Red down the far slope of the ridge, and at its base moved cautiously toward the corral. At least he could advance as long as he had cover. The ground here, he noticed, was covered with an odd type of loose rock. Kirk picked up a fragment, examined it curiously, then threw it away.

Farther on he picked up another fragment, scratched it with his thumb. It wasn't limestone; it wasn't flint; it wasn't shale.

It was volcanic ash!

The fact alerted Kirk. He looked again at the steep, truncated cone which reared directly back of Goff's cabin.

Volcanic ash, he knew, can come only from a volcano. The floods of many thousands of years may hack it into small fragments, but it's still volcanic ash.

262

That cone with a flattened top! Perhaps if one were up there, he could look down into the bowl of a crater.

Kirk remembered another such cone, higher than this one, not more than a hundred and fifty miles northeast of here at the head of the Cimarron. A perfect volcano so long extinct that the bed of its crater was a bower of wild cherries. Men called it by the Spanish word for wild cherries, Capulin, and had talked of making it a national monument. Its bowl, they said, was snug and habitable. Could this be a miniature Capulin?

A hollow hill threaded with mine tunnels? What a hide-away! Certain it was that a fugitive outlaw named Donlin had ridden from here two nights ago, by the evidence of a roan horse.

Kirk drew back under cover and crossed the ridge again. On its far side he advanced obliquely, not toward Goff's cabin but in a direction to circle the cedared cone back of it.

The going was rough, and most of the time he had to walk, leading the bay. Piñons gave way to cedar. Everywhere the same volcanic ash crunched underfoot.

When he reached the base of the cone he was a quarter-way around it from Goff's. He followed the foot of the slope until, he estimated, he was a full diameter from the mine cabins. There he tethered Red, took a carbine from the saddle scabbard, and began climbing afoot.

The steepness, in places, made him pull himself from cedar to cedar by hand. Twice he started a rock slide and waited, breathless, till the noise subsided. There

263

wasn't much chance, though, that Goff would hear from the other side of the hill.

He arrived finally at the top. It was an old volcano, all right. Lying flat on the lip of it, Kirk peered down into the verdant bowl of its crater. Capulin brush grew down there. The inner walls were sheer. The oval bed of it lay not much more than a hundred feet below Kirk. At one end of the oval stood a flat-roofed cabin.

No human life was in sight; but plenty of signs told Kirk that people lived there. A woodpile had a bright ax by it. A beaten path led from the cabin door. Kirk's eye followed it to the mouth of a tunnel in the opposite wall.

That would be the side toward Goff's. An old mine drift evidently connected the outer world with this crater.

The door of the crater cabin opened, and two men came out. They were bearded and gun-slung. They didn't go anywhere, merely picked up some horseshoes and began tossing them at pegs. They were just taking exercise, apparently, and waiting for the sun to shine down into the bowl.

Kirk could have potted both of them with his carbine. But there might be others inside.

In a little while another man came out. This one was young, with a pale, discouraged face. He was in frayed shirt sleeves and wore no gun. Kirk saw him carry a bucket to a seep of water, fill it, and return into the cabin.

Mark Lindsay! Kirk hadn't the faintest doubt of it. He was imprisoned, unarmed, among armed outlaws who could come and go at will. Were the two men pitching horseshoes the ones who had fled, night before last, from a chore of sabotage?

Dealing with them must wait. First there was Goff and whatever crew he kept at his exposed horse ranch.

Kirk began sliding down the outer slope. From cedar to cedar he descended, toward his tethered horse. When he was halfway there, the bay snorted. Something had frightened it. Kirk took warning, dropped flat and rolled into the next spread of cedar skirts below. At the same instant came a rifle shot. A bullet spanked into the rocks where Kirk had been a second ago.

He crouched against the cedar, whipping up his carbine. Something moved, not far from his horse. An Indian in buckskin breeches and ragged felt hat. He was raising his rifle for a second shot.

Kirk drew a bead and fired. The Indian pitched forward; the rifle flew from his hand and he lay spread-eagled on the rocks there.

Kirk slid on down to the foot of the slope and ran to him. It was a breast hit. The Indian was dead.

Probably he was Goff's scout and sentinel. Had the two shots been heard by Goff himself? Or by outlaws in the crater? Kirk didn't think so. Sound would hardly carry through a rock mountain. Or, if heard, the hearers might think the Indian had merely bagged a couple of squirrels.

Kirk took the Indian's rifle, tied it to his saddle. He mounted, retracing his way cautiously around the hill.

On the far side of it he sighted Goff's cabin. It was quiet. Smoke curled from its pipe chimney. How many were in there? If they were depending on the Indian for a sentinel, they wouldn't be alert. On this side of the cabin there was no window. Kirk dropped his reins and advanced afoot toward it.

Step by step he closed in, carbine stock at his cheek. No sound from the cabin. Nothing to indicate life there except a warm chimney.

Reaching it, Kirk flattened himself against the outer wall.

In a moment he heard voices.

"Hand me my pipe, Jake."

"Here you are. Where's Chaco?"

"He went to chuck some firewood into the hole."

At least two men were in there. Kirk slid along the wall to a corner. Rounding it he saw a window. He got below it, raised his head a little, and peered in. Two men. One was Stumpy Goff. The other man had his back to Kirk. Morning sunlight streamed in through an open door.

Kirk laid aside his carbine and drew his forty-five. Two quick steps and he was framed in the open door, covering both men.

"This is the law, you guys."

The man with his back to Kirk twisted around, shooting. Kirk's squeeze of the trigger sent a slug through his head. Across the table Stumpy Goff made no resistance. His fleshy face turned the color of milk, and his thick, hairy arms went slowly up.

Jake Orme slithered to the floor, gave one convulsive curse, and then lay still there. Kirk stepped over him and searched Goff for a gun.

Goff wasn't armed. "What's the idea?" he asked.

"A roan bronc," Kirk jibed. "Remember? You tried to trade it off on me one time. Was it you killed Carmencita to keep her from tipping me about Lindsay? Or did you have the Indian do it?"

Goff gave a blank stare. "It wasn't me," he mumbled.

"Lie flat," Kirk ordered.

He found ropes and trussed the fat man. Looking through his pockets he found a heavy brass key. "What's this for, Stumpy?"

Again the blank-stare. Kirk could get no further word out of him.

There was bound to be a shaft or adit, somewhere, leading to the crater. Kirk had already seen its other end. He went outside and surveyed the hill slope. There was no visible opening.

A stable of sorts backed against the cliff, and Kirk went in there. It had no horses. But a box stall at the rear had a manger top-heavy with hay. The hay was old and dusty. Any horse eating it would get the heaves. So it was here to cover something. Kirk pulled it away and saw the mouth of a tunnel.

He went back for his carbine. Also he took Jake Orme's six-gun. There was a lantern in the cabin. Kirk lighted it and went back to the stable. Stooping, he moved warily into the tunnel.

An oaken door stopped him. The big brass key fitted its lock. Kirk passed through and on. After a dozen twists of the tunnel he saw daylight ahead. He extinguished the lantern and left it there.

At the tunnel exit he looked out into the crater. Two men were pitching horseshoes in front of the cabin, but they weren't the same two men. Both were belted with guns. It meant that at least four outlaws were here. There was no present sign of Mark Lindsay.

Kirk kept just within the tunnel and out of sight. He waited half an hour. When he looked out again, the horseshoe game was over. The players had gone inside. Chopping sounds drew Kirk's eyes to a pile of wood about forty yards from the cabin. He saw Lindsay using an ax there.

Kirk couldn't risk calling him. But the capulins were in full leaf, and a fringe of them reached almost to this tunnel. Kirk made a quick dash and got in a screen of foliage. Through this he made his way toward the woodpile.

Boughs crackled as he pushed through. A carbine and two forty-fives hampered him. He kept alert eyes on the cabin, but no one came out. After slow, torturous progress, he arrived within twenty feet of Mark Lindsay.

Kirk spoke to him in a hoarse whisper. "I'm a friend, Lindsay. I got a gun for you. Don't say anything. Just edge over this way."

Lindsay stiffened, ax poised in midstroke. His eyes turned toward the cherry brush. Through the leaves he saw a face he didn't know. Then he saw a hand holding out a gun, butt forward.

Kirk saw him look nervously toward the cabin. "Easy does it, Lindsay. You're leavin' this deadfall. Chris is waitin' for you in town."

A faintness made Lindsay sway. He steadied himself by leaning against the ax handle. Sweat broke over his prison-pale face.

Then he dropped the ax and walked slowly toward Calloway. With a furtive look over his shoulder, he stepped into the screen of brush.

Kirk handed him a forty-five. "Take two if you can use 'em. I got a saddle gun."

"I can use 'em." Mark's hands closed eagerly over the grips of two six-guns. "How did you get in?"

"Never mind. How many in the cabin?"

"Only four, right now."

"Feel up to a gun fight?"

"I been waitin' for one a long time." A fierce fire burned in Mark's eyes as he turned, a gun in each hand, toward the cabin.

"Okay," Kirk said. "Let's go."

They advanced, elbow to elbow. "Is there a back door?" Kirk whispered.

Mark nodded. "A kitchen door. That's where I take the wood in."

"You go in there. Just like you were bringing in wood. Don't let 'em see your guns till you hear me whang in at the front."

Mark went to the rear of the cabin, Kirk to the front. Kirk waited outside a minute, giving Mark time to flank them. Then, carbine poked out in front of him, he kicked open the door and stepped in.

He was keyed up for a finish fight — but not a shot was fired. Mark Lindsay had beaten him to it. Mark stood just inside the kitchen door with two level guns.

269

Four men in a poker game sat staring, hands slowly going up. Mark had them covered, and their shock of surprise was complete.

"Nice goin', Lindsay." Kirk punched his carbine between the shoulder blades of the nearest outlaw.

"Shall I call the posse in?" Mark asked.

Kirk caught the cue. "It won't be necessary, Lindsay. We can handle 'em ourselves." One by one he disarmed the four men.

The illusion of a posse in the offing made tying them up easy. When they were secure Kirk said to Lindsay, "Round up all the keys and we'll lock 'em in here."

"There's only one key," Mark said. "And Goff keeps it in his pocket." But he made sure of it by a thorough search.

"So we can chuck Goff in here with 'em," Kirk decided. "Let's go."

They went out through the tunnel. At the outside cabin Kirk untied Goff. "We're putting you on ice, Stumpy."

They herded the fat man into the tunnel and through the oaken door. Kirk searched him again to make sure there was no second key. "Okay, Goff. If this *calabozo* was tight enough to hold Lindsay, it'll hold you. We'll let Alfredo pick you up tomorrow. So long."

At the corral Mark selected a horse and saddled it. Kirk's watch said only a little past noon as they hit the trail for Las Vegas.

"What were they holding you for, Lindsay?"

"Only Goff was holding me," Mark explained. "Those other guys were just boarding there. Goff aimed to use me to get a payoff from Vogle."

270

"Adam Vogle of Las Vegas?"

"That's the guy. Get an earful of this, Calloway." As they jogged along Mark recited the entire sequence of Vogle's treachery.

Kirk whistled. "Gee, that fellah's billed to marry the sheriff's sister! The sheriff calls him a fine *caballero*."

"He's a fine, four-timing killer, Calloway. It was him knocked off the whole CLC outfit in the bunkhouse."

By the time they were halfway to town, Kirk was able to tie every thread. It was Vogle who'd poured that gunful of lead into Kirk and Carmencita. And as prospective husband to the heiress of the Linked Hearts, it must have been Vogle who'd tried to throw the big wager to Alfredo.

"Soon as I hit town," Mark said grimly, "I want a showdown with that guy."

"Leave him to me, Lindsay."

"No, he's my meat, Calloway. You've done enough."

"You're out of practice," Kirk protested. "And we know he's fast or he couldn't 've beat the whole CLC outfit to the draw. So *I'll* gun it out with him. You doll up and walk in on your girl."

They were still debating it when, near sundown, they rode into a small Mexican plaza just out of Las Vegas. A barber's sign caught Lindsay's eye and he pulled up. "Here's where I grab a shave, Calloway. If I bust in on Chris lookin' like this, she'll think I'm Father Time."

Kirk went with him into the shop. A jolly little Mexican barber applied his art, transforming Lindsay. Stepping clean-shaven from the chair, he looked boyish and handsome. "You'll knock her dead." Kirk grinned.

"She'll be at the hotel, you say?"

"She's a cinch to be there. Because I sent her a note yesterday, and she'll want to know how I came out. That'd hold her in town all right."

Sight of a cantina across the street reminded Kirk that he was famished. "What say we grab a plate of frijoles? Been livin' outa my saddle roll for thirty hours. And I don't want to shoot it out with Vogle on an empty stomach."

"You don't have to, Calloway. I'll take him on myself." They crossed to the cantina and ordered supper there, still debating as to which would take on Vogle.

Kirk argued: "I'm a deputy and you're not. He lives at the hotel and he'll be in his room when we hit town. If you walk in on him, he'll go for his gun. Better he shoots it out with the law than with you, Lindsay."

But Mark was obstinate. "Look, Calloway. I've been buried alive for seventeen months. All on account of Vogle. He was the gink who planned the CLC steal that got me shanghaied. If it hadn't been for him I'd have been there to meet Christine when she drove in from Iowa, like I promised. We'd be married by now. So I got more call to take on Vogle than anybody else."

"What about me?" Kirk countered. "He pumped me full of lead one time. *También*, I got to think about Alfredo Baca. Means I got to get it over with before Alfredo hears you're back. Why? Because Alfredo's sheriff, and he never ducks a duty. He'd go after Vogle himself. Which he shouldn't, because Vogle's engaged to his sister. It's embarrassin' for a guy when he has to kill his sister's fiancé."

Mark had heard all about Alfredo. Boarders had come and gone from the crater, bringing in news from the outside world. Mark had even heard about Alfredo Baca's sensational bet with a cattle king named Harper.

A grim smile crossed Mark's face. "Okay. You want a showdown with Vogle. So do I. He's at the hotel right now. So's Christine Dunbar. When we hit there, one of us goes to Christine's room and the other goes to Vogle's. I'll cut you for it, Calloway. Odd or even."

CHAPTER
TWENTY-SIX

A Death and a Wedding

Mark called the cantina man and asked for a deck of cards. When it came, he shuffled it and placed it neatly in front of Kirk Calloway. "Call it," he invited. "Odd or even."

"Alfredo lost with odd." Kirk grimaced. "So I'll try even."

"Cut."

Kirk parted the deck in the middle, inverting the top half. The card he exposed was the eight of diamonds.

"So Vogle's my dish," he said. "Let's go."

It was dark when they rode into Las Vegas. The town was jaded, spree-fagged, drowsing off its hangover after riotous celebrations. Hitchracks held only a few horses, and stores, except for the saloons, had already closed for the night.

Calloway and Lindsay dismounted at the livery barn, tossing reins to a hostler there. "Sheriff Baca in town?" Kirk asked.

"Don Alfredo? No, señor. He has gone out to his rancho."

It suited Kirk exactly. Alfredo could hear the bad news about Vogle after it was all over. Kirk went with

274

Mark Lindsay to the plaza, and they entered the hotel there.

The lobby was almost deserted. Mark went forward to the desk and asked eagerly, "Is Miss Dunbar still here?"

The clerk nodded. He didn't recognize Mark. "Top of the stairs and turn right. Her room is the third door."

Kirk asked, "Is Adam Vogle in his room?"

"Yes, Mr. Calloway. Top of the stairs and turn left. His room is at the front corner that way."

They went up together. At the top of the stairs, Kirk faced Lindsay and gripped his hand. "Here's where the trail splits, pardner. *Buena suerte.* Third door to the right, the guy said."

With his face flushed, Mark turned right down the corridor. Kirk, turning left, strode toward its opposite end.

After a few steps he stopped and looked over his shoulder. He saw Mark Lindsay stop at a door, heard Christine's voice say, "Come in." He saw Mark open the door and bound in, and heard Christine's glad cry. Then only silence.

Kirk went on to the far front-corner room. He knocked.

"Come in," answered the relaxed voice of Adam Vogle.

Kirk went in, closed the door, stood with his back against it. Vogle was seated, fully dressed, just as he had come up from supper. He tossed aside a Santa Fe paper and looked at Kirk with an unalarmed smile.

The smile froze when Kirk announced bluntly, "I found Lindsay. I just brought him to town."

Vogle didn't get up. His broad face turned three shades grayer, and it was half a minute before he could summon an answer.

"Lindsay? You mean that CLC man who disappeared? Glad you found him, Calloway."

"No you're not, Vogle. Because he knows all about those six thousand CLC cows. Which reminds me. Soon as the courts confiscate the property you bought with that money, we can make restitution to the Crown Land and Cattle Company. Then we can hang you for killing four men in a bunkshack, not to mention Carmencita."

Vogle still remained seated. His eyes flicked to a window and then back to Calloway. They dropped to the forty-five at Kirk's hip. "I don't know what you're talking about." His voice was cracked and false. "You're mixed up, some way."

"I *was* mixed up. Plenty. So was Alfredo. So was Rosita. They thought you were a fine *caballero*. Get your hat, Vogle. I'm taking you to the *carcel*."

At last the man stood up. He looked beaten and old. "I'll report this insolence to Alfredo Baca," he said. "He'll fire you when he hears about it. He's my friend."

"He'd drill you just as quick as I would. Get your hat."

Vogle's low-crowned, wide-brimmed hat hung on a rack in the corner. He turned and went to it. His back was to Calloway. As his left hand reached for the hat, his right slipped slowly under the left lapel of his coat.

An armpit gun was there. Vogle whirled, firing. His bullet smashed through the door by Kirk. Kirk drew. Wrist against hip, he fired once. Vogle's knees buckled,

276

and his chin sagged. His knees hit the floor first, then his outspread hands. Red spurted from a hole between his eyes.

Kirk took a key from the door. He went out, locking it behind him. Occupants of adjacent rooms poured into the hall. The lobby clerk came dashing upstairs.

Kirk handed him the key. "Vogle's in there. Dead. Don't let anyone in. Get word to Pancho at the jail. Tell him to bring the coroner and take over. I'm pretty much all in. Anybody wants me, I'll be in my room."

In his room Kirk took off his gun belt. He shaved and changed clothes. Voices hummed from the hall. He could hear Pancho chattering a report to the coroner.

Kirk sat down and lighted a cigarette. It was all over now. But he was tired. A succession of gun fights and hard rides had sapped him, drawing him out fine and leaving him kitten-weak. He leaned back now, relaxing, mulling over details of his report to Alfredo. They'd have to send a posse to the crater, of course, to pick up Goff and his crowd. Whether or not one of them talked, the case was wrapped up.

Three cigarettes later someone came in. Kirk turned, expecting to see Pancho. But it was Mark Lindsay.

Lindsay sat down on the bed.

Kirk passed him the makings, "When'll the weddin' be, *amigo?*"

Lindsay rolled the smoke awkwardly. He spilled some of the tobacco. "I'm outa practice, kinda; didn't often get any makings in that hell-hole of Goff's."

"I said when'll the weddin' be?" Kirk prodded.

277

Mark gave him a queer look. "Why don't you go in there, Calloway, and find out?"

Kirk gaped at him. "Whadda you mean, Lindsay?"

"I got to tell you something, Calloway. About me and Chris. We were boy and girl on adjoinin' farms. Then the cowboy-bee stung me and I came west. After three years I got lonesome. I wrote Chris and asked would she come out and marry me. I picked out a couple of homesteads for her and her father. Fixed it up to meet 'em in Vegas. When I walked in on her just now, she hadn't seen me for five years."

Kirk stared at him vacantly.

"She's loyal," Mark said. "She came into my arms and cried like a baby. She said we'd get married right away. I told her you'd brought me to town and had gone down the hall to settle up with Vogle. She kissed me. But it was a sister kiss. I didn't know it until —"

"Until what?"

"Until we heard two gunshots from Vogle's room. They said things to us. They said either you'd killed Vogle or Vogle'd killed you. I looked at Chris and saw what it meant to her. For a minute she forgot I was there. Then we heard people in the hall say Vogle was dead. I saw her face when she heard that. It was like sunlight breaking through clouds. She threw her arms around me and kissed me again. But it wasn't me, really. It was you."

Mark stood up and took Kirk's arm. He looked down, grinning. "Don't just sit there starin', you big lummox. On your feet."

278

He jerked Kirk Calloway up, pulled him out into the hall.

"After you pass the stairs it's the third door on the right." He gave Kirk a little push. "Just knock there, pardner, and see what happens."

It was still July when the chapel bells rang in Las Vegas. A score of carriages and twice as many saddle horses were hitched close by. Stockmen and railroaders were there. *Ricos* were there from the ranchos, and *pobres* from the plazas.

Inside, every bench was filled. Old Calvin Harper was on hand with his full crew. The entire county was there, it seemed, solemn and sleek. A fragrance of flowers filled the place, and not a gun was in sight.

Strains of the wedding march sounded from an organ. In slow cadence, down the aisle, marched Alex Dunbar with the bride on his arm. Christine was beautiful in her long veil and train. Las Vegas had never seen such a gown. Women in the pews marveled. How could it have been made ready on such short notice? Only the mistress of the Linked Hearts could have told them. Rosita Baca was a realist, and practical beyond her years. Such a creation, even if made to honor Adam Vogle, must not go to waste.

So a girl from Conchas Creek wore it now. And back of her came the bridesmaid, Rosita herself.

Waiting at the altar stood Kirk Calloway. Beside him, straight as a ramrod, stood his best man, Mark Lindsay. Mark's eyes smiled at the bride and then went beyond her to fix softly on Rosita. She'd make a lovely bride herself, Rosita.

The organ played on, swelling to crescendo under a master's touch. His slim, artistic fingers flowed over the keys, and the chords he struck there had all the harmony of sweetness and courage, of pride and loyal amity, which ruled his own life. Only Colonel Harper, at the moment, noticed him. Everybody else was looking at Christine and Rosita.

Colonel Harper took off his glasses; a mist, somehow, had clouded them. He wiped them, put them on again, blew his nose vigorously. Again his gaze fixed, wistfully and a little enviously, on his best friend at the organ. For the organist was none other than that companionable *caballero*, Don Alfredo Baca, the sheriff of San Miguel.